the *Goodness*

*Someone of Substance*

—————— BOOK ONE ——————

# PD JANZEN

THE GOODNESS
Copyright © 2021 by PD Janzen

ISBN: 978-1-4866-2127-9
eBook ISBN: 978-1-4866-2128-6

Printed in Canada

Word Alive Press
119 De Baets Street Winnipeg, MB  R2J 3R9
www.wordalivepress.ca

**WORD ALIVE**
—P R E S S—

MIX
Paper from
responsible sources
FSC   FSC® C103567

Cataloguing in Publication information can be obtained from Library and Archives Canada.

*For my dear friend Laura.*
*She not only encouraged me to publish this book,*
*but she wouldn't let me give up when my own doubts overwhelmed me.*
*Thank you from the bottom of my heart!*

# *Acknowledgements*

IT'S TRUE—ONE PERSON CAN'T WRITE A BOOK. ONE CAN PERHAPS DO THE typing, but there are many other people involved.

I want to acknowledge my husband, Brian, who dislikes being mentioned in any of my writing but still encourages me, even if I don't listen to him. Thank you for praying for me and going it alone so many times when you could see I was in "writing mode." Your patience is amazing and always has been.

To my three children I say thank you for surviving this imperfect parent (not your dad—just me) and rising above that. You have inspired me more than you'll ever know, and now your children are doing the same. You're all so precious to me.

To the many nurses and doctors I've worked, laughed, and cried with for over thirty-five years: I hold the greatest respect for you. I'm in awe of your dedication to other people's wellbeing—very often above your own. So many of you have helped me to not only become the nurse I am but the person I am as well. May God bless each of you in a special way.

Thank you to the many people at Word Alive Press who had a hand in crafting this novel. A special shout-out to Jen—the calm voice of encouragement on the other end of the phone; Ariana—the person in charge of putting it all together; Kyla and Kerry—thank you for teaching me so much through the editing process; and everyone else who I don't know by name but appreciate so much. I couldn't have done this without you!

My greatest thanks and praise go to my heavenly Father for blessing me so much—with my family, my friends, and my church. I thank Him for telling me to "sit down, shut up, and write" when I didn't know how.

God has truly given me all good things—not only when I see them as such but even more when I don't. He knows the whole picture, and I praise Him for His goodness—especially through the rough stuff.

# Prologue

"ALL RIGHT, DEAR," SAID THE NURSE, STANDING NEXT TO HER YOUNG PATIENT'S bed. "Only a few more pushes left, and the baby will be born."

"I can't!" screamed the fifteen-year-old girl, clearly distraught with the pain she was in.

"Yes, you can," said the nurse calmly and with encouragement in her voice.

The girl's mother, a middle-aged woman standing on the opposite side of her daughter's labour bed, huffed. "You got yourself into this. Just push hard and let's get this over with."

The nurse pursed her lips and tried to ignore her patient's clearly lacking-in-support person.

When the next contraction came, everyone in the room braced themselves. The girl's shrieks could be heard down the hall, even with the case-room door tightly closed.

The nurse leaned close to the girl's ear and whispered, "Put your lips together. No noise and push past the pain, honey. It'll be over faster if you do that."

The girl glanced at the nurse, with pain and sorrow etched on her face. Tears ran down her cheeks, but she finally nodded and did as she was asked.

Beside her, her mother rolled her eyes and pinched her lips in frustration.

*So cold*, thought the nurse, staring at the mother. *She's still your daughter, even if she disappointed you.* She wished she could say it out loud.

The baby's head crowned with the girl's next push, and the nurse quickly instructed her to pant. The doctor found no cord around the baby's neck and with one more push the tiny baby was born. As soon as the baby started to cry, a nurse took it from the room.

"You did a great job!" praised the nurse before taking the girl's blood pressure. When she was done, she continued, encouragingly, "You should be proud of the work you did today."

"Proud?" spat the girl's mother. "That's a laugh. There's nothing to be proud of here."

The girl looked away from her mother, eyebrows pinched. The nurse smiled at the exhausted girl, trying to show sympathy.

"She doesn't need stitches," interjected the doctor, throwing a sterile green towel over the girl's legs and pelvis. He was clearly uncomfortable with the tension in the room and spoke to the nurse before leaving. "I'll write orders, and when she's stable, she can go home."

"Can I go home now?" the girl whispered, her words slurred from exhaustion.

The nurse poured warm water into a basin. "Not yet, honey. We have to check on you and make sure you're all right before you go, and there will be some paperwork to do first."

The girl nodded, closed her eyes, and laid her head back on the pillow as the nurse checked her uterus and flow.

The nurse's heart ached for the young girl. She'd come into the hospital in active labour, having had little prenatal care and with only her angry mother by her side. From the history they gave, the girl's pregnancy was unplanned, and she hadn't told her mother about it until at least halfway to her due date.

As the nurse watched their limited interaction, she thought it must have been like living in a nightmare when her mother found out. The wrath she seemed to impart on her daughter in the delivery room was harsh—the nurse couldn't imagine what her home-life was like.

Nonetheless, here they were. They had hidden the pregnancy from the girl's father and planned to give the baby up for adoption. During admission, the mother had done most of the talking. She'd made it clear that they didn't want to know the baby's gender, and neither one of them would be holding it or seeing it. When the nurse had asked her patient if that was what she wanted, the girl had simply looked down at the blue hospital gown she wore and nodded.

"It's not up to her," her mother had snapped. "She's underage—a child, really. You'll be answering to me."

The nurse had taken a deep breath, feeling her blood pressure rise but trying to keep her anger in check. "Well," she'd answered back, sounding calm, "your daughter is my patient, and I need to know what her wishes are too."

After that, both mother and daughter had fallen silent.

Shortly after the birth of the baby, a social worker was called. When the social worker came out of the room after visiting with the girl and her mother, the nurse asked, "How is she? Her mother is really mad. Does this girl really want to give up her baby?"

The social worker looked perturbed as she brushed past the nurse and sat at the desk to begin writing her notes. The nurse stood and stared, waiting for an answer. When the social worker ignored her, the nurse cleared her throat, crossed her arms, and waited.

The social worker looked up and sighed. "This is what they've decided. Her mother has the right to make the decisions, and the girl says she doesn't want to take the baby home."

"That's probably because her mother's standing over her forcing her to agree," said the exasperated nurse. "Couldn't you talk to her alone? The story might be different."

"Look!" replied the social worker. "She's fifteen. She can't take care of a child, and her mom knows it. They don't have the means for it, and this is the best plan. What could a fifteen-year-old know about caring for an infant? It'll all be dumped on her mom, and her mother knows it!"

The nurse fell silent, knowing at least some of that was true. If the poor girl had only her mother for "support," how could she possibly stand a chance? It was just so heartbreaking.

The patient was quiet every time the nurse assessed her over the next few hours. Although her mother didn't leave her side, they hardly spoke. Papers were signed and before the nurse's shift ended, the young girl was physically ready to be discharged.

The nurse helped her young charge to the bathroom one last time before sending her on her way. When they were alone for those few minutes, the girl asked shyly, "Would you please... tell me one thing?"

"Anything," answered the nurse, looking at her patient's sweet face.

"Can you tell me if it was a boy or girl?" she whispered with doubt in her eyes. "I won't tell my mom."

Tears filled the tired nurse's eyes as she replied, "You had a baby girl, honey."

The girl nodded and softly whispered, "Thank you."

# Chapter One

THE BUILDING WAS AN OLD BROWNSTONE IN AN OFTEN THOUGHT OF "POOR" side of town. The office inside smelled of old smoke and the typical smells of aging wood in buildings with squeaky floors that you don't want to look to closely at—especially in the corners.

Helen sat in the waiting room of Boss Agency, a PI firm, crossing and uncrossing her legs so often she had to stand to adjust her skirt. As she sat again, settling with keeping her legs uncrossed, she fiddled with the handle of her purse and licked her dry lips. She opened her bag, unzipped the inner lining, and fumbled for her lip gloss. She was just uncapping it when a balding man stepped out of his inner office. He greeted her with a smile and motioned to her to move inside his space. She forgot her dry lips, replaced the cap on the gloss, and quickly stood.

"Come in," he said. "I'm sorry. My secretary didn't come to work this morning because her son is sick, and I must say, I'm a little lost without her, Mrs.—"

"Please call me Helen," the woman interrupted, twisting her wedding ring nervously. She had spoken with this man on the phone, but this was their first meeting face to face, and somehow, she'd imagined things differently but didn't know exactly how.

"I'm Melvin Boss. Please sit," he said as she entered his office. He motioned to the chair across from his old mahogany desk. "Sit," he repeated, smiling, when Helen hesitated.

Helen nodded and sat on the edge of the seat that was offered her. Her throat felt dry and her hands clammy.

"Helen, it's okay," Melvin said. "When you asked me to find this person, I didn't know where to start, to be honest. But I think I did it."

"Really?" Helen blurted, in disbelief.

Melvin smiled. "Really."

Helen looked down, not sure what to feel. She had both hoped and not hoped for this result. She wasn't sure about anything now. She looked up and let her breath out, not realizing she'd been holding it.

"When she tried to contact me a few years ago, I was so scared that I just ignored it. I didn't want to have anything to do with this, but ... over the last ... well ... I just have to know," Helen finished in a rush.

"And now you will, Helen. For what it's worth, I think it's a good thing," replied Melvin.

He handed the envelope toward her. She didn't take it immediately but rather stared at it. The contents in this envelope would change her life—and others' lives—forever. Could she go through with it?

"What do I do now?" she asked, battling the panic inside her.

Melvin looked at Helen with an empathetic smile. "Well ... taking the envelope would be the first step."

"Oh!" stammered Helen as her shaky hand accepted it. "And now what?"

"That's up to you. After you read the documents, you decide what to do with the information," he offered. "Everything you need to contact this person is in there, Helen, but you can take your time."

She nodded, staring down at what she was holding. Then she squared her shoulders and looked up. "What do I owe you, sir? I'd like to take care of that now."

"Normally that would be great," replied Melvin, "but like I said, my secretary isn't here, and I don't really take care of that." He looked embarrassed by the admission and quickly added, "We don't mind billing you. That way you can have some time as well—"

"I don't need time," stated Helen, "and I'd like to pay you now, if possible. Surely you take cash?"

Most clients preferred to pay in cash, and now Melvin wished he'd taken more notice of his secretary's administrations.

"Okay," he replied. "Let me try to find your bill and a receipt book or something."

He left his office, and Helen waited while she heard him scrounging around his secretary's desk. Soon he returned, bill and receipt book in hand.

With the transaction complete, Helen's purse was lighter, but her mood was not. Her mind swirled with more questions and anxiety. She had thought this was a good idea when she began, but now she wasn't sure of anything.

"If you need anything at all, Helen, please feel free to call," Melvin said, holding out his hand.

Helen took his hand and shook it. "You seem to be a nice man. Thank you for everything you've done to get this information, but I think our transaction is done now."

"That's fine. I'm just saying — my door is open," replied Melvin.

Helen thanked him again and left.

He watched her as she quietly closed the door behind her. Then he stood to watch out the window of his third-floor office until she exited the building. He'd been in the business of watching people and learning about them, for someone else's information and money, for years. So many people, so many searching, so many hurting. He wondered what Helen would do with the information he'd found and where it would lead her.

After she was out of his line of vision, he turned toward his desk, sighed, and wondered if he'd done the right paperwork in accepting the payment for services rendered. He guessed his secretary would tell him when she got back.

# Chapter Two

I AWOKE TO THE SHRILL RINGTONE OF MY PHONE. WHY IS IT THAT WHEN choosing a pleasant ringtone, it's anything but when you're startled awake?

"Hello," I answered with frustration after dropping the phone onto the carpet twice before successfully speaking into it.

"Hello," replied a rather terse voice that I, in my haze, didn't immediately recognize.

I glanced at the clock to see 11:00 a.m. I'd slept for three hours. I fleetingly thought that when I found out who was on the other end, I would phone them at 1:00 a.m. and see how they felt about being disturbed from their deepest sleep cycle. Instead, I tried to sound … well … at least awake.

"Can I help you?" I asked.

"Help me?" the woman paused. "This is your mother, Trish Holmes, and now I can prove you don't call me and never come over anymore. You don't even know my voice!"

I sighed. "Give me a break, Mom. You just woke me up."

"It's eleven o'clock in the morning! What are you still doing in bed?" she said accusingly.

"I'm a nurse, Mom. I just got off nights," I replied, trying for patience.

"Well," she huffed, and I could tell by the pause that she was thinking of an excuse as to why it was only right for her to call and my fault to be sleeping. She didn't disappoint.

"This is not my fault. You never talk to me. If you did, I might know your schedule, and this sort of thing could be avoided."

"Right ... it's my fault," I started accusatorially, but then thought better of it. To shorten the conversation and get back to dreamland, I had to change tactics. "Sorry, Mom," I continued, trying to fake it. "What can I do for you?"

"Nothing much, except ... please try to come home this weekend, or maybe the next. I'll take whatever works for you." She paused. "Your dad and I would like to see you."

She knew if she used my dad, I might be more apt to go, but she also sounded more insistent than usual, so I suddenly felt more awake.

"Is something wrong?" I asked with concern.

"Now why would something have to be wrong for us all to be together, Trish?"

She sounded hesitant, nervous perhaps, and accusatory all at the same time. I was too tired to get into it, so I acquiesced.

"Okay, Mom. I'll look at my schedule when I get up and I'll text you."

She sighed but agreed.

I tried to return to sleep. Unfortunately, I was too awake, so I tossed and turned until, finally, I got up. I wasn't going back to work that night, so I thought maybe three hours of sleep would be enough. Often it had to be.

I started coffee and showered. It felt wonderful except for the headache and nausea that all too commonly followed a night shift. When you work late hours, the "hungover" feeling usually hits at 2:00 or 3:00 a.m. It did last night too, as I was doing the final stage of care on a newly delivered mother. Now it was back. I turned on the television, and a panel of arguing women on some talk show came on. I turned it off. The coffee was done and smelled heavenly. Caramel flavoured coffee with cream. Wonderful.

I must've dozed on the couch because I woke up, startled by a buzzing text, a few hours later.

*Wanna do supper?* the text asked. It was from my best-friend, Trent.

*Sure*, I texted back.

# Chapter Three

AS A REGISTERED NURSE FOR ALMOST EIGHT YEARS, I WORKED ON A BUSY Labour and Delivery unit in a large city with many surrounding rural communities.

Trent and I grew up in the same rural town, went to the same school, and were each other's best friend our whole lives. We were, in fact, born within days of each other, and our new mothers met each other in the hospital. They became friends, and Trent and I did as well. We'd always been there for each other—in the sandbox, on the swings, later through crushes, through breakups, and all the things one thinks are so important in those younger years. Then we ended up in nursing school together. Trent lives down the hall from me. He is quite chagrined that I haven't at least a fifty-two-inch screen taking up half my living room area, like he does. I'm quite content with a small TV, since I don't have much time to watch anyway. I've explained this more than once to him, but he doesn't grasp it. He thinks I'll "find a man" much more expediently if I bring him to a more inviting "man cave-like" place. I laugh at Trent. He's such a bachelor.

Trent and I planned for Chinese. It was a hole-in-the-wall café, but sometimes the best food comes from the most unassuming places. This restaurant always turned out delicious food, and this night was no different.

I hadn't fussed getting ready, and he hadn't either. Both of us wore jeans and T-shirts. I'd put my brown mid-length hair into a messy bun earlier and it was already escaping its clip, but that's the great thing about friends—

they truly don't care what you look like. I wasn't that hungry, because I was sleep deprived, but I woke up once I started sipping my Diet Pepsi.

"What's up, Trent?" I asked, picking up on an excited vibe from my friend. With sisterly fondness, I looked at the tall, attractive blond man sitting across from me.

Trent shifted in his seat. "I've been offered a job away from here, and I think I'll take it," he said in a sudden rush.

I felt my throat constrict and looked down at the table between us, saying nothing. Trent and I had come to the city together after we graduated with our nursing degrees. We were looking for more exciting experiences than our small town could offer and, although the city was just short of two hours away, we couldn't wait to get out. He worked in Emergency and I worked Labour and Delivery. He'd been my friend through thick and thin, and although we weren't romantically attracted to one another, he was the closest person in my life. When I had a bad day, I vented to him. When I had a good day, I laughed with him, and vice versa. When I had all the in-between days, he'd always been there for me, and I for him.

I looked up at Trent, and his expression appeared to be almost apologetic. I immediately felt a twinge of guilt in thinking only of myself. Maybe this was his unlikely idea of a dream job and he thought it was in God's plan for his life. Who was I to be upset about that?

"Where?" I asked, trying to smile without much success.

"Back home," he replied, and my jaw dropped. "I know what you're thinking," he rushed on, "but hear me out. I know when we were younger, we just wanted to get outta there, but I've been thinking ... and changing, I guess."

I waited, taking a sip of my drink.

He continued. "You know I've been talking with Melissa again and, well, I thought I'd just throw an application in at the hospital in town and see what happens. It turns out they have a position available, and I'm looking at this as a sign that maybe I need to pursue this relationship with Mel. It seems like everything's falling into place."

"Well ..." I paused, unsure of how to react.

I wanted to tell him that of course the hospital had a position for him. Trying to get quality staff in a rural hospital was challenging, much less someone with Trent's experience and background. They'd be crazy not to hire him. Instead, I lashed out. "I'm a bit hurt that you didn't share this with me before now, Trent. I mean, how long have you been thinking about it? It must've been a while if you already have a job lined up. And really? Back home?"

I was sorry I'd said it as soon as it was out, which is typical of me much too often. I could see he was hurt by my reaction and that it was time for me to try apologizing.

"I'm sorry, Trent," I said, feeling guilty. "It's your life, and I had no business saying that." I paused. "It's not about me," I squeaked out, although I felt it should be.

My religious teaching really kicked in then, and I said the most piously understanding statement I could think of. "I'm sure you prayed about it and God's answered that."

He laughed as he placed his hand over mine, seeing right through me.

"I know you believe that, Trish, and so do I, but right now they're just words coming out of your mouth to try to make me feel better." He smiled, pausing. "Listen … I know when we came to the city, we thought we'd stay forever, and maybe that's still okay for you, but I think my path needs changing. No … I know it needs changing. I'm almost twenty-nine, and it's time. I hope you understand. I'm not moving to hurt you or because I hate it here. I just know this is the right move for me."

My eyes teared up as I nodded. "Okay. I'll just miss you so much. You're my best friend."

I looked away from his deep brown stare and tried to get my act together. After a few deep breaths, I looked back at his face and said, "I am happy for you. You look happy, and I'm glad. You know I only want the very best for you, Trent."

He smiled. "I know."

"I just wish you'd be happy here," I admitted.

He laughed again as the waitress served our food. It was a quiet meal, which was unlike us, but it needed to be.

We said goodnight early and I hugged him before leaving him in the hallway of our apartment complex. I wondered then why I'd never been romantically attracted to him. He smelled nice and wasn't bad to look at.

It might have worked, but there had never been the "spark" people spoke of. That was important too, or so people said. I'd had a couple of "boy" friends but nothing serious enough to amount to anything more than a few dates. I was so focused on my career that I didn't mind not having a "special someone."

I don't know why I cried so much when I got back to my empty apartment. Maybe some of it was sleep deprivation, maybe because I'd called my mother back and agreed to go home for the long weekend, maybe just from sadness or loneliness, but one thing I knew—my life would never be the same again, and change was coming.

# Chapter Four

IT'S FUNNY, IN A NON-HUMOROUS SENSE, HOW GOD WILL SEND A SITUATION into your life that brings into perspective how small your problems really are compared to some. This happened to me during my very next shift.

I had two days off work after Trent's news, which was a perfect time for me to have my own forty-eight-hour pity-party. I didn't see Trent much over that time because no matter what I'd told him, I was still hurt that he hadn't filled me in as he made his plans to move. Between that and the mourning, I slept a lot and my days off sped by.

My next shift was a busy day shift with inductions, a few spontaneous labours, and three elective C-sections that all went fairly routinely. At the start of my shift, I was assigned to a labouring patient who had come in during the night. She laboured quickly and was soon ready to push.

"Push," I whispered into Stephanie's ear. "You can do this. Put your lips together and push right down into your bum."

My young patient looked at me as her contraction grew in its intensity and nodded, ready to go again. She took a deep breath, closed her eyes, and bore down deeply.

Suddenly she broke. "It buuuuurrrns ..."

"I know," I quickly acknowledged. "That's the baby's head stretching everything down there, but you have to push past that pain. You can do it, Stephanie. Push!"

She listened and the baby's head began to crown.

"Now pant," I said directly into her ear. "You don't want to tear."
She panted as I directed.

"Now push a little," I encouraged. She did. "Now pant." She did.
We did this together a few times. Her control was amazing.

The small head slowly emerged as I said, "Now stop and breathe. The baby's head is born. The doctor's just checking for a cord around the neck. Try not to push."

I wiped Stephanie's forehead as she laid her head back on the pillow, took a deep breath, and waited.

"Okay," said Lisa, the young on-call obstetrician. "Let's have the rest of this little one. You're doing great. Can you give me one more push?"

"Just one more?" Stephanie asked.

"Just one more big one," I promised, squeezing her hand.

With a deep, guttural groan from Stephanie, the rest of the baby emerged. We waited, as we always do, for the cry—the music of the delivery room. It took only a few seconds before a very angry scream from the small new person filled up the whole space.

"Remember, I don't want to know," said Stephanie with an edge of panic in her voice.

"We know," I soothed while nodding at the other nurse beside me, who was caring for the newborn.

The cord was cut, the baby wrapped in a warm blanket and whisked away to the nursery as quickly as she'd been born. Not our usual practice.

Stephanie was a nineteen-year-old patient who had successfully hidden her pregnancy from her parents and all those close to her. She considered herself very lucky that her parents, with whom she lived, had recently left for a distant holiday. She'd gone into labour soon after they left and was relieved that she started the birthing process at such an opportune time. Her plan was to have the baby, give it up for adoption, and be back home by the time her parents returned.

I pitied her but also admired her strength. She was in college and knew the plans and goals she had set for her life. She had told me she had said no to going out that night, but her friend had talked her into it. Too much alcohol and one weak moment threatened to end all she'd planned so well.

She could have ended the pregnancy prematurely but instead chose to give life to the baby inside her.

I didn't know why she chose not to tell her parents. All she said was that they had always been good to her and she couldn't bear to put them through it. She just wanted this chapter of her life over with, and the way I saw it, she loved that baby enough to give someone else the greatest gift anyone can give another.

Later that day, Stephanie was stable enough to go home. Before leaving, she asked me if she could see the baby, although she still didn't want to know if she had given birth to a boy or girl. I carried the small bundle to her before she left the hospital. She peered at the cute little face as I cradled her little one in my arms. A curl of auburn hair escaped her beige stocking-net toque, and I noticed a small birthmark in the shape of a perfect heart on the far side of her left cheek, which only made her seem sweeter. Stephanie saw it too and her eyes teared as she gazed at the miracle she'd help to make. Mine did too.

She looked at me after a minute or so and simply said, "Thank you."

I nodded and took the baby back to the nursery, but not before I told Stephanie that I thought she was the bravest, most loving person I had ever met.

Before placing the baby back in the hospital bassinet, I prayed for their safety and that God would protect them both with every blessing.

Stephanie left the hospital after signing the many papers it takes to give up a child. A few days later, people from Social Services would come to retrieve the baby from the hospital nursery. She would live with a foster family until her adoptive parents would be chosen.

I wondered if Stephanie would finish college and if she'd ever tell her parents about the baby. I wondered how many times she would think of the child she gave up as a gift for someone else to love.

After my shift, I stopped by Emergency on my way out of the hospital. Trent was working the opposite twelve-hour night from my day shift and, although he seemed busy, I waited until I caught his eye.

"Hey, you," he said, coming toward me. "What's up?"

I looked up at his familiar face—the face I'd laughed with so many times and cried to as well.

"I guess ..." I started, battling tears. "I just want you to know ... I'm sincerely glad for you. I'm so glad you're happy and moving on. You know ... the way God is calling you to. For real."

Before he could answer, I reached up, kissed his cheek, and hugged him hard. Then I left before he could say much, or I'd fall apart. I felt better and more at peace. He was a good guy, and I hoped that he and Melissa would find love and joy together, and I knew our hospital at home was getting the best ER nurse ever.

## Chapter Five

I WON'T GET INTO THE DAY TRENT LEFT BECAUSE TEARS WERE INVOLVED, AND I felt ridiculously embarrassed by the river I cried. For a while after he was gone, I slipped into a funk I couldn't climb out of, but after a couple of weeks, I decided to kick my own butt, pray for strength, and throw myself into my work. I worked my full-time rotation and as much overtime as the hospital needed. I became a working machine, which has been one of my "go-tos" in times of stress and is more than achievable in the medical profession.

As we know, on Labour and Delivery, the worst things usually happen in the middle of the night with a full moon shining. There may have been studies done to disprove these suspicions, but most nurses would agree that they seem factual. I was at the end of a stretch of five twelve-hour shifts when the worst night of my career happened.

It had started as a "quiet" shift, a word we nurses never say out loud on our unit. Although I'm not a superstitious person, and I believe that God is ultimately in control, I also know that using the word "quiet" on nursing units seems to stir up immediate trouble. A few women had come in before midnight and were progressing normally in their labours. My small, blonde, thirty-five-year-old patient was in active labour when she arrived and appeared to be coping extremely well.

I reviewed her history and noted that two years prior she had given birth by caesarian section to her first baby, who was in a breech presentation at that time. The baby had been over eight pounds, and the mom had been counselled about the risks of having the baby vaginally. She had opted, due to her baby's rump coming first, for an elective C-section, as most women do these days. Unfortunately, their first baby had serious abnormalities that we in the medical field call "incompatible with life." Tragically, as prenatally diagnosed, he had died a few hours after birth. I had so many more questions for her and her husband but kept them to myself. This time, their baby appeared to have a normal anatomy and was in a cephalic (head down) position.

Stacy wanted to deliver vaginally this time, something we call a Trial of Labour After Caesarian (TOLAC). There are definitely risks to this, the most important being the rarity of uterine rupture from the scar's weakening presence, but as it had been two years since the C-section, the risk was much lower. Watchful waiting and prudent assessment would be my responsibility.

"You're six centimetres dilated already," I told them, delighted. "You're doing great!"

Stacy and her husband looked at each other, smiling.

Grant was a dark-haired man with a few crow's feet around his blue eyes, which deepened when he smiled. He spoke gently to his wife.

"See, honey? I told you you're doing great! This baby is coming soon," he said, excitedly taking her hand. He looked at me then with concern in his eyes. "Is the baby okay too?"

"Yes," I assured him, nodding.

Stacy teared up. "God is good, Grant. He's giving us our baby. Finally."

I've learned to believe that often you can glimpse the strength of a relationship by what you see in the Labour and Delivery suite. Stressful times tend to show the truth. The labour room can be a sort of litmus test. This couple had been through an unimaginable loss and had stuck it through. Many people's relationships, as studies have shown, suffer greatly after a loss, especially one as devastating as theirs had been. However, a healthy relationship full of hope and love filled the room with promise and joy that night.

Grant and Stacy were the patients a nurse treasures. Both were completely in this for each other, and soon, the newest member of their family. It was refreshing to see and humbling to be a part of.

Stacy's vital signs and the fetal heart rate monitor strip were normal. I started her IV as a colleague, Anne, put the chart in order.

The anesthesiologist came soon after to give Stacy an epidural, and about ninety minutes after I first met them, they were settled in.

I had just covered Stacy in a warm blanket when she said, "I feel pressure."

"That was fast," I laughed. "Sounds good. Maybe you're fully dilated already."

I examined her and felt no cervix, but with the epidural taking more effect, she had no urge to push. I phoned her doctor and, as is usual, we decided a "passive second stage" would be appropriate. The baby's head would descend mostly on its own while Stacy was still comfortable, and the epidural was working effectively. Then, when birth was imminent, she would push her baby into the world.

I explained it all to Stacy and Grant, and they were agreeable to the plan. The baby couldn't have looked better on the monitor, and I sat in silence beside them as she nestled under the warmth of the flannel blankets.

I turned down the lights and we waited. Stacy soon dozed, the epidural taking full effect and dulling the previous sensation of pressure.

I smiled at Grant and he smiled back. I studied him a little between entries I made in her chart. He seemed like one of those rare guys who was equally as gentle as he was strong.

"We've waited for this day for a long time," he whispered, catching my eye when I glanced at him.

"I'm sure you have," I quietly replied before looking down at the pen poised above my nurse's notes.

"When the ultrasound showed that everything was normal, I think we cried tears of joy for days. We couldn't believe it." He wiped his hand over his face as some loose dark hair drooped over his forehead. He swept it back.

"You've been through a lot," I offered, looking up again. "You only deserve good things."

"I don't know if we deserve good things, but I believe God is granting us one."

He looked directly at me, still holding his tired wife's hand, and continued. "We can't know if what seems bad to us is really good in the bigger picture.

Only God can see it all, and He is good all the time. Sometimes what we see as the absolute worst is Him doing good for us."

I couldn't tell if he was reciting something or really meant what he said, but my heart skipped a beat, and I couldn't help but stare at him. This couple had lost a child—one of the biggest heartbreaks anyone can experience, yet he saw it now as if it had been a "good" thing from God?

Grant saw the question on my face and continued. "I'm not saying it wasn't hard. It was the most awful thing we've ever been through. Trevor … our son … was so perfect on the outside. You'd never have known that something was wrong. When he was born, we didn't actually believe what the doctors told us, but …" He sighed. "They were right."

He stared down at Stacy, who still appeared to be sleeping. "His heart wasn't normal." He stopped then and faced down.

My mind reeled, and I wanted to ask more questions and say again how sorry I was, but I couldn't find my voice. I ached for this couple and their pain, but I turned to my charting instead. As I checked the fetal monitor and jotted down the baby's normal heart rate, Stacy stirred. When I looked toward her, she was staring at me with big, round eyes.

"Something doesn't feel right," she said, grimacing and placing her hand just above her pubic bone.

After a few years of experience, a Labour and Delivery nurse knows those words can mean many things. Sometimes it's simply because the pain is so much greater than a woman expected, and she thinks she'll be overcome with its enormity, but after the baby is born, all becomes well again. There are other times, however, when a patient says those words and things, indeed, are not right.

Stacy wasn't supposed to be in pain. She was supposed to be numb. My heart rate increased, and my senses heightened with her words. I checked her vital signs, glanced at the baby's heart rate again, and palpated her uterus. All seemed well.

"I'm going to check how low that baby's head is, and we'll see if it's time to push," I smiled, breathing easier.

She smiled but looked very uncomfortable and restless.

"Stacy," I said as I slipped a glove on for the exam, "what exactly are you feeling?"

"I don't know," she answered. "There's pressure, but something's burning …"

Her scar! I peeled back the covers and saw the trickle of blood.

When I was a newly graduated nurse on the Obstetrical unit, a more experienced nurse told me, "In an emergency, you must retain your composure. Think of a duck." I must've appeared puzzled as she explained. "When you see a duck resting on water, it appears to be sitting calmly, but underneath, those legs are moving like crazy to keep it afloat. That's how you must compose yourself … calm on the outside … even if you're feeling panic on the inside."

"Grant," I said, outwardly calm, "would you pull on the call-light please? It's time to have this baby, and we need some extra hands."

My heart raced as I opened up her IV fluids. Stacy hadn't needed any augmentation for her labour, so her body alone was causing her contractions. They didn't seem to be too close or long. Nothing could be slowed down. I put a wedge under Stacy's hip to keep her from lying directly on her back. By now, Anne and another nurse had come into the room. After calling the doctor, we started pulling Stacy's bed apart to ready it for the birthing position.

Grant sensed my urgency and asked if everything was all right.

"Yes," I answered. "Everything's fine for now, but the baby's ready to be born. This is good." I felt like I was trying to convince myself. I started to silently pray, as I often do when something is worrisome.

Dr. Nelson came bustling in and in his usual, jovial way said, "So guys, baby's coming, huh?"

I didn't hesitate. "Stacy's BP has dropped a bit; she's trickling and feels burning over her scar."

"Hmm," acknowledged the doctor, pulling on his protective gown quickly. "How's the baby?"

"Looks good." I smiled as Grant looked directly at me. He looked worried, and I wanted him to feel encouraged.

Dr. Nelson examined Stacy, and the vacuum extractor was placed on the baby's head to expedite the delivery. Stacy pushed as our most experienced physician pulled. It was only two great pushes and the screaming baby girl filled the room with her song. Grant and Stacy both burst into tears of joy as she was placed onto her mother's abdomen.

The placenta came out with some difficulty but appeared to be whole.

Stacy looked pale but grinned from ear to ear. She needed a few stitches, but when those were finished, we put her bed back together and I tucked her and her daughter in with warmed blankets once again.

"How are you doing?" I asked, smiling at her as I felt her uterus and assessed her flow of blood.

"I'm so totally great!" she replied as she held her infant, skin to skin on her chest, with Grant by her side. They both couldn't stop smiling and cooing at the beautiful child they held.

"Good," I said smiling, watching them adore their new baby.

The next time I checked on her, Stacy was trickling a bit too much blood, so I increased the rate of her IV again, which had Oxytocin added, as was our standing order. After the placenta had been delivered, she'd been given other medications as well, to assure she wouldn't bleed too much. Dr. Nelson had left the room a few minutes before, and I now informed him of the excess bleeding.

"She should settle down with all the meds we've given her. Watch her closely and keep me posted if you're concerned, Trish," he told me over the phone before hanging up.

At her next assessment, I noted that Stacy's blood pressure was even lower, and her pulse was high. I assessed her bleeding again and was dismayed to see a large amount between her legs, pooled there in the few minutes since I'd checked her last. My hand immediately went to the top of Stacy's uterus and I was startled to find it had risen high in her abdomen. I pressed down and many large clots, and even more blood, gushed out. No matter how much I massaged, which is the first line of defence with a postpartum hemorrhage, her uterus wouldn't firm up. I kept massaging the boggy organ when Stacy spoke again.

"I don't feel right," she managed weakly as her head drooped to the side.

As Grant stayed by her other side, near the call-bell, I told him to pull it again and immediately positioned the bed into a Trendelenburg position, placing Stacy's head lower than her body.

"Stacy," I commanded as I opened up her IV with one hand while continuing uterine massage with the other, "stay with me."

Stacy tried to open her eyes and nodded slightly, groaning from the discomfort of having her uterus massaged so firmly.

Other nurses came into the room. Dr. Nelson was called immediately and came running. He wanted to assess the uterus himself and took over the massage while I pulled the nursing baby from her mother's chest, bundled her quickly, and handed her to Grant. I ushered him over to the recliner, and he sat with the baby until a nurse from the newborn care area took her to the nursery. Her weight, height, and physical assessment, usually done in the room with the parents, would be done there instead so that Grant could stay with his wife.

"Stacy's bleeding a bit too much, Grant," I said calmly, "and we're trying to stop it."

Dr. Nelson started barking orders after examining Stacy more thoroughly.

Grant looked petrified. As everyone hurriedly prepped his wife, I spoke as I worked. I explained that Stacy would have to go to the operating room. I told him that we suspected her old scar had torn, but we couldn't know that unless the doctor took a good look inside and then fixed it that way. All the while another IV had been started, vital signs taken over and over, and the uterus massaged as Stacy was prepared.

What seemed like forever took only minutes, and soon we were running down the hall with the semi-conscious Stacy on the bed. The operating room was ready.

Grant stayed close to Stacy as he and the rest of us ran. Before he left her side, he leaned over and kissed her almost blue-white cheek. She whispered something to him, and he nodded.

The OR staff took over in a frenzy of hurried activity. The door shut, and Grant and I stood outside the room, suddenly quiet. This poor man had watched as we readied his wife for surgery. He'd signed consent forms that, in the urgency of the moment, he probably hadn't read. He trusted us with caring for the love of his life, and although nothing had been done incorrectly, something had gone horribly wrong.

"How come you're not going in there?" asked Grant as we turned away from the operating room to walk back to the delivery suite.

"I help with C-sections in our OR, Grant," I replied and then paused. "But if something gets more serious, like ... if they have no choice and have to do a hysterectomy, the staff from the main operating room have to help with that."

He nodded slowly. "That's what the big word was on the consent, wasn't it?"

"Yes," I breathed, nodding. "It means they'd take her uterus out ... but maybe it won't happen. They can't tell until they put Stacy to sleep and take a good look."

I had seen many postpartum hemorrhages, and in most cases with uterine massage and proper medications, most of the bleeding stopped within minutes. If the bleeding became life-threatening, the uterus was removed, and the patient's bleeding would cease. Usually after that, and with some blood transfusions, the patient would stabilize. On that night, the bleeding didn't stop. A hysterectomy was performed as blood transfused into Stacy as fast as it left her frail body.

Over two hours later, Dr. Nelson came to find me. My shift was ending shortly, and I was giving a report to the day staff when he entered the report room. The Labour unit was bursting at the seams, so my patient load hadn't ended with Stacy's exit to the OR.

"Trish," he said quietly.

I knew by the stricken look on his face that she must have had the hysterectomy, which would be terrible news for the new parents. They had told me they were planning for a larger family.

"Yes, I'll be right there," I answered, quickly determined to finish my report.

"Trish," he repeated a little louder.

I stopped mid-sentence as the feeling of foreboding increased.

"Where's the dad?" he asked.

"Grant?" I whispered.

"Yes," Dr. Nelson answered, his face pale.

"He's in the labour room. I'll come with you," I said.

The usually happy older doctor said nothing else as we walked toward the room that, only a few hours ago, had been a place full of joyous celebration.

"Hi, Grant," I said as we entered. "How's that baby doing?"

He was holding the bundled baby girl in his left arm as his right fingertip stroked her cheek gently.

He looked up at us with a content smile. "She's pretty perfect. How's Stacy?" he asked, moving to stand up.

"Don't get up, Grant," said Dr. Nelson with a serious tone. He pulled up a chair and sat directly in front of the new father. Then he paused and took a breath.

Grant looked first at the doctor and then me. "You guys took so long I thought maybe you'd gone out to eat or something," Grant stammered nervously, trying to make sense of our serious expressions.

All I could think of was how devastated he'd be, finding out the child he held would be the only one he and his wife would achieve together naturally, and my heart hurt for him.

"Grant," started the doctor, clearly emotional. "I'm so sorry but ... I'm going to have to tell you the worst news you'll ever hear, and let me just say how incredibly sorry I am."

A tightness I had never felt before infused itself into my whole body, and I felt blood drain from my face.

"Stacy ..." Dr. Nelson paused and then sighed before continuing. "Well ... she bled too much, and we tried everything modern medicine has, but ..." The doctor choked and his eyes filled with tears.

"But what?" Grant and I blurted out in unison.

Grant looked at me, startled. I looked at Dr. Nelson in disbelief, somehow knowing what was coming next but wanting to stop him. He couldn't mean what he was trying to say. This couldn't be happening!

"Stacy's ... gone," Dr. Nelson finished. "There was just too much bleeding and ... we couldn't save her."

Grant's face went white, and his body sagged in the chair. I grabbed for the baby, who was starting to cry, afraid she'd be dropped. Grant didn't seem to notice but covered his face as soon as she'd been taken from his arms.

I couldn't hold back the tears as I stared into the small, round face of the dark-haired newborn. My tears fell onto the pink blanket she was so perfectly bundled in.

Dr. Nelson spoke to Grant in low tones, trying to explain that in the last few minutes before the baby had been born, and unbeknownst to us, Stacy's scar had torn apart. It wouldn't and couldn't stop bleeding.

As I stood watching, I felt like I was floating in a terrible dream somewhere above ... everything.

Dr. Nelson moved his seat beside Grant, who wept as the doctor's arm engulfed his shoulders. I tried to speak my condolences but couldn't find my voice. I stood holding the baby as my arms started to shake.

I remember Anne came in after that, as well as a few other staff, some to help Grant and some to help me. I don't know who took the baby from my grip, but the next thing I knew, I was in our break room sitting on the couch in a stupor, with my colleagues surrounding me. I said nothing to anyone. I had only tears for my lovely patient, her husband and child, whom I'd had the privilege of caring for, if only for such a short but sweet time.

The nursing unit manager, Katherine, came in shortly after to speak with me about taking some time off for stress-leave and asked me if there was anyone I wanted her to call. I thought of Trent but then remembered that he was gone.

I shook my head and said, "No. I'll be fine. I just have to take a minute and then I'll go see him."

"See who?" she asked. "I can get whoever you want to come here."

"Him," I answered, shaking my head. "Grant."

"The patient's husband?" she queried. "You don't have to do that, Trish. Social Services and a grief counsellor are speaking with him now. They'll take care of everything for him."

"No," I said with a firm tone I didn't feel. "I need to finish this. I have to see if I can help him and his baby and—"

"Trish," interrupted the senior nurse, who had always been such a good mentor to me and was now my boss. "I know what you're saying, but not only is your shift over, this is devastating for you too and ... it's probably best if you don't see or talk to him again."

I looked at her with confusion and then dawning realization.

Katherine looked away. "It's awful for all of us. Mothers just don't die nowadays."

"Apparently they do," I blurted out.

I needed to see Grant, and I felt that although empathetic to my plight, Katherine was in my way. I knew something about legalities, but all my heart and mind could focus on was the heartbroken man in a room down the hall. I stood up and walked to the door of the break room.

"What will you say, Trish? You can't make it better," she called after me.

I paused and turned to look at her. "I don't know ... but at least I can say I'm sorry."

After the doctor had given us the news of Stacy's death, I had left their room too abruptly. As much as Stacy had been my patient, so too were Grant and his daughter. I had to at least give him my condolences.

The Social Services worker was leaving as I reached the room.

"How is he?" I asked stupidly, before thinking. How did I think he'd be?

"He seems to have a strong faith—that's for sure. But he's in shock," the young man said, walking away.

I nodded and softly knocked on the door.

"Come in," I heard from inside.

"Hi, Grant," I said as I entered the now brightly lit room. The sun had come up sometime between the bad news and this moment, and it seemed like, as is with sorrow, time had moved without me.

"Hey," he said as he stood up quickly, almost knocking over the chair he'd been in. He turned to straighten it.

"Don't worry about the chair, Grant. How are you doing?" I stammered lamely. How did I think he'd be doing? His wife had just died during what was supposed to be the most wonderful time of their lives. Why couldn't I think of something intelligent to say?

"I'm ... overwhelmed," he replied, sticking one hand in his pocket and the other through his hair.

Why had I insisted on coming back to talk to this man? I had nothing of use to say to this grieving new father. How could I have possibly been so full of myself as to think I could help him in any way?

"I'm sure you are," I acknowledged as I let go of a breath that I didn't realize I'd been holding. I felt a bit dizzy and took a deeper one, thinking I should sit but knowing I should go. I noted his red-rimmed eyes and started to tear up again. I had to leave.

"I just wanted to tell you how incredibly sorry I am, Grant," I managed to choke out. "I just want you to know that … from the bottom of my heart."

He looked at me for a long while, and I was feeling almost uncomfortable in his stare when he spoke again.

"Thank you," he said slowly as he looked down and then up again. "Thank you for everything you did."

I teared as our eyes met, and underneath the undeniable grief, I saw something else there that alluded me. I shook it off, knowing he was, as the social worker said, in shock.

As I left the room, I thought of what Grant had said earlier—about God being good no matter what we see in our circumstances. I was sure he wasn't seeing any goodness from God that day. I knew I wasn't.

## Chapter Six

"IT'S NOT FOR ME TO SAY ONE WAY OR THE OTHER," I SAID. "I'M NOT MAKING THE decision. How could I? I've never had to make these choices, and neither do I care. Besides," I added, glancing at the paint samples on the coffee table, "I'm no good at this."

I sat across from my mother in my childhood home—an expansive house with every amenity known to man. My mother looked perturbed, as she often did in my presence, and set her teacup down too forcefully on the ornate coffee table. This brought her focus to the cup and she examined it closely before turning her attention back to me.

"That's it!" she huffed, satisfied that her china hadn't cracked. "I don't know what's wrong with you, but clearly you care nothing about your family or being here. I just want one opinion. Is that too much to ask for?"

"Mom ... I don't care about stuff like painting and decorating. You are so much better at that than I am. Go with what you like."

I softened when I saw the hurt come over my mother's face. Her home had always been more important than anything or anyone, in my opinion, and today proved no different. Now I'd be made to feel guilty over my reaction.

It had only been two weeks since the worst shift of my life, and my patience level was at an all-time low. It wasn't a good time to be back home for a day, much less the weekend I had promised. I hadn't told anyone about Stacy, but there had been questions from a few family members and non-medical friends who had heard through an unrelenting grapevine of the tragedy in the hospital I worked at. Keeping with confidentiality rules, I had not admitted to anything.

I scrambled to think of something else to talk about. I needed to turn the tedious subject of paint and blind colours into what I deemed something of validity. "I thought when you invited me out here that maybe we could have a real conversation," I said quietly.

"What do you mean?" questioned my mother with what I thought was brief panic on her features.

"Well," I continued, "I got the feeling on the phone that maybe there was something you needed to talk about. Something important?"

She paused and looked down at her unfractured teacup.

"Mom?" I queried, starting to feel concern. She didn't look up.

I crossed the room to sit beside the woman who had tried her best to raise me right and do right and always appear right. I placed a hand gently on her shoulder. "Tell me, Mom," I coaxed gently now, feeling genuine concern.

Somewhere between my touch and the words I'd said she thought better of something and sat up straighter. She shook my hand off her shoulder and stood up.

"It's fine," she proclaimed too loudly. "This is silly. I'm fine." She paused, clearly searching for what to say next. "I'm worried about the fundraiser at church is all, but I have no reason to be. It will all go well, and the children will be given what they need, and all will be fine."

I had never known my mother, who had been in charge of uncountable church affairs, charities, and fundraisers, to be nervous or worried about any of it. Ever. She was the most organized and "together" person I knew. I was sure that there was something else but decided not to push.

"I don't know why you'd want to be burdened with my worries anyway, Trish. You have enough of your own—working in the city and living alone. I'm still not really in agreement with that."

Knowing she was trying to bait me with the age-old subject of my leaving home, and since she was clearly not going to tell me what was really bothering her, I stood up and gathered our cups.

"Okay," I said quietly and headed for the kitchen.

I placed the teacups carefully in the sink and turned. My mother was staring at me and asked, "Are you all right, Trish?"

Had she really sensed something was off with me, or was this her trying to turn the attention onto me instead of herself? I couldn't tell.

"I'm fine," I answered, echoing what she'd said in the living room.

"Okay," she said softly, knowing, as I did, that neither of us were "fine."

• • •

Later that evening, ignoring the cold, I decided to go for a walk. Our smaller town's quiet streets lent to wonderful strolls when one could really think and breathe in freshness that, in the city, isn't possible. My father, who I favoured in many ways, including our darker colouring, had been working the weekend and had just opened the garage door. He pulled past me as I began my stroll.

"Hey, punk!" he greeted through the window he'd opened when he saw me. "Want company?"

He parked inside the garage as I walked to join him beside his SUV.

"Sure, Dad," I smiled. "I have a bone to pick with you anyway."

"On no!" he said, feigning fear and backing away as if to get back into the vehicle he had just jumped out of.

"My question," I said as we hugged, "is why Mom insisted I come home to visit my parents, and here you are, getting off the hook?"

He laughed, as was always his way, and shrugged as the hug ended.

"Just lucky, I guess," he joked, winking. "But seriously … it couldn't be helped."

He pulled a jacket from the back seat and shrugged it on. Then he grabbed his bag from there and shut the door.

"I'm sorry," I said. "It always falls on you, Dad."

"Not always," he smiled. "Just this weekend, which is rough because I've missed you. Maybe we'll have some time now."

"We better walk fast," I chided and then added, "Tell me about your day, Dad." His work had always intrigued me.

"I'll just drop my bag," he said, leaving it in the garage on the stair instead of throwing it inside. He looked at me. "It can stay there for now."

He told me that one of his partners was away, and the doctor who was supposed to cover call on the long weekend had been called away unexpectedly because her mother was dying. Of course he'd stepped in. He always did and always would.

I watched the man who had inspired me to become a nurse. He was tall and handsome in every way, but maybe that's how all girls see their daddies, if they're around ... or maybe more so if they're not.

Dad had been a little disappointed I hadn't pursued medicine as a physician, but I truly hadn't felt that particular calling. I wanted to be beside the patient's bedside, and when I'd watched the nurses my father worked with, I knew that was exactly where I needed to be.

He locked the garage, and we started our walk down to the street, arm in arm.

"Had some serious stuff today, actually. Bad GI bleed and an MI," said my father. "Flew them both out to your hospital."

My father had been one of the three general practitioners working in our medium-sized rural town since before I was born. When I was small, I thought he was probably as close to God as anyone could be on earth. He had always been so dedicated to the people of our town and, my mother and some would argue, more dedicated to them than to his own family. I, on the other hand, respected his work ethic and could relate to him on a level my mother couldn't.

"Aren't you tired after working all day?" I asked.

"You know me, Trish. Kind of like you. Peas in a pod. Never stop working and energy to spare."

We strolled in comfortable silence.

"You're quieter than I remember you," he observed.

"Oh, not you too!" I exclaimed, smiling. "It hasn't been that long since I've been home."

"No?" He gazed upward, appearing to be thinking deeply while counting on his fingers.

"Stop it," I laughed and then sighed. "I know I don't come home very often, Dad. I'm sorry."

"No, you're not," he said, "so don't lie and say you are."

"Hey! I was taught to apologize with the best of them, so I'm good at it … even if I don't really mean it," I retorted.

My father was quiet while he thought.

He put his arm around my waist, and I put my head on his shoulder as we slowly walked, enjoying each other's presence.

"Were you involved with the patient that died?" he asked softly, breaking the moment.

I stopped short and looked up into his face. Of course he'd know about it—with probably more details than most people knew. He was a senior physician on boards that developed practice standards and things I didn't even know about. The medical grapevine, although confidential, needed to know details of anything with a "bad outcome." Cases, policies, and procedures are reviewed thoroughly in situations like these—for legal reasons as well as learning purposes. I had been to many conferences where cases with the worst outcomes were presented. We, the audience, would ooh and aah over things that were possibly missed or done incorrectly—judging what someone else could have done better to change the outcome. Names were never used, but notes on charts were discussed, so when you heard the details it seemed easy to judge and depersonalize the actions.

Suddenly I felt sick and moved away from my dad to stand facing him. Stacy's case would go there too. Doctors and students would dissect what we—I—had done that night. It was as if my dad had read my mind.

"Did they talk to you yet?" he inquired seriously, with sympathy in his eyes.

"Yes," I answered. "My manager and the Chief of Obstetrics. We all had a debriefing as well, with everyone there."

"What did they say?" he asked.

"Say?" I asked, confused.

"About fault, Trish," he answered, as if I were a bit simple. "Who are they blaming it on?"

I paused. "Well …" I stammered. "No one."

"Oh honey," he said, in obvious disbelief of my naivety. "I'm so glad you've never been involved in the ugly side of medicine before this, but now … you might be." He seemed to be talking more to himself as he continued. "Maybe I should have told you about this before you went into this crazy profession, but I always hoped you'd get an easier job—with small chance of litigation. But no, you had to choose obstetrics—"

"Dad," I said, cutting him off, "what are you talking about?"

He looked at me, thinking. "Oh, honey," he said. "I'm sorry. I'm putting the cart before the horse. I just … want you to be careful. You probably didn't do anything wrong, but—"

I interrupted. "Dad, I didn't do anything wrong!"

I couldn't believe what I was hearing from the father who had always only encouraged me and made me feel like I could do anything I dreamed of.

"I know, I know," he repeated. "I'm just being realistic, Trish, and you need to be too."

I stared at him, not knowing what to say.

He continued as he looked at me. "I know you think you didn't do anything wrong, and you probably didn't, but lawyers are paid to find the things done wrong—sometimes even when there's nothing there, unfortunately."

I shook my head, my mind reliving vignettes of that night again, but now with questions about everything. When the counsellor had talked to me the day after Stacy died, and during the debriefing with the other staff a day later, everyone seemed encouraging and supportive, but my father was right. Of course there would be an intense inquiry. A woman had died. Maybe I'd be sued. Then I thought of Grant.

"Dad," I said. I was about to give him details of the night when he stopped me.

"Listen, sweetheart," he interrupted, holding his hand up to stop me but suddenly sounding sad. "I've been there. This might not be easy for you—what may be coming. I'm just saying be careful who you talk to about any of this. If you're lucky, no action will be taken, but honestly, it's doubtful. A young woman died, Trish. I'm so sorry you were involved. Wrong place, wrong time."

I didn't know why it happened right then, but an overwhelming peace suddenly overcame me. It was the strangest thing. I'd never felt that way before. I thought, fleetingly, that maybe it was what a nervous breakdown felt like just before the crash.

I smiled as my Dad looked at me with new concern. "Dad," I started gently, "I don't know what's going to happen, and maybe it won't be good, but I do know one thing. This may sound strange, but … I know I wasn't in the wrong place. It's an awful thing, and I cry almost every day about that patient, but I have to believe that I was her nurse for a reason. God put me there, and I have to believe something good will come out of this."

I put my hand to my forehead and stepped further away from my dad. I couldn't believe I'd just said that after I'd questioned God over and over ever since that night, as to why He had allowed me to be that couple's nurse.

My dad was quiet for a short while as we slowly walked back toward their home.

"I know one thing as well, Trish," he finally said, breaking the silence. "I love you—no matter what—and when you need me, I'm here for you, sweetheart. Not everything we taught you was right, Trish." He suddenly looked more tired than I'd ever seen him.

"Dad," I said, "you did a great job raising me. No parent is perfect, but they do the best they can. You've always been great."

I stopped to hug him before my father looked at me and very seriously said, "Then why can't you see that your mom did the best she could too? After all, she was there much more than I was."

I turned my face down and said, "Maybe that was the problem."

"Hey," my dad replied, raising my chin so I had to really see him. "She loves you, honey, and she's so proud of you."

"Yeah, well," I said, doubtfully, "you haven't told her about this, have you?"

My dad looked disappointed. "You know this is all confidential, Trish. Of course I haven't told her."

"I'm sorry, Dad," I apologized, knowing he was telling me the truth and I shouldn't even have asked. "What's going on with her anyway? I feel like there's something she's hiding from me."

I felt him straighten a little, but just as quickly he looked at me with his usual reassuring smile and said, "She's fine."

"Really?" I questioned, looking up at the man I adored. "She said the same thing, but somehow I can't help but think there's something going on."

"Honey, she's fine," he said with a reassuring smile. He clearly was avid to change the subject when he continued with, "Why don't we go inside and see if any WWE is on TV?"

My dad had always loved watching wrestling, and he had taught me to like it, after he'd explained the backgrounds of some of the players. I don't know if it was because I spent that time with him or that I really believed him when he told me it was the "best sport on earth," but some of my best memories with my dad included the wrestlers of the WWE.

I agreed as we walked into the warm house. I wanted to believe him about this too—that nothing was wrong with my mom. I did. But you know that still, small voice of God? That voice was speaking loudly.

# *Chapter Seven*

I MET TRENT AND HIS GIRLFRIEND, MELISSA, FOR COFFEE THE NEXT DAY BEFORE I left for home. It was so good to see him, and it was nice to reacquaint with Melissa. She was a few years younger than Trent and me, but we'd met in youth group at our church when we were teens. We'd never hung out together because, in your teens, a year makes a huge difference in who you spend time with. As adults, however, age doesn't matter, and I couldn't help but like her. She seemed a perfect fit for Trent. Where he was often calm and quiet, she was high-spirited and chatty.

I sat across from them and watched them interact as we visited. They clearly adored each other, and although I felt slightly nauseated (as someone who has no one does in the presence of people in love), I also felt an element of peace about Trent leaving me behind. He was in love and was enjoying his new place of work, and that sincerely made me glad. I felt genuinely happy for him.

Time flew as we talked and drank our cappuccinos. I got to know Melissa better because she was more than glad to do her part in the conversation. I was more content to listen, which is not usually like me, and Trent must've picked up on that.

"You know," he said as we stood in the entrance of the restaurant before leaving, "we could use a good obstetrical nurse here too. I'm sure I could talk to the management to hire you if you'd like."

"Are you joking?" I asked, not laughing. "You know more than anyone how I couldn't wait to get out of here."

"Listen," Trent said, grabbing my arm. "Before Mel gets back from the restroom, tell me what's up with you."

I hadn't told him about Stacy. I wanted to—him being my best friend and all—but when I'd picked up the phone numerous times during the past weeks, I'd always hung up again. He was with someone else. It seemed weird, somehow, to call a guy who was clearly in love and going on with his life. I didn't want to come between that, even if it was innocent enough.

"I'm fine" was clearly becoming my "go-to" answer, and I went with it.

"Oh?" said Trent, skeptically. "You must have me mixed up with someone who doesn't know you at all. Out with it." He looked at my pained expression and suddenly, with realization, a look of sadness clouded his features. "You were her nurse," he stated softly.

Of course he'd heard of the maternal death in our hospital too. News of some deaths get around quickly enough, but a rare death, such as Stacy's, even faster.

My eyes filled with tears, and I nodded. Trent immediately pulled me to one side and enveloped me in a tight embrace as I cried into his shoulder. I'd cried since that fateful day, but I wished then that I had cried much more, because maybe the deluge would've been lessened.

Minutes later, Melissa came up behind me. "Oh no!" she crooned with genuine concern. "What's wrong, Trish? Are you okay? What happened?"

I pulled away from Trent and brushed away my tears. He rescued me and told Melissa that I was a little homesick and tired from working so much. It was nothing that serious and she shouldn't worry. Aside from the "homesick" part, none of it was a lie.

I quickly thanked them for meeting me, said goodbye, avoiding their eyes as much as possible, and ran to my blue Rav4 parked just outside.

Only Trent followed me and knocked on the window. When I opened it, he leaned in and insisted, quietly, "Call me tonight and we'll talk."

I nodded and took off.

That night we talked into the wee hours of the morning. He had dealt with death many times. So had I, but this was different. I told him all about it—every detail—without mentioning names. I confided in him how I was struggling with God.

"You know, Trish," he said, "he wasn't wrong."

"What do you mean?" I queried.

"The dad," he said, not knowing he referred to Grant. "God *is* good ... all the time."

"I know we were taught that God is good, Trent, but I can see nothing ... *nothing* good about this—any way you look at it. A man lost his wife, and a little girl lost her mother."

Trent was quiet as he softly replied, "I know, Trish. It's awful. It's okay to feel angry. God has big shoulders. He can handle it, and so can I."

At the end of the conversation, I felt compelled to apologize for the crying I'd done in the restaurant, and we remembered a time, years before, when I had first cried in front of Trent. He, normally thoughtful and serious, had laughed and said, "You were right. This is not your best look." I had punched him in the arm then and we had laughed together.

Tonight, as our conversation ended, I appreciated Trent even more for his long-standing and supportive friendship.

# Chapter Eight

IT HAD BEEN OVER THREE MONTHS, AND KYLIE STILL HADN'T HAD ONE GOOD night of sleep. Neither had Grant, and he was becoming exhausted. Not only did Kylie's fretful nights awaken him, but the ongoing dream did as well. It had awoken him again tonight. In it, Stacy called out to him, reminding him of the promise he'd made before she died.

Grant closed his eyes and listened for Kylie's cry. Now as he listened to the silence, he knew he should be relieved, but instead, loneliness gripped him. His eyes welled with tears as he thought of Stacy. He had loved her fiercely and with a love that had been fought for and earned through prayer and hard work. So many times since her death Grant had asked the Lord "Why?" Why had it all happened?

He'd loved his wife so much, through everything, but now he was alone. He knew God was with him, but it wasn't the same as having another, tangible, real, warm ... person ... the person he loved. Grant shook his head. He had to get his act together. He knew that. If it hadn't been for his mother and people from his church helping, he was sure he would have completely fallen apart by now. He could see God's hand in all the care he'd received, but still he asked ... why?

• • •

Grant had taken some time off after Stacy's death, but being the owner of the company, he needed to return to work on a regular basis.

His mother, Sandy, was playing with Kylie one day. "Grant," she said, "we'll be fine. You'll go to work, and I'll babysit, and it'll be okay."

Grant took a sip of his coffee, looking haggard. At thirty-three years of age and sitting in his mother's house, he wished he were young again when his problems were so much smaller.

After their son, Trevor, had died Grant didn't think there could be a greater sadness, but he'd woken up in the dead of night many times over the last few weeks wishing God had taken him instead of his sweet wife. He knew Stacy would've been much more capable of caring for Kylie. She had been good at many things. At least now he knew how to make a bottle of formula for his daughter and change her diapers, but that was about it.

"Thanks, Mom," Grant nodded. "I appreciate it. Kylie likes you more anyway."

"Oh Grant, that's not true," replied Sandy. She sat across from him in an over-stuffed chair and turned her attention to the baby girl in her arms. "Is it Kylie? You love your daddy very much, don't you?" The little girl stared at her grandma with bright blue eyes. "I'll even take her some nights, Grant, when you need more sleep," Sandy offered.

"You've already done so much for us, Mom. I know it's time I climb out of the funk I've been in and carry on. I have to get organized, but it's all so overwhelming. Stacy would've been so much better at this. I'm not … at all." He paused.

"Oh honey," assuaged Sandy, "be patient with yourself. You haven't been a parent before. It's tough work and—"

"I'm alone," finished Grant, his shoulders sagging.

"Well, not completely alone," said Sandy, "but you are a single parent, yes, and that's not easy."

Grant saw the sadness in his mom's eyes and felt a twinge of guilt. Sandy had been widowed at a young age, leaving her with two young boys by the age of twenty-eight. If anyone could understand how Grant felt, it was her.

"How did you do it, Mom?" Grant asked again. He had asked her that more times than they both could count in the last weeks and months.

"Honey," Sandy sighed, standing up with Kylie and speaking in no uncertain terms, "it's time for that question to stop."

Grant looked up from swirling the coffee around in his cup.

"My boy, you're stronger than you think. I've asked myself over and over why God would even allow such a thing, but I don't have an answer. Why would He take Kylie's precious momma away? Why would He take your dad away? It all makes no sense, but ... it happened ... and I know, like me, you must go on. You will forever grieve for her, Grant. I will grieve for her and so will Kylie someday. That will never stop. I still think of your father, even wondering how things would be different if he were still here, but God gives me the strength to go on."

Sandy took a deep breath, put Kylie in her baby chair, crossed the room, and sat down next to him. She put a hand gently on his shoulder. "You can do this. You have a beautiful daughter who is depending on you in every way. I've seen how you love her deeply, but right now you're scared. Kylie can sense that. You must tell yourself you can do this because ... you can!"

Grant's eyes teared up as he pushed the hair that had fallen over his forehead back. "I don't know if I can, Mom."

Sandy sighed again as she straightened next to him. She ached for her hurting son but had to forge ahead.

"You can, Grant. You're not one to give up. I'm going to pray for you and Kylie and then you'll go to your new home and pray some more. Tomorrow, when you get up, you'll bring Kylie here and go to work. This is your life, and you're going to live it."

Sandy's hand didn't leave Grant's shoulder as she prayed for him. She prayed for strength, for peace, for sleep, and that they would praise God even through the storm they were in.

Grant was quiet as he left with Kylie, but he thanked his mom for taking so much of the responsibility for her, and himself, over the last weeks. Her faith in her Saviour had always been unfailing, and although she'd assured Grant that she often hadn't been strong, he had rarely seen that. Sandy had always taught him and his brother that God was their very good Father, *all the time*. Although he didn't feel strong, he knew he had to be. He couldn't let his mom or Kylie down.

When he got home, he bathed the little girl who looked so much like her mother and gave her the bottle she became impatient for. As she fell asleep in his arms, he gazed at her, taking in her dark hair. She had blue eyes like him as well, but her facial features were all Stacy's.

Not knowing if she could hear him, he looked up at the ceiling and whispered, "Stace ... she's so beautiful. You'd just love this little girl. I promise ... I won't let her down."

Then, as he gently placed her in her crib, Grant prayed. He hadn't prayed in a while but felt compelled. "Please help me, God. Help me be strong and not to let her down."

Sometimes God's grace shows up in very small things. When Grant next heard the squeal of his baby girl, the clock said 6:00 a.m. They both had slept for seven hours straight, which, as we know, is golden when you're a new parent. For the first time in over three months, Grant thanked God for being good, at least in this small thing.

# Chapter Nine

SOMEHOW, I ALWAYS THOUGHT I'D BE FIRST TO GET MARRIED, BUT WHEN TRENT called, out of breath with excitement, I knew I was wrong. I had just lay down on my very old brown couch, clipped my hair high on my head, and turned on the television. There was a movie I'd been wanting to watch and decided tonight was the night. My big orange bowl of buttered popcorn was beside me on a TV table, and I had just poured a can of Diet Pepsi over ice. I could hear the sound of carbonated bubbles popping as the phone rang.

"When's the date and how'd you propose?" I queried after Trent's breathless "hello."

"Oh c'mon!" he laughed. "How'd you know?"

"You forget … I know you too, bud," I answered, smiling. He'd been calling more frequently recently, asking a lot of questions about what "girls" liked and other suspicious sounding questions, so it didn't take an Einstein to figure it out.

"Well …" He paused, knowing it would be killing me to wait for details I had to know.

"Well what, Trent? Out with it!" I laughed, sitting up straight and almost knocking the whole bowl of popcorn onto the rug, instead of just the few puffs that fell. I picked them up as he laughed.

"I had the ring on me, but she knew because she said *yes* before I could even get the whole question out," answered Trent. "That's Melissa."

I laughed on and off as he set the stage of their special night. He again reminded me how much he thought all the women in his life seemed to be of the impatient breed. I couldn't dispute that because I knew it was so true of me.

"July wedding, Trish, and you better be ready to stand up for me," stated Trent. "I can't do it without you."

"I wouldn't miss it, Trent. Ever. But it's only three months away. That's fast!"

"Yeah, well, maybe impatience plays a part here too, but ... when you know, you know." I could hear Trent grinning over the phone.

"Tell Melissa if she needs anything to please call me. I'd really like to help," I said with genuine sincerity. If I couldn't plan my own wedding, the thought of helping someone else seemed like it would be fun.

"I will, Trish," promised Trent, "but I have a feeling the whole thing's already planned out."

I giggled. "I wouldn't be surprised. She must be so excited."

"That's an understatement," laughed Trent. He sighed. "I'm so pumped, Trish."

I smiled and lay back on my couch, imagining being there with Trent. He sounded so together in every way. I couldn't help but feel a bit envious of all he had as I listened to him tell me about their plans.

• • •

Three months later, the day broke with the sun shining and the weather forecast promising it to continue. The bit of rain that happened overnight had passed and just a few puddles remained with the glimmering sun shining off of them.

"Are you sure you're ready for this?" I smiled, laughing at Trent, who was struggling with his tie. "Forget how to tie a tie, church boy?"

"Ha ha," he replied, looking in the mirror and continuing to try to figure out the tie. "Droll. Very droll. If they let me wear a stethoscope instead, I wouldn't have this problem."

"How about this dress?" I said, adjusting something at my waist that wasn't quite comfortable. "Give me scrubs any day."

The dress wasn't horrible, as attendant's dresses often have the reputation to be, but it was form-fitting and much more snug than I was used to.

Trent, now seriously concentrating on getting his tie just right, replied softly, "Can't get married in scrubs I guess."

We were in one of the small rooms at the back of the church. Melissa and her bridesmaids would be in one of the others. These were spaces that had been appointed as "get ready" rooms where people would prepare themselves before entering the main part of the church. They were used for many things, even prayer, but mostly to prepare for things like Christmas plays, baptisms, and, like today, weddings.

"Here," I laughed, walking closer to him. "Let me help."

"No. I got this. Just nervous I think," he continued, starting over with his tie.

"Where are the guys who are supposed to be helping you?" I asked, looking at the small wall clock and seeing that the wedding was minutes away.

"They went to get something," he said. "Besides, you're my best man. You're supposed to help me the most."

"Thanks a lot," I said, rolling my eyes.

"Okay ... best woman?" he said, glancing my way. "Melissa worded it right in the bulletin. I don't know what your title is."

I laughed at him. "I know what you meant." I paused. "And, for the record, I offered to help."

"Yes, you did," he said slowly, looping the tie around itself. "But ... I think I've got it now."

I smiled as I watched him. I would miss my best friend, but over the last few months I'd grown so fond of Melissa, I didn't mind much anymore.

She was so welcoming and gracious in letting me help with some of the plans that I couldn't help but love her. I hadn't realized how many details went into a wedding celebration, but Melissa seemed to forget nothing, and when issues came up, she rolled with the punches.

She had chosen a beautiful colour theme of off-white, muted pinks, and deep burgundies. Her enthusiasm was contagious, but mostly I loved when she talked about Trent. I could see how much she loved him, and that meant so much to me. Maybe it wasn't my place, but I felt I was leaving my best friend in great hands.

Trent turned from the mirror and walked toward me with the half smile that was his trademark. He grabbed me in a quick hug.

"Don't make me cry," I warned, stepping away. "My mascara will run."

"Ha!" he laughed, rolling his eyes. "Like I haven't seen that before."

"I don't care about you," I said as I pushed past him and approached the mirror. "It's everyone else who doesn't need to witness it."

The signal to start was a knock on the door, and Trent's groomsmen laughingly stumbled into the room.

"Not a good sign," I whispered to Trent.

Trent shook his head, rolled his eyes, and smiled again.

Trent's brother and his friend started the procession. I walked up the aisle after the two men and before Trent. The bride's attendants came after.

When the music changed, announcing her entrance, the congregation stood, and all eyes were on Melissa as she strode slowly down the aisle on the arm of her father. She seemed to glow with the brightest smile possible on her face.

I glanced at my childhood friend, standing straight and tall beside me. I had never seen him smile so brightly as he stared at his bride. I suddenly felt overwhelmed with joy for them, and by the end of the ceremony, no matter how much self-talk I'd silently done, everyone in the congregation had seen me cry.

• • •

The reception was held in a large outdoor tent. The sound of laughter from the crowd echoed across the ranch where Melissa had lived her whole life. The meal was amazing, but I wasn't very hungry. As is often tradition, the head table was set up on a platform so that the bride and groom could be seen by everyone, and they, in turn, were able to view their guests more clearly as well. Feeling like I'm being watched while I'm eating is not my favourite thing. I feel rather anorexic when on display.

I was continuing to play with the food on my plate when the toasts started. Trent didn't insist I do a toast, as is tradition for the "best man" to do, which was a relief, since I knew it would only end with me crying and embarrassing myself in front of a room full of mostly strangers. Besides, I'd done that like a champion already during the ceremony. Trent's brother, Matthew, was the biggest comedian in their family, and his toast to Trent, as well as his welcoming of Melissa into their family, had everyone rolling.

When he came back to sit beside me, I smiled and said, "Thanks. I needed that."

"Not having fun?" he chided.

"No! It's not that!" I replied. "Yours is the only toast where I didn't have to fight tears while I was listening to it. The others are so … heartfelt, shall we say." I took a big breath. "Not that there's anything wrong with that," I quickly added, hearing how pathetic I sounded.

"And I could have said so much more," he said dryly with a sparkle in his eye.

"I'm sure," I laughed and nodded.

By the end of the evening, my cheeks hurt from smiling, not only because of what seemed like hours of picture-taking, but from meeting and greeting so many people, some of whom I hadn't seen for years, and many I'd never met before. Although I greeted many, I couldn't have possibly mingled with all of Melissa's family and friends.

"Trent," I said, getting his attention after he'd broken away from the small group he and Melissa were talking to. "I think I'll go if that's okay."

The band played on, so we had to talk loudly to hear each other.

"Already?" he asked, looking at his watch and then glancing back to me. "Oh!" he added, realizing time had flown.

"Yeah," I laughed. "It's late. I better go. Too many nights awake are catching up with me."

"I get it," he nodded, and I knew he did.

"Oh no you don't." Melissa had joined us and now grabbed my arm. "You can't go yet, Trish. I need you to meet one more person. Please?"

Of course I couldn't turn down the bride, so I laughingly agreed.

She looked around. "He just said goodbye. He must be outside already," she laughed, leading me outside the tent. She turned her face from mine and yelled, "Hey! Wait!"

She started pulling me quickly toward the back of a man reaching to open the door of what I assumed was his white Silverado. He slowly turned toward us, but his face was still in darkness due to the late hour.

As we walked closer, Melissa kept talking to him. "What's your hurry, man? You haven't met Trent's friend. Grant! I want you to meet Trish."

My feet and heart stopped as the man's face became clear. Grant and I stared at each other, both of us recognizing one another and not knowing what to say.

He regained his composure more quickly than I and said, with surprise in his tone, "It's you, right? From the hospital?"

"It's you," I managed back in a whisper, nodding.

He came toward us and stopped when he reached a comfortable distance in front of us.

"I thought that might be you in the line up," he smiled.

He held out his hand to shake mine. It was warm and strong, and when he let go, I felt sorry he had.

"You know each other?" asked Melissa in surprise.

"Well…" we said at the same time and smiled.

What could I say in a moment like this? I met him when his wife died? I suddenly felt very uncomfortable and thought I might panic, but Grant took over and simply said, "Mel, we met when Kylie was born."

He looked at me with a kind smile that immediately made me feel strangely at ease.

"Oh!" said Melissa, excitedly, clearly unaware of all the circumstances of our first meeting. "I thought you didn't know each other, and I wanted you to meet. Trish, Grant's my cousin. He's a great guy, and I guess you know he's got a daughter," Melissa continued, her voice fading into the background.

Grant and I just stared at each other while Melissa kept chatting. I knew I wasn't concentrating on what she was saying, and I doubted Grant had been either when he interrupted, ignoring his cousin.

"How've you been?" he asked me with concern in his voice.

"Good," I replied and then asked, with the same concern, "How have you been?"

"Well, I won't lie. It's been hard," he answered, looking down at his feet.

"I'm sure," I managed, my heart aching as I watched him. I wanted to comfort him in some way, as I had wanted to on that horrific night.

When he raised his head he was smiling, which caught me off guard. "But God has been really good to me and Kylie. She's really cute."

I couldn't help but let out a relieved laugh. "I'm sure she is. Is she here?"

He paused then, with a small smirk on his face, and said, "No. It's pretty late for a baby."

"Of course," I said, feeling stupid.

He watched me for a second and added, "She was here, but she went back to the city with my mom earlier."

"Pics?" I managed, more brightly, trying to save face.

"Yes!" he exclaimed, scrambling for the phone in the pocket of his suit jacket.

As he scrolled to find pictures, I looked around and realized Melissa had left us.

"Here," he said, stepping closer to me and holding the phone so I could see the pictures of a most adorable baby girl.

"She looks like Stacy," I breathed and felt him straighten. I thought I'd done something wrong, and my eyes flew to his face. "I'm sorry."

"No," he said as he looked into my eyes. "Don't be sorry. I just can't believe you remembered her name."

"Of course I remember her," I said, looking down again at his phone. "How could I ever forget her?" Tears filled my eyes as I added, "Kylie looks like her."

I tried to step away, suddenly uncomfortable again.

"Don't," he said quietly, touching my arm so I wouldn't leave. "I think you've got me wrong. I just ... I'm just really moved that you remember us."

I turned toward him, trying so hard not to cry but not succeeding. I looked up at him anyway and simply nodded.

He scrolled through a few more pictures of Kylie, some of her alone and some with a woman I didn't recognize.

"That's my mom," explained Grant as he proudly showed off his daughter with her smiling grandmother. He talked about where a few of the pictures had been taken and how she'd grown and how much he reminded her of Stacy too. "Now she at least sleeps through the whole night, so I usually keep her at home with me. When I go to work, my mom has her most of the time. Thank God for moms."

I nodded, not sure I'd agree with him but trying nonetheless. When I had first seen him tonight, the tragedy had passed over me again in vivid memory, but he seemed so relaxed and at peace as he chatted about his daughter that I relaxed as well.

"You seem happy," I blurted out, immediately sorry I'd said it. Why did I seem to have trouble speaking intelligently around this man?

He didn't seem to notice but smiled and said, "I am happy, Trish."

I felt foolish as I stammered on, but I couldn't stop myself. "It's just … it hasn't been that long."

"True," he agreed and nodded. "It seems like yesterday sometimes." He paused, pushed his hair over his forehead and looked deeply at me again, as if he saw into my soul. "I guess I've just accepted what's happened and, hey," he shrugged, "I've gotta carry on for Kylie."

"Yes … of course," I agreed, nodding. "Good for you. You're obviously strong."

"Not me," he grinned, shaking his head. "God … and my mom. They've both helped a lot."

I just nodded. He wasn't putting on an act of bravado. He really meant it.

We chatted more and he asked about my job. I felt so at ease with him and soon I even laughed a little at his humour.

"Well," I finally said, "I better get going. I think I was going to leave an hour ago."

"Yeah, me too," he agreed. "I haven't stayed out this late for a really long time."

"Baby cramping your style?" I hinted, not sure if he'd find it all right but chancing it.

"Absolutely," he laughed, and I felt relief.

As much as I knew I should leave, I didn't want to, but it was time.

"Maybe I'll … see you again sometime," I ended as I smiled and turned to walk away.

He paused, as if thinking. "I hope so, Trish."

I turned back to look at him and we both nodded as he got into his truck. I walked toward my Rav and waved as he drove away. I thought of going to say one last goodbye to Trent but then thought better of it. It had been a good day, but it was over.

## Chapter Ten

AFTER THE EXCITEMENT OF THE WEDDING AND THE LATE HOUR, I WAS exhausted. I stayed at my parents' home that night instead of making the two-hour trek back home to the city. With the little sleep I encountered, however, I wished I'd just gone back. I hadn't dreamt about her for a while, but that night Stacy was forefront in my dreams. I fell into a restless sleep just before dawn and awoke to the smell of coffee and something baking as the sun peeked through the blind.

My mother was bent over the oven, pulling something fragrantly sweet from it, when I came down the stairs. She closed the door and turned off the oven as I sat at the kitchen island across from her.

"Good morning, sleepyhead," she smiled in greeting.

"Morning, Mom," I managed with a yawn.

"You were busy yesterday. You must have been tired. I'm sorry if I woke you. Did you sleep well?" she asked.

I yawned again and stretched, thinking about my answer. Years ago after I'd first moved away, she'd been compelled to change the mattress in my childhood room. I had told her my new one in the city was much more comfortable and I didn't sleep well here anymore. The new mattress was too firm for my liking, but I wasn't going to tell her that after her good intentions.

"I'm good," I said, smiling at her. "What did you think of the wedding?"

"It was beautiful, of course," answered my mother. "I wasn't sure about being outside in that tent, but they were fortunate the weather was so kind. The mosquitoes weren't as bad as I thought they'd be either, which was lovely." She was pouring icing sugar into a bowl and paused. "You certainly looked beautiful, Trish." She paused again. "I wanted to tell you that at the wedding, but you were so busy with all your friends I couldn't get a moment of your attention."

Such a seemingly nice compliment and then ... that. Guilt with breakfast.

"I'm sorry, Mom. I was a little busy standing up for Trent and all," I quietly replied. I was still feeling tired and didn't need any drama.

"Yes," my mother continued. "What did they call you in the bulletin? A groomsman? Seems strange to me. Why can't the women have women stand up for them and men have men? It's so confusing now."

I couldn't help but laugh. "Mom, it's important to have your closest people stand up for you at your wedding, whether they're male or female. I've been Trent's best friend since we were babies. Of course he asked me," I said.

I stood up and poured coffee for myself from the maker on the counter before returning to my seat. She stirred milk into the small bowl of icing sugar and then added some vanilla flavouring. A small amount of melted butter went in too before she started mixing the icing for the cinnamon buns she'd baked.

"And," I added, "I was a grooms-woman. Not a groomsman. I know I don't have much up here"—I gestured to my rather unimpressive breasts—"but I'm still a woman."

For some reason I wasn't as easily irked by her off-handed comments this morning, and I laughed at my own remark.

"You're not as funny as you think you are," she said, but she smiled just a little while shaking her head. "So much has changed. But I was serious when I said you looked pretty yesterday. You did."

"Thanks, Mom," I said, knowing that she was trying.

"What time did you and Dad come home?" I asked.

"Between eight and nine sometime," she replied. "You know me—not a late-nighter—and your father needed to go back to the hospital to see someone who wasn't doing well, anyway. You know ... the usual."

I picked up on a sad tone in her voice and suddenly felt sorry for her. She had always seemed unscathed by my father's absence, but had something changed? I didn't know if it was just in the tone of her voice or the way her shoulders seemed to droop a little this morning, but I had the same feeling I'd had when I was home last.

"Are you okay, Mom?" I asked quietly, feeling genuine concern.

She straightened up and immediately answered, "Of course. Why?"

"Nothing," I paused. My mother and I had been so far from each other emotionally for so long, and I couldn't remember another time I'd actually felt sorry for her. At this moment, however, that feeling was profound, and I didn't know why.

As I sat by the large counter island across from her, she kept her eyes down, concentrating on sprinkling even more icing sugar into the bowl of frosting. "Mom," I said, now determined to have a real talk with real results, "something is bothering you. I know it. I want to help. Really, I do."

She stirred, much more furiously than I thought icing deserved, but she finally looked up with tears in her eyes. She left the spoon in the bowl and placed both hands flat on the counter. Her shoulders slumped again. This was not like my mother.

"I need to tell you something, but I don't know how," she whispered.

"Okay, Mom," I said, feeling very ill at ease.

I had never seen my mother falter. Ever. Even as a child, teen, or adult—no faltering. Sometimes I thought she'd been born without emotions, but I'd asked my dad, the respected physician, and he told me it was unlikely. Then he'd laughed. When I was a kid and fell down, she was there for me, but not often with sympathy; rather, she'd say, "Get up. It's not that bad." Many times I felt her embarrassment was more important than my suffering. Being the klutzy person I was, and am, she was embarrassed … a lot. She was a "stiff upper lip" parent, and sometimes I wondered if her roots came from British royalty. She would've made a perfect queen—always demure, always "together," always stable, and never emotional. Almost cold.

I didn't know how my parents fit together at all. My father was full of feelings and life and fun—at least, that's what I saw, but what does a kid really know about their parents' relationship?

Now my mother's watery eyes gave me great pause, and for a fleeting moment I thought of walking away, but my curiosity got the better of me and I pursued the conversation.

"You can tell me anything," I quietly said in my "nurse" voice, placing my hand over hers. She pulled away, picked up the spoon, and started stirring again. I had just wondered if it was possible to over-stir icing when she stopped and took a deep breath.

"I was going to wait until later, when your father comes home, but I suppose you'll want to leave before then, so I might as well tell you," she said quickly with a nod of decisiveness.

Instead of continuing, however, she began to ice the fresh buns.

I tried to wait but the child in me couldn't stand it any longer. After a few seconds, I blurted, "Are you and Dad getting a divorce?" There! I'd asked it. All these years I'd wondered how they could be together and couldn't see any reason why my wonderful father had chosen to stay with my stern mother. Now, if they were breaking apart, my world, perhaps, would make more sense.

"No!" exclaimed my mother, clearly chagrined that I would jump to that conclusion. "No, we're not divorcing, separating, or anything. We are perfectly fine, young lady. That is not what this is about."

"Oh," I said. My state of confusion was overwhelming. What could my mother possibly need to tell me that would be more serious to her than that?

She sighed and kept sighing as she finished icing the cinnamon buns, making sure all of it was dispersed evenly on each. She then rinsed and dried her hands as I watched and waited. She walked to the china cabinet, which was full of … just that. It was expensive bone china that, she once told me, had been crafted in England centuries before. I dropped a piece once as a child. I'd tripped with it when I was helping to set the table. We rarely used the sacred china, but someone of importance must've been coming for a meal. Although the plate had been unscathed, I'd been sent to my room to think about what I'd done as my father consoled my mother. I had never again been asked to set the table if the china was involved. That may have seemed like a punishment … to her.

She pulled an unopened envelope from the drawer. I saw the envelope shake slightly before she turned to sit at the kitchen table.

"Come and sit here, Trish." She motioned to the chair across the table from hers.

"Okay," I replied tentatively. "I have to say, you're being really mysterious, Mom. You're scaring me a little."

My mother looked at me with a soft, sad expression that I'd never seen before. Now my eyes teared. Why, when I was raised by such a stoic and almost stern woman, did I have to turn out to be such an emotional wreck?

"I know I don't say this often, but I want you to know that I love you, Trish, with my whole heart."

I stared blankly at her, my heart beating loud and fast in my chest. I suddenly felt that I knew what was coming next and, again, I couldn't wait.

"You're dying," I blurted out, my eyes spilling over.

My mother's brow furrowed with a familiar look of frustration as she gazed in my direction.

"Oh for goodness' sake, Trish. I'm not dying!" she exclaimed. "If you would just listen for a change instead of jumping to conclusions, I may have a chance to tell you. Quit being so dramatic."

There she was! The mom I recognized. Suddenly I felt more comfortable in this uncomfortable conversation, but it didn't last long.

Her demeanour changed again, almost immediately, as she said softly, "I'm going to tell you something about me that I've told very few people. It will come as a shock I think, but I need to tell you because I'm not strong enough to carry on with this, but I think you will be."

I felt so confused that I lost all empathy and, suddenly, just wanted her to spit it out.

"Okay, just tell me," I blurted out a bit defensively, but I quickly softened again as I looked at her sad expression.

"All right, I will," she said, taking another deep breath. She placed a hand over the envelope and pushed it toward me. "Years ago, I had a baby I gave up for adoption, and the information about her is in there."

I blinked. And blinked. Up until that time, there hadn't been many times in my life when I'd felt lost for words. My mother must've been getting worried because this time she grabbed my hand.

"Wh ... at?" I finally stammered.

She talked quickly in response. "I know this is shocking, Trish, but it feels good to have said it. I've been battling with this for a while—really my whole life, if truth be told—but it's time," she sped up as she spoke. "She tried to contact me years ago, but I just couldn't respond, and then I tried but she hasn't communicated back, so I hired a private investigator who apparently found her, but I haven't had the strength to open the envelope. It's been quite a while, and I just thought you are always so strong … and maybe you could open it and, I don't know, correspond with her and find out—"

"Stop!" I held up my hand to stop her mid run-on-sentence. "Mom! Please stop!"

We stared at each other, our own heavy breathing the only thing audible in the room. I had so many questions, and I needed some answers, but I didn't know if either of us was ready for all of it. I didn't think I was.

I stood up abruptly and said, "I have to shower. I need a moment, Mom."

She looked hurt but nodded.

I ran up the stairs in shock and hopped into the shower. As the warm water poured over me, so many questions bombarded my mind. Did my dad know? Did Mom's parents know? Maybe she'd been like Stephanie— the patient who'd come in and delivered a baby all by herself and never told anyone. What other secrets hadn't she told me? Who was the father? Who was this person—this sister I'd never known about? Where did she live? Was she normal? What was normal anyway, besides a setting on your dryer?

I shook my head to clear my rambling thoughts. My mind reeled in every direction, some of it making sense and some thoughts having no sense to them. By the time my lengthy shower was over, I had a weak grip on myself and decided, after finishing all my ablutions, to go back downstairs and continue this important conversation with my mother—a woman I suddenly felt I didn't know at all.

# Chapter Eleven

SANDY SMILED INTO KYLIE'S FOOD-COVERED FACE AS SHE FED ANOTHER spoonful of baby cereal into her mouth.

"You like that stuff, don't you?" she spoke in a higher voice, as most do to small children.

Kylie giggled and spat out some of the cereal, indicating she'd had enough.

"Hey," Grant greeted both as he entered the kitchen.

Sandy ignored Grant and spoke again to Kylie. "There's your daddy. He was partying yesterday and had a late, late night with a long drive home, sweetie. Just like we did, but way earlier." She laughed.

Grant smiled, coming over to Kylie and rubbing her hair with his hand. "And Daddy's thankful to Grandma for taking care of Kylie at the wedding and afterwards."

Sandy glanced at Grant. "Not like you to be out that long, but I was glad I took my own car."

Grant didn't reply but went to the cupboard to look at the breakfast choices.

"Not that I'm complaining, sweetheart. I'm glad you enjoyed yourself and stayed out to have some fun for a change. I'm assuming you had fun?" she hinted.

Grant shrugged. "Yeah, it was okay. Saw a lot of people I hadn't seen for a while. It was good. Nice wedding."

Sandy sighed. "It was beautiful, wasn't it? Melissa couldn't have been more radiant." She paused before adding, "I wish Joe could've come."

Grant stopped and turned to look at her. "I'm sorry, Mom, but I'm kinda glad he couldn't," he said quietly.

"I thought we'd dealt with this, Grant. It's over," she replied.

"He wanted me to sue everybody, Mom," he said, angrily. "He didn't know anything about it, and all he could think of was 'Where's the money?' Joe's crazy."

"But when you explained that everyone did everything they could to save Stacy, honey, he dropped it," she said, surprised that his reaction was still that strong toward his brother. She thought this was behind them. "Let's not ruin a nice morning by hashing out things that are over. Okay?"

Grant turned back to stare at the boxes of cereal.

"I think that man Melissa married seemed really nice too," continued Sandy, hoping her son would focus on the wedding they'd been talking about.

Grant was sensitive when it came to his younger brother. Their lives were so different, and he couldn't understand why Joe seemed so aimless. Sandy was sorry she'd mentioned she missed him.

"Trent's a nurse, right? Not a usual job for a man, but I guess it's getting more common," Sandy stated as she started to wipe down Kylie. Sandy stopped and stared at her son, who was still gazing into the cupboard. His expression had changed, and he looked almost ... pleasant. She smiled. That was her Grant. He blew hot and cold, just like her.

"Yeah, he's a nurse," he answered, glancing at his mom.

"Would you like me to make you eggs or something, or is toast and cereal all right?" queried Sandy, arching an eyebrow.

Grant didn't answer right away but seemed to be thinking.

"Grant? What's wrong?" asked his mom, pausing after wiping Kylie's face.

"Huh?" said Grant, breaking from his stare. "Oh! Sorry, Mom. Just thinking."

"Deep thinking for a breakfast decision," observed Sandy, smiling as she wiped the tray in front of her granddaughter.

Grant smiled too and nodded, closing the door to the cupboard. He couldn't decide.

Kylie grinned up at Grant as he lifted her from the highchair.

"Hey, sweet one. How was your night?" he asked, sitting at the table with her on his lap.

"She partied hard at that wedding too, apparently, because she fell asleep on the way home and didn't even wake up when I put her in the crib," answered Sandy for her granddaughter.

"Thanks again, Mom, for always taking care of this sweet kid," smiled Grant, bouncing Kylie gently on his knee. A few colourful toys were on the table and she was having fun grabbing at them.

"You know I love it," assured his mom, now pouring coffee for herself and her son.

"Can I ask you a question?" Grant said.

"Of course," answered Sandy. "Anything."

"You know how much I loved Stacy, right?"

Sandy nodded as she brought the coffee to the kitchen table and sat across from her son.

He continued. "I still do, and I miss her like crazy. When Kylie smiles, I think of her every time. She's been on my mind a lot, but—"

"But what, Grant?" queried Sandy, feeling sorry for her hurting son.

Grant took a deep breath and spilled it. "I've been feeling really guilty about this all night, but for the first time since she died, I think I felt something for someone else. Not anything crazy, but … am I wrong?"

Sandy's eyes teared as she reached across to place her hand over his. "Oh Grant," she breathed. "Honey, that's okay."

"Is it?" asked Grant with a doubtful look.

"Yes," answered his mom. "I've been praying that if God doesn't want you to be alone, He should send someone for you. This is good, honey."

"But, Mom, Stacy hasn't been gone all that long, and as nice a feeling as it was last night, I have just as much guilt for even thinking anything like this," said Grant.

"Listen," stated Sandy, pulling her hand from his and placing both her hands around her warm mug. "God has a plan for you, Grant. You've never been one to sit and do nothing, so this doesn't surprise me." She smiled and sighed. "Just ... be sure you're done grieving before starting over."

He looked at her, questioningly.

She looked down and then up again. "Grant, you're so much like your father. You're strong and patient, and you try to be everything for everyone around you. You're the least selfish person I know, but..." She paused. "I'm still concerned that when you don't let your true feelings out, they'll build and—"

"Mom, I'm fine," he said in a matter-of-fact tone. "God's got this. He's my strength."

She nodded and then slowly smiled. "Well, I'm pretty sure God doesn't want you to be alone for the rest of your life."

"You're alone, Mom," interrupted Grant, placing a toy closer to Kylie so she could more easily grab it.

Sandy stopped, smiled, and then continued. "I'm clearly not alone, Grant." She motioned to Kylie. "But if you're talking about marrying again, you're right. God didn't bring another man into my life after your dad died when you were little, but that could change any time."

Grant raised his eyebrows. "What are you saying, Mom?" he asked. "Did you meet someone?"

Sandy blushed and looked down at her hands.

"You did!" he laughed. "Who?"

"Don't get ahead of yourself. You first," she lifted her head, with her eyes smiling.

"No way," he replied. "Who's the guy, and how long has this been going on?"

Sandy laughed as she gave in and told him very little about the new man she'd met. He'd been coming to some of the events at church for a few months. They'd gone out with a few other people and a friendship had formed. He came from a background unlike her own, but they had some of the same interests, and their relationship was growing.

"Who is he? Have I met him?" asked Grant, trying to think of the new faces he'd recently seen at church, but he couldn't begin to guess. Their church was large, and most Sundays he was busy with running Kylie to and from the nursery.

"You probably haven't met him, Grant," answered his mother evasively. "But I'll be glad to introduce you sometime."

"Well, I hope so. If he's going to fall in love with my mother ... which he will," he added pointedly, "I've gotta check him out."

"Enough," laughed Sandy. "Enough about that. It's nothing serious, and if and when it becomes that way, we'll talk more about it." Her smile lessened and she continued. "Grant, tell me about her."

Now it was Grant's turn to redden a little. He shook his head. "I don't know, Mom. It's kinda weird," he said.

"It's always a little weird, Grant," Sandy replied, trying to make her son feel more at ease. He didn't find it easy to talk about his personal life, and Sandy had never pushed. She prayed many prayers for her sons, mostly that they'd make wise decisions. She didn't think talking at them helped much. God could do the work, and He had in Grant's life. Stacy had become a wonderful partner for him. Sandy was thrilled when they married and was devastated by her loss, but that didn't mean God didn't have another person in mind for Grant and Kylie.

"She was there when Stacy died, Mom," Grant blurted out, brushing his falling hair from his face again.

"What?" asked Sandy, confused. "She was there?"

"Yeah," nodded Grant. "She was the labour nurse. She was there when Kylie was born."

The more he spoke, the more uncomfortable with the whole situation he felt. Why had he even mentioned this to his mother? It wasn't like anything would come of it.

Sandy knew her son and knew he was battling with his thoughts. "Stop thinking so much, Grant," she said. "Your guilt is misplaced."

"Ya think?" he asked with his brow furrowed.

Sandy smiled. "Yes!"

Kylie balked, becoming bored with the toys. Grant turned her to face him and grinned at her, which immediately turned her face into a sunbeam for her daddy.

"Maybe you're right," he said. "Nothing will happen anyway."

"Hmm," pondered Sandy. "Don't throw out a possibility just because you think it's weird, Grant. God is all about loving weird."

# Chapter Twelve

I STARED AT THE YELLOWY-ORANGE ENVELOPE ON MY BEDSIDE TABLE. IT looked different to me since speaking at length with my mother. After her confession, I phoned my manager at work, telling her a family issue had come up. I asked to have a few more days off, and Katherine was very gracious and granted me my request.

I stayed for another two days, and my mother and I talked and talked and cried and cried and even laughed a little. We had never conversed as much in the entirety of my life as we did in those two days, and I left home feeling different toward her.

She told me about being fifteen and finding out she was pregnant. She said little about the boy involved, except that he was two years older, wild and fun, and so appealing that she was swept away by his charisma. She didn't blame him and made it very clear that she hadn't been pressured or raped. She didn't say much else about him except that her parents had disliked "his type" immensely. They'd seen him only once and were not impressed, which made him all the more appealing to my mother. He and his family moved away not long after their short-lived relationship, and she had never heard from him again. She didn't tell anyone about the pregnancy because, even though she suspected it, she hadn't been to a doctor.

My eyes teared and spilled over when she told me about the frightening experience of telling her mother about what she suspected when her pants didn't fit any longer. I had never known my grandmother because she'd passed away when I was very small. From what my mother shared, I couldn't help but picture a militant drill sergeant, strict and unbending.

As my mother explained a bit about her upbringing, the thought crossed my mind more than once that it explained so much about her. She was raised by a strict, no-nonsense, almost mean maternal figure. Compared to what she'd had as a mother, mine seemed almost warm and fuzzy now.

"So," my mother sighed, "after it was over, I knew I had a baby girl. That's all. I didn't find out what she weighed or what her length was. I didn't even get to see her—"

"I can't believe it, Mom," I said, with anger rising. "That was so unfair. It wasn't like it was 1905. It was only 1980. How could the staff at the hospital not help you?"

"Trish," my mom continued, "my mother was with me the whole time. She was the boss. I wasn't of legal age to have a say. I couldn't sign any papers for myself. My mother had to. The only time she wasn't with me in the hospital was when I'd get up to go to the bathroom. A nurse helped me then. I remember she wore a white hat with two black stripes—not like now when none of you wear hats. I've actually thought of her often—the nurse. She was so kind." Looking right into my eyes, she said, "I think you'd be like her, Trish, when you're with your patients. She was so sweet, and I could tell that she felt sorry for me. She was the one who told me the baby was a girl. My mother forbade me to know even that, but because of that nurse, at least I could imagine my baby as a girl, wondering where she was and praying she had a good family to care for her."

"Wow," I breathed, swallowing the huge lump in my throat. My mother had been through such a traumatic event and now was sharing it with me. I couldn't help it. I got up, walked across the living room, and hugged her. Both of us cried and hugged. I couldn't remember if that had ever happened before, but it was good.

Over the two days I spent at my parents' home, I rarely saw my dad. He was busy with work, but my mom shared more and more information. She had told my father about the baby shortly before they married. She shared about how incredibly scared she'd been—scared he would leave her, scared the wedding would be called off, scared that other people would find out, scared. My father, as I would have expected, didn't care about her past. He told her that he loved her "no matter what" and "heaven and earth could move" and still he would love her. That didn't surprise me. That was my dad and, although I could never before figure out why he loved my mom, and maybe still couldn't, some things made a little more sense now, though.

I stared at the envelope and picked it up off the table beside my bed. Mom and I had discussed opening it together, but she decided that she would rather leave it in my hands for the time being. This frustrated me in a way, but on the other hand, I understood. She was overwhelmed, and I couldn't blame her after what she'd been through. Before I left to come home, she told me that she'd appreciate it if I would consider carrying on with finding my sister. I told her I'd agree to take the information but may need some time to think about contacting her. My mother said she understood and told me to take as much time as I needed.

"After all," she said, "it took me many years to even try to find your sister. You can take all the time you need."

I left then, but every night since, I'd stared at the envelope, wondering but not having the fortitude to actually open it.

I sighed. I wanted to call Trent but knew that he and Melissa were somewhere on a beach enjoying the sun, sand, and being together in their new life. I smiled thinking of all the fun they must be having on their honeymoon. I put the envelope back on my nightstand and picked up my cell, instead dialling my dad.

"Hey, kiddo," he greeted over the line. "I don't have a lot of time. Just going in to do a little surgery but go ahead and shoot."

"Oh, it's okay, Dad." I sat up in bed. "We can talk another time."

"No, honey. Tell me what's on your mind," he said.

"It's nothing really. Just staring at this envelope and wanted to bounce a question off you."

"Whether you should open it?" asked my dad. I could tell he was engaged now.

"Yeah ..." I paused.

"Hey," he said, "take your time. Maybe Helen shouldn't have dropped this on you, honey, but maybe it's for the best. It's tough on her. It's been a long time, but I think she still relives a lot of it."

"I'm sure I would too, Dad. It's a bit crazy," I agreed, lying on my back and staring at the white ceiling of my apartment bedroom.

"I really appreciate your understanding in all of this too, Trish. Your mom told me she was so proud of how you took the news. I think that's why she asked you to do this for her. She knows you're strong."

"Honestly, Dad, I'm kinda nervous about who I'll find. We don't know anything about this person. Are we ready for this? It could be anyone, from a princess to a drug addict," I said with concern.

"Well, I doubt she's a princess, hun," he said, attempting to lighten my mood. "Not a lot of those around."

"No, probably not," I agreed, smiling to myself.

Then more seriously he added, "I hope she's had a great life, but if not, maybe she needs our help. Who knows? Not knowing and guessing is probably worse than the reality, Trish."

"You're right, Dad," I smiled again as I heard my father being paged in the background.

"Gotta go, honey, but I just want to be very clear about one thing." He paused.

"What's that, Dad?" I asked.

"Whatever happens and whoever you find, know that I love you."

## Chapter Thirteen

GRANT PUSHED HIS HAND OVER HIS FOREHEAD AND THROUGH HIS HAIR. KYLIE had been fussing all evening, and he had finally got her settled after much pacing and praying. When she got like this, which was thankfully more infrequent lately, she tested his patience but when she'd finally rest, he'd stare down at her and feel the overwhelming love that only a parent can understand.

He muted the episode of *CSI* playing on the TV and picked up his phone.

"Hey, cousin!" exclaimed Melissa on the other end. "Nice to hear from you!"

Grant smiled. "How was the honeymoon?" he asked.

"Super fantastic!" exclaimed Melissa. Grant could hear how excited she sounded and felt that his call was misplaced. Bad timing, perhaps.

"Listen … congratulations again. Just thought I'd call and say that." Grant hesitated.

"Thanks," laughed Melissa. When Grant didn't continue, she asked, "What can I do for you, Grant?"

"Uh …" he said, thinking.

"Seriously, Grant, it's not like we talk that often. Not that I mind hearing your voice or talking or whatever, but do you want something?" she hinted.

"Well," he replied, "I was just wondering if you have your friend's number? You know… Trent's friend?"

"Trish?" asked Melissa.

"Yeah ... Trish," Grant said tentatively, now convinced this had been a bad idea. He didn't like people knowing his business—especially personal business. "I just thought I'd give her a call and say hi," he continued quickly, wishing he'd just watched TV and gone to bed.

"Just to say hi, huh?" Melissa teased, knowing that he'd be uncomfortable if she made too big a deal of this. "Sure," she said, matter-of-factly. "I'll text you her contact numbers."

"Thanks," Grant said. "I appreciate it. Say hi to Trent for me."

"I will, Grant," agreed Melissa.

After hanging up quickly, Grant let his breath out and flopped onto his back on the couch. He watched a few minutes of the episode he was sure he'd seen before and then glanced at his phone. Melissa had wasted no time in texting the numbers for Trish. Grant turned off the TV and walked to his room. He'd sleep on it.

● ● ●

Melissa, on the other hand, squealed with delight after quitting the call and ran to tell Trent all about Grant's request.

*Chapter Fourteen*

AFTER THE WEDDING AND WITH THE BOMB DROPPED ON ME BY MY MOM, I AGAIN decided work would be cathartic and threw myself into it. As good as my bank account felt, I was tired. When overtired, some people drink more coffee, some people experience increasingly more unfiltered speech, and some people laugh at inappropriate moments when they should maintain their professionalism. I do all of those things.

It was during this time, when my mind was in overdrive, that I cared for a couple I will never forget. I've taken care of many a farmer's wife in labour, and one thing that many farmers tend to do, much to my chagrin, is compare their partner's birthing process to cows or other farm animals. I realize that the physical process is similar but being of the belief that human beings are made in God's image, I have a constitutional issue with being compared to any animal.

So when I learned that my patient's husband was a veterinarian, I didn't know what to expect, but I was prepared to speak out in advocation for my patient's dignity if necessary. I was so relieved when not once did he make any comparisons to an animal, bovine or other, during his wife's first stage of labour. She had then gotten to fully dilated, without incident, and was nearing the end of an exhaustive hour of pushing. As often happens, when a woman has given all she's got after hours or even days of pain, my patient basically gave up.

"I can't do it anymore!" she yelled, stopping mid-push.

She'd been doing so well with her control and determination that her sudden outburst caught us all off guard. I immediately started in with the words of encouragement I'd said so many times to help women finish the last leg of the race.

"Listen, you're just about done. Only a few more contractions. You're amazing, and you can do this," I breathed near her ear.

These words are often convincing enough to get the job done, but this time she wasn't about to be placated. She started losing it at everyone in the room, including her husband, and when the next pain hit, her volume went up. Suddenly, without warning, her husband leaned over her, and with his face as close as he could get, took a deep breath and forcefully blew into her face.

She stopped yelling immediately, shocked by her partner's action. After a very short pause, she looked at him directly and loudly proclaimed, "What the heck was *that*?"

He backed up just a little, shrugged his shoulders, and defensively replied, "Well, it calms the animals when they get outta control."

The room went silent.

As the doctor regrouped, very professionally, and began talking calmly, I, unfortunately, couldn't contain my laughter. I tried turning away, but even that didn't help. The other nurse in the room thankfully maintained her decorum and tried to speak above my giggling.

After the baby was born, the excited couple didn't appear to be too worse for wear, but I wondered if she would question her husband again someday about his unusual action.

*Don't judge, don't judge, don't judge* looped through my mind as I smirked, thinking about it again.

"You need a break," stated Melanie, my colleague.

"You're not wrong," I agreed.

"Go for one," she continued, smiling. "I've got this. You're tired, Trish. Nine deliveries and three C-sections in less than eight hours—we all need a break. You go first. I think some of the other girls are already in the break room."

"Thanks," I nodded. "I won't be long."

I couldn't help but smile again as I walked to the room, where I heard laughing from a few other nurses.

"Hey, Trish!" said Shauna.

I hadn't seen Shauna for a long time. Our schedules hadn't lined up for working or church-going together lately. We'd texted often, but as everyone knows, that's not the same as face-to-face visiting.

"Hi!" I replied, flopping onto one of the chairs across from her. "What's up? I've missed you."

"Yeah," she agreed. "We're kinda like two ships passing in the night lately."

She was a cute blonde with endless energy, but tonight even she looked tired.

"Yeah, it's too bad," I agreed. "Anything new on the boyfriend front?" I asked, thinking about the pastor we'd met the last time we were at church together.

"Well," she said with a confused look on her face, "honestly, I don't know. He's nice and all, but I'm not sure I can live up to his expectations. I guess you'd say it's a work in progress."

"Hmm," I mumbled, feeling a little sorry for my friend.

"It is what it is," she said, shrugging.

She didn't continue and I didn't push.

I shared my "vet" experience and admitted my embarrassment for not keeping my emotions in check. The other nurses laughed as I got up to grab a granola bar and the phone out of my locker. I glanced at it, noting the time of 4:00 a.m. We'd been so busy that this was the first time I'd picked it up, and I noticed a few messages. I scrolled through and noted my dad had texted. There was one from Trent and one from an unknown number as well.

"Hey, Trish, are you coming to the fall barbecue in a few weeks?" asked Shauna.

"Already signed up, Shaun, and I'm bringing my usual—chips and dip," I smiled.

She knew that I was cooking-challenged, so I wasn't surprised with her reply.

"As expected," she smirked.

Dad had texted that he loved me and was just checking in. He'd texted four hours ago, so he was probably just getting home from the hospital then. I would text him back when I got home in the morning, since his phone was probably on. I didn't want to disturb him now.

Trent's text said, *Hey! Anything new?*

That had come to my phone an hour ago. He was obviously working a night shift as well.

I texted back, *Nope.*

As I sat back down, his text came back: *Nothing?*

*Nope,* I sent back. *Except really busy shift. Lots of babies tonight. You busy there?*

Trent: *Not too bad.*

Me: *Good for you. First shift back after honeymoon?*

Trent: *Third. Honeymoon seems like a long time ago already. Talk soon?*

Me: *For sure*

I laid my head on the back of the chair. Sometimes it wasn't wise to sit down after running full speed for hours. My fifth night shift in a row felt like it had caught up to me.

I'd just about forgotten the unknown number when my phone vibrated again. I groaned, feeling too tired to even deal with texting, but peered at the display. It was from the same unknown number as earlier in the evening. My eyes focused on the first message, sent at 10:00 p.m.

*Hi. This is Grant Evans. Wondering if you'd like to meet for coffee sometime.*

I sat up straighter and suddenly felt a lot more awake. His first text had been sent six hours ago, and now another?

*No pressure. I met you again at Melissa and Trent's wedding. Mel gave me your number. Hope that's OK. Again, no pressure.*

I didn't realize I was holding my breath until it escaped my lips.

"What's wrong?" asked Shauna, looking up from her cell phone.

"Nothing," I said, shaking my head and trying to seem nonchalantly vague. My heart was beating faster and now I was really awake, not knowing what to text.

"You know," another nurse was saying, "some of the new interns are coming to the barbecue too. Could be fun."

The other nurses, including Shauna, began talking about a possible volleyball game, but I couldn't pay attention. When Grant texted, I hadn't answered in the evening. Had he been up all night, or did he usually get up this early? Maybe he thought I was ignoring him, since I hadn't texted back earlier. Suddenly I didn't want it to be that. Normally I would have thought more about it, but I found myself typing quickly.

*Hi. Sorry I didn't text earlier. I'm at work and it's nuts. I'd love to meet you!*

I pressed "SEND" before I could think it through. Now that I reread my reply, I chastised myself for sounding too excited. What was wrong with me? An exclamation mark? Love to meet you? I groaned without thinking.

"Seriously, what's wrong?" queried Shauna with concern.

"Oh!" I exclaimed, blushing. "Nothing. Really. Just tired groans," I smiled at her.

The other girls, thankfully, ignored me, but Shauna didn't look convinced. I jumped a little when my phone buzzed again. It was from Grant. *Great*

I couldn't help myself and texted, *Are you usually up this early?*

Grant: *Nope*

Had he been worried because I hadn't answered earlier, or was his baby awake? I told myself to stop guessing and think of what to text back, but I still didn't know what to reply when my phone buzzed again.

*Hope work is good. I'll text later?*

I couldn't help the smile on my face as I quickly typed, *Great!*

I stared at the exclamation mark, which I tended to often add to the end of my sentences without thinking. I erased it before pressing "SEND." I didn't want to look desperate.

The other girls were leaving the break room, and I hopped up to join them, not realizing I still had a grin on my face.

"Good news at four in the morning?" asked Shauna.

"No," I answered. "Just glad we're three hours away from being done and off for a couple of days."

"You and me both, Trish," she agreed. "You and me both."

When I got home from work, I checked my phone a few times until I passed out in my room. I slept well, from exhaustion I suspect, but woke up at 3:00 p.m. and immediately checked my phone for messages. No texts.

I felt a twinge of disappointment, but as I had picked up the phone, the envelope it had been resting on fell to the floor. I picked it up and sighed. Before anything else, I needed to stop procrastinating and deal with this. It was time to find my sister.

## Chapter Fifteen

I HAD TRIED CALLING THE TWO PHONE NUMBERS WRITTEN ON THE INFORMATION in the envelope a few times, but they hadn't been answered. As I stood outside the listed address, I felt very nervous but took a few deep breaths, prayed for wisdom and strength, grasped the envelope tightly, and rang the bell.

As I stood on the stairs of the small home, I noticed the flower beds along the front. They looked like they may have started well but had succumbed to an overgrowth of weeds. It was a cute little place, and I especially liked the painted green door. I reached up to knock again but before I could a tired looking woman with brown hair, much like my own, opened the door, balancing a baby on her hip.

"What?" she asked abruptly. "I'm not going to buy anything."

Her eyes weren't like my brown but rather a bright green, which would've been beautiful if not rimmed between puffy lids and the bags underneath them. I felt sorry for her as I stood staring at the woman whom I suspected shared my DNA.

I stammered, explaining that I wasn't selling anything but needed to ask her some questions. She looked suspicious but stayed at the door.

"This will seem strange," I started, suddenly realizing I hadn't planned out exactly what I'd say when facing my sister for the first time. I just had to hope that she would be receptive to my declaration, so I dove in.

"I believe … you may be my sister," I half-blurted out.

She stared at me, looking as though I'd grown a horn and began laughing. "Go on," she smiled, clearly not convinced but curious enough to hear me out.

I tried to explain, in no great detail, about my mother's unexpected pregnancy and that she'd given up a daughter over thirty years ago. I opened the envelope and showed her the transcript with the phone numbers and her address.

"Well, hun, I'm sorry to disappoint you," she said, softening a little, "but that's not my name."

She pointed to the paper with her free hand. "I'm not … Natalie Carr."

"Oh," I said, thinking. "Well, would you know this person, by any chance?"

"No." She shook her head. "But I haven't lived here that long."

The baby started to fuss, and the woman became distracted.

"I'm really sorry. I wish I could help you," she said, sounding sympathetic, probably from the look she saw on my face. "I hope you find her."

I thanked her and she closed the door before I could walk down the front stairs. I got into my Toyota and dialled my mother.

"Mom, I looked into this mystery sister of mine, but I've met a dead-end." I explained the phone numbers that yielded no answers and my interaction with the woman at the given address.

"Oh, I'm so sorry, Trish. I didn't expect that. The man who gave me the information seemed so nice, and I thought he knew what he was doing. I'm sure he was on the up and up, but I've had the envelope for awhile."

I suspected the guy had ripped off my mother and doubted I'd even get an appointment, if I could contact him at all. After all, she'd found his number in the yellow pages and had simply dialled him up.

I sighed. "Mom, could you give me his number? Maybe I could make an appointment with him."

I could hear my mother rustling papers or, more likely, flipping pages in the phone book.

She gave me the name and number to call, and I immediately dialled it after ending the call with my mother.

"Boss Agency," answered a cheerful, female voice.

"Hi," I began. I gave her my mother's name after explaining that she had hired a person there to locate someone but that the information given was incorrect.

The woman was friendly and assured me that the man she worked for was honest and had integrity. She suggested we make an appointment together. I agreed and set a date and time and called my mother back. Two days later, we sat across from the PI my mother had seen months before.

Melvin Boss looked up from his copies of the information he'd found and shook his head.

"Seriously, this has never happened to me before, Helen," he said with sincerity, "but let me try again. It has been a while. Some people change numbers for various reasons—can't pay the bill being the most popular—and people often move, especially those who don't pay bills." He looked apologetic and then added, "Don't worry, Helen. You won't have to pay me any more than you have. I'll dig deeper."

I could see why my mother had defended this man. His credentials appeared legitimate and, unless my radar was off, he seemed genuinely concerned.

"I'll call you as soon as I learn anything," stated Melvin.

## Chapter Sixteen

MY MOTHER HAD BEEN UPSET, BUT WE ENDED THE MEETING MORE HOPEFUL that Mr. Boss would get the information we needed. She had travelled into the city to meet me, and now she apologized for not being able to stay to visit or treat me to dinner.

"I have a meeting at church tonight, and since I'm the chairperson, I must attend. I'm so sorry, Trish."

"It's fine, Mom," I replied. "We'll do it soon. It's been a long day anyway. I'm going to lay low and veg tonight."

"Okay, sweetie," she said as she waved goodbye.

I left my mother, thinking I'd go home and turn in early, but now that the search for my sister had stalled, my thoughts wandered to other things. Over the last days, I'd thought of Grant but had begun to doubt that he would text again. I tried to reconcile that in my mind. It would probably be too weird to pursue any kind of friendship with him. We'd both be reminded of that night constantly, and where would that get us? Not healthy, anyway. But then I thought of his eyes and how deeply he'd looked at me after I met him again at the wedding and … my phone vibrated, startling me. I'd just started my Rav to begin the ride home. It was him.

*Sorry I haven't texted. Still interested in coffee?*

Me: *Yes.*

I couldn't help but smile. So much for thinking it was weird.

Grant texted, *Great. Tonight too early, or are you working?*

Me: *No coffee if I want to sleep ... ha ha.*

Grant: *OK. Another time?*

I didn't stop to think. *Supper instead? Still good for tonight if you are.*

I waited while berating myself for probably seeming too forward. I had to wait a few minutes, which made me second guess my reply even more so, but then his reply produced a sigh of relief and another smile.

*Even better*

He texted a suggestion of where and when, and I raced home to get ready.

After trying a few outfits, I settled on jeans and a pink shirt with some lace on the neckline and sleeves. Casual restaurant, casual clothes.

He must've gotten there quite early, because when I arrived five minutes before the agreed upon time, he was already seated. He stood up beside the booth when he saw me enter. I noticed he was in jeans as well and had on a blue shirt with a small striped pattern. When he stood, I noticed he was probably an inch or two taller than I and had wide shoulders and a nice physique. He looked like he probably worked out; if not, he'd been blessed with a great metabolism. Although I felt a bit guilty checking him out, I justified it by reminding myself that I wasn't blind and should be appreciative of all God's creatures. Such a good Christian girl.

The restaurant was full and loud. Some kind of jazzy rock format played in the background.

"Hi," we greeted each other in unison.

We commented on our punctuality as we sat across from each other in the booth.

Grant looked apologetic and said, "Hey, I'm sorry I didn't text sooner. Kylie had a cold coming on the night I texted, but I thought she was just grumpy. I knew by morning that something else was going on, though. I took her to the doctor because she'd never been sick before, but the doc just said she'd get over it in time. It took a few days but she's better now. My mom said I shouldn't have rushed to go to the doctor, but what do I know?" He shrugged.

I smiled. "Sick kids are scary. So many things can go wrong, and at Kylie's age she can't tell you what's hurting. I don't work paediatrics for a reason." To be honest, sick children had always intimidated me a little.

Grant laughed and added, "You work with brand new babies, though."

"Not really, unless there's absolutely nothing wrong," I explained. "When there's anything wrong, we call the Neonatal Intensive Care Unit. They come running and take over all the baby care. That's the advantage of working in a large city hospital."

He nodded, still looking a bit confused.

"So she's better now, you said?" I asked, wondering where Kylie was as well.

"She was pretty miserable for a few days, but she's doing a lot better. I felt so sorry for her. The poor kid could hardly breathe. She's not quite back to herself, so my mom took her for the weekend while I get caught up at work. She's pretty happy with Grandma," he smiled.

"You work all weekend?" I asked, wondering about his job.

"That's the way it is when you're the boss," smiled Grant, "but it's great when you need time off too."

I was about to ask more questions, but Grant was looking around. "You know, it's not usually so noisy in here. If you want to go somewhere else, we can," he offered.

I shook my head. "This is fine. Really." I paused. "Unless you want to go?"

"No," he smiled. "The food's really good here, and I'm starving, if that's okay."

"Absolutely," I grinned. "I'm not allergic to noise. Labouring women aren't always so quiet."

He smiled and looked down at the menu the waitress had put in front of him. "Right."

I felt foolish immediately, staring at my menu as well. How insensitive could I be? *Bring his memory back to that, Trish. Really smart*, I inwardly berated myself.

"I'm sorry, Grant," I said, flustered and blushing. "I didn't mean to bring up—"

He looked back up swiftly. "Trish," he started, confidently, "I just want to get past something here."

I sat nervously, not sure what to expect.

"What happened to us that night was awful. Terrible, actually ... something no one should ever go through. After I saw Stacy lying there, so white, my heart broke in a million pieces and I thought I would never heal."

An understandable pain crossed over his features and he stared down at the table again.

"For months I couldn't get myself out of the funk I was in," he continued as my eyes teared. "I was good for nothing. I was a bad son and a useless father to Kylie. I turned away from God. I was so mad and wrapped up in the unfairness of it all. My faith faltered big-time, I'm ashamed to admit."

I didn't know how to reply, so as he paused, I said nothing but just waited, feeling deep empathy for his pain.

He looked up at me then and continued. "But I realized, eventually, that I had to go on and live what I really do believe. I needed to rise above my depression and get back to all of them—God, my daughter, my family, and friends." He clasped his hands together on the table in front of him. "My mom showed me some tough love, and here I am—maybe not completely healed, I guess, but stronger than I was."

I smiled with sympathy, and the corners of his mouth lifted slightly too as he looked at me.

"And I know," he continued, "that it couldn't have been easy for you either, Trish."

Suddenly I couldn't breathe.

"This isn't about me," I managed to whisper, fighting tears and wishing I hadn't agreed to meet him in this noisy restaurant, or in any restaurant. I'd been unconsciously playing with a napkin on the table when he put one of his hands over one of mine.

"Of course this concerns you too. It must've been awful for you," he said with intensity.

A wave of nausea swept over me as my mind raced. Is this why he wanted to meet me? To discuss the night his wife died? My father had warned me not to talk to anyone about it, but that had been so many months ago, I'd almost forgotten. He'd said people would question me, and that had happened many times at the hospital, no doubt in fear of Stacy's "case" being litigated. The few weeks after that horrible night had been a nightmare that I didn't want to relive. I felt that I'd just started to breathe again at work and was just getting my confidence back, and now this.

It was like he read my mind, or maybe he saw the impending panic attack about to take place directly in front of him.

"This isn't about blame, Trish," he said, looking worried and shaking his head. "I'm not saying this well."

"I don't know what to tell you, Grant," I rushed, trying to move my hand from under his. "Maybe I should go."

"No," he pleaded, holding on tighter. "What I'm saying is ... many times I've wondered about you ... how you've been after that night. I'm sure you were questioned and worried about me suing you or the hospital. I mean, some of my friends, and even my brother, wanted me to. It was crazy—all the pressure. But even when I got so angry about Stacy dying, that was never an option in my mind. I just knew the doctors and nurses had done the best they could. I knew you did, because you came and saw me later. You didn't have to do that, and you looked so ... upset." He paused, his gaze never leaving mine, and then he said, "What I'm saying is, I'm guessing I wasn't the only one going through a horrible time after that."

I felt the tension in my shoulders lessen as his eyes bore into mine, and I started to cry—not a tear or two, but a full-out cry. I thought I'd cried over Stacy's death and the details of that awful night so many times that I'd have none left to give to it, but I was wrong. I don't know how long I wept, but Grant got up and came to sit next to me at some point. He put his arm around me, and we just sat—me crying and him waiting.

I eventually stopped and became more aware of my surroundings again, and nothing less than complete mortification set in. Not only was I embarrassed about my lack of strength and what a wreck I knew I looked like, but I also noticed that the two napkins on our table were now a shredded, wet mess. I assumed that I'd blown my nose, which I was sure was very red—not the appealing look a person goes for when in public ... or with a guy ... or ever.

"I am so-o sor-ry," I finally said, with the staggered breath you get after weeping uncontrollably.

The waitress, who had come and gone a few times, now returned and appeared noticeably uncomfortable, but she asked what she could bring us to drink.

"I've got to go. Seriously," I whispered. "I am so sorry, Grant."

Unfortunately, he was sitting beside me, so unless I wanted to escape under the table, I would have no way out.

"You know," he said, as if a brilliant idea had entered his mind, "if we just sit here and order something calmly and rationally, the whole restaurant will soon forget what they just saw."

I couldn't help it. I was tired and stressed, so I fell to one of my go-to reactions. I started laughing. It wasn't appropriate, but neither was completely melting down. I am so glad that no one held a mirror in front of me right then, or I would have probably opted to dive under that table after all.

"Do you work tomorrow?" he asked me.

I shook my head.

Grant looked up at the waitress with his arm still around me and smiled. "We'll both have coffee."

I looked down and couldn't help but smile a little too.

Before our food came, he moved across to the seat opposite me, and I quickly excused myself to go to the washroom. I wasn't impressed with what I saw in the mirror but figured it could've been worse as I dabbed cold water onto my puffy eyes. I figured that since he'd seen the worst, I might as well stay and tough out the meal.

We talked about so many things—some involving Stacy and Kylie—and the time flew. Before we knew it, the restaurant was almost empty. He was funny and at ease, and it didn't hurt that he was ridiculously handsome. His dark, wavy hair fell over his forehead, but it didn't seem to bother him as he often brushed it away. He had piercing blue eyes. He laughed easily, and very small wrinkles would form beside his eyes when he did so. It was in the way he looked directly at me that made my heart skip a beat during our time together that night.

"Excuse me," the waitress chimed in. "We're so sorry about this, but we'll be closing shortly."

He nodded, smiling at her. "You can bring me the bill."

"Oh, that's okay," I said. "I'll pay for mine."

Grant smiled. "That won't be happening, Trish," he laughed. "I asked you out, and I'm a little old-fashioned that way."

I don't know why but I blushed and felt strangely warm inside. He wasn't like the other guys I'd been out with before—not that I had much experience—but still, he seemed so different. Maybe because he was in his thirties instead of his twenties.

He paid the bill and we walked outside together. He asked me where I'd parked, and I pointed to the west parking lot. He walked me to my Rav, and we stopped in front of it.

"I had a nice time, Grant, but I really have to apologize for the meltdown," I said uncomfortably.

"Hey!" he said casually. "It was nothing. Kinda my fault. I freaked you out."

"That wasn't it at all, actually," I said quietly, looking at my feet. "No one ever said what you did tonight ... that you knew it was awful for me. After Stacy died, all I could think of, every day and night, was what happened to you guys and how horrible it must've been for you." I looked up at his face and continued. "Being questioned and having to go through every detail over and over ... well, I thought I might break. They offered "debriefing" and counselling but then they'd call me into another meeting, and I'd have to explain everything I did, again." I paused, remembering the feeling of doom that loomed over me for weeks, maybe longer. Maybe even until now. "I asked about you and Kylie once, and the person in charge of the meeting told me that in no way should I ask about or try to find out how to contact you. They would take care of it, he said. I had to trust them because I was scared, but I'm sorry about that too. I really am."

Grant looked like he might cry now, which made me feel even worse for him. He sighed instead before saying, "I don't know a lot about the health care system, Trish, but I know hospitals fear being sued when something bad happens, but they should be ashamed of themselves if they aren't supporting the nurses who do the hard work. Maybe sometimes things are done wrong and should be investigated. I suppose that's someone's job, but I want you to know this—from the bottom of my heart—I know you did everything you knew how to prevent Stacy's death. And I think Dr. Nelson did too, and all the other people involved. I know it. I just do." He shrugged.

I nodded and tried to look down again, but he gently lifted my chin and again gazed into my eyes. "I don't want you to feel bad about this anymore. Ever. It's really over, Trish. If it makes you feel any better, I knew Stacy really well. She didn't always have an easy life, and she wouldn't want either me or you to live with this pain and sadness."

My breath caught with his closeness and I glanced at his mouth, suddenly wishing I could kiss it. Then, of course, I knew I was being very inappropriate and broke my gaze from his. I stepped back. He seemed like such a nice man—understanding, compassionate, and kind—but he wasn't mine.

I thanked him again for supper, got into my vehicle and drove away.

## Chapter Seventeen

I DON'T KNOW IF IT WAS FROM THE COFFEE OR THE EMOTIONAL "DATE," BUT after waking for the fifth or sixth time, I wished I were at work instead of tossing and turning at home. I finally got up, went to the bathroom, and stumbled to the cupboard that held analgesics, vitamins, and other medications I took as needed. Nothing looked like it would help for sleep, but I took a Tylenol anyway.

I had just dozed off again when I heard my phone vibrate.

The text was from Melissa: *Hi! I'm in the city for appointments. Have time for breakfast?*

I sighed, feeling tired, but willing to give up the prospect of more sleep to spend time with her.

We met at a popular breakfast spot and both ordered coffee.

Melissa had brought wedding and honeymoon pictures, and for the first part of the visit she regaled me with stories of the hikes they'd gone on, the warm ocean they'd swam in, and a boating expedition they'd been on. That was great for her but not so great for seasick Trent. Her eyes shone brightly when she talked about the trip.

We laughed about Trent and compared a few notes about him. I felt genuinely happy for them.

After we ate, Melissa sighed.

"Can I ask you a personal question?"

"Sure," I said, stirring some cream into my third cup of strong coffee.

"Did my cousin call you?"

I stopped stirring and looked up at her.

"Yes."

"And?" she continued, grinning.

I decided to be vague about the date. "We went out last night."

"Oh!" Melissa sounded surprised. "That was fast."

"Fast?"

"Well, yeah. As excited as I was when he asked for your number, I didn't actually think he'd carry through. At least, not so soon. My mom said he's been in a bad way, but I thought it was a good sign when he texted."

She paused, clearly waiting for me to say something more, but I wasn't sure what to share.

"C'mon, tell me about the date. At least a little. I'm so glad you said yes!"

I looked down, trying to decide what to divulge. "It was ... nice."

"Just nice?"

"Well ... interesting."

I could tell she was thinking about what to say. "He's been through so much, Trish," she finally began. "I worry about him. First their son, Trevor, dying, and now Stacy ... I mean, how much can one person take?" She took a deep breath. "Why is it that some people seem to get so much tragedy in their lives, and others seem to skip through life with hardly a problem?"

We were both quiet for a moment.

"I don't know, but maybe the answer is in the word seem," I said. "Everyone has problems, and some are more visible than others. Some are definitely more tragic for sure, but everyone's problems are huge to them, I suppose. And yet you're right about Grant and Stacy. I don't know much about the circumstances surrounding Trevor, except that something grave happened. I can't even imagine."

Though I was curious about Grant and Stacy, I didn't know if I should ask Melissa about any of the circumstances in Grant's life.

Melissa, however, was more than willing to share some without being asked.

"Grant and I are cousins through my dad and his mom, my Aunt Sandy," she said. "I'm younger than Grant and his brother, Joe, but our families did some ranching together. We saw each other a fair bit. Those boys couldn't wait to leave when they finished high school, although Joe loved the ranch more than Grant did. Their dad died when they were really young. Grant was about six and Joe was two. Don't get me wrong ... they learned about everything ranch-related, but Grant's heart wasn't in it. He left for the city as soon as he graduated high school, and no one was surprised." She paused, thinking back. "But the city wasn't really a great place for him. I won't get into the details, but he kinda went crazy for a few years trying to find himself, I guess. Nothing too bad, though."

She looked sad and I remained quiet, waiting.

"Anyway," she started again, "after a few years he grew up and decided to continue the business his dad and mine started once. I've never been exactly sure of what he does, but I know he's a good businessman, because my dad employs him, and now Grant sort of runs the financial end of the ranch. He doesn't do the ranch work, like with the livestock; he crunches numbers in the city, buys and sells, and makes a lot of money for our family. His business—GR-Jo Holdings—was originally started for Grant and Joe, I think." Melissa shrugged. "I know he makes a good living. I don't know much about it. I was into the ranching part. I'm not a numbers girl."

I smiled. "I'm the same. I can figure out my own budget, but that's it."

"Another thing we have in common, Trish. We could be sisters."

"I wish," I said sincerely. The more I got to know Melissa, the more I liked her.

"Do you like ranch stuff?" she inquired.

"I wouldn't know." I shrugged. "I know nothing about that kind of life. Although I wasn't brought up in a big city, I wasn't exposed to farm life either."

"Oh, you'd love it, Trish," said Melissa enthusiastically. "It's busy for sure, but there are moments ..." She looked like she was thinking back on a wonderful memory, and I was quiet, not wanting to interrupt her.

Then, like she was divulging a huge secret, her eyebrows lifted, and she looked at me. "There's this beautiful little spot about a ten-minute walk from the yard site at my parents' place. We hung a swing from a huge tree overlooking the stream. It's a perfect spot. Seriously, I've gone there so many times to think and pray and, well, just ... be. In the silence, a person can really figure things out. I've made some really great decisions sitting there." She sighed.

"But getting back to Trevor." She paused. "I know Grant and Stacy found out about all the problems he had in the middle of the pregnancy sometime. They were told then that they should opt to end it, but Stacy really believed that God might make a miracle happen or something. Her faith was amazing. I think she thought if she carried the baby to the end, though, that maybe all would be well. I don't know exactly, but the doctors turned out to be right, and he died. It was awful for them."

Melissa looked down and quietly added, "I probably shouldn't have told you that. Maybe don't mention that to Grant."

"I don't think that'll be a problem, Mel. I doubt I'll be seeing him again, actually," I said, smiling on the outside.

Since she had shared so much with me, I decided to tell Melissa a little about the time I'd shared with her cousin. She laughed when I told her how I'd fallen completely apart in front of him and the entire restaurant, and how embarrassed I'd been. I didn't give all the details, but I told her that what he'd said, and the fact that he didn't run away screaming meant a lot to me.

"Don't laugh so hard," I said, smiling as she shook. "It really wasn't funny."

"Well, I know you have a hang-up about crying in front of people, so it's kind of even more funny picturing it," she said. "That's just your pride, you know."

"I'm not proud," I said, feigning hurt. "I'm just very self-aware."

She laughed again and looked at her watch. "I've got to run. I have a doctor's appointment I'm going to be late for."

We both stood and hugged our goodbyes.

"Thanks so much for meeting me," Melissa said. "This was fun."

I nodded in agreement and we parted.

# Chapter Eighteen

I BELIEVE THAT THERE ARE TRUE, FAITHFUL, LOVING CHRISTIANS IN CHURCHES, but there are also the "attenders but pretenders" in every church. I think I fall somewhere in between. I want to be a person of substance. I really do. You know—loving, kind, and faithful—but often I fall short and feel, according to my closest friends, an inappropriate amount of guilt when I do. I can't help the guilt. I was raised that way.

I hadn't attended church for quite awhile due to my work schedule, the wedding, and, if truth be told, just plain laziness, so when Grant texted and asked if I wanted to go with him the next time I was available, I accepted.

It was two weeks later when I met Grant at the church he and his mother, Sandy, attended. He met me in the foyer ten minutes before the service was about to start. Kylie beamed as he held her on his hip.

"Oh my goodness, what a big girl you are," I gushed, looking into the bright blue eyes of his baby.

"I guess you haven't seen her for a while," Grant smiled.

She bounced, cooed, and drooled, her bib looking quite drenched.

"Listen," he said, "I'll just drop her off in the nursery and I'll be right back."

He was just stepping away when the woman I recognized from the pictures he'd shown me came toward us, and Kylie reached out to her.

"Mom," Grant smiled as Kylie was taken happily by her grandmother, "This is Trish. She's a friend of mine."

Sandy smiled as I saw her eyebrows heighten. "Hello. Welcome," she offered with her hand outstretched as soon as Kylie was settled on her hip.

"It's very nice to meet you, Mrs. Evans," I said, shaking her hand.

"Call me Sandy, for goodness' sake, Trish," she said easily.

"Cute granddaughter," I continued.

"Isn't she?" Sandy agreed. "Couldn't be cuter, this grandma says."

We all talked to Kylie, and it was like she knew she was the centre of everyone's universe, as all children should be to someone.

"Grant," Sandy said, "I can take Kylie to the nursery. You go enjoy the service."

"Thanks." He smiled in appreciation as she walked away.

Grant introduced me to a few more people on the way to "his" usual seating area. One thing about regular church goers—you pick a pew, and you stick with it. I've noticed that most people prefer consistency like that. In my church, I prefer to sit on the far end of the bench, in the last pew on the right-hand side. My reasoning, to be brutally honest, is that this affords me the chance to quickly escape after the service ends.

In most churches, escape time is around noon. I don't often eat a big breakfast, or any at all, so I'm pretty much feeling famished by lunchtime. If I can concentrate at all on the sermon (my pastor, although very learned, isn't exactly what you'd call "expressive"), by the end I'm anxious to eat and can only think of that. That's probably not something most people will admit, but there it is.

Grant, however, was very comfortable sitting in the second bench from the front, which I felt was entirely too close. He must've read my mind, because he leaned over and said, in not much of a whisper, "Don't like the front?" as soon as we were seated.

I thought I'd shown a complete air of nonchalance, but apparently, he hadn't been fooled.

"I'm not really into being the centre of attention. I'm fine, though, if this is where you like to sit," I replied, trying to look relaxed. It bothered me that he seemed to be able to read me so well.

"Don't worry," he smiled. "You're not the centre of anyone's attention," he added, gesturing up.

I looked up and saw the worship band entering the platform. They were all dressed pretty casually and looked like they were excited to play and sing. I relaxed as the music started. I may not have any musical talent, but I've always appreciated music.

The band started with a song I recognized, and soon the congregation was singing and rejoicing, some with their hands in the air and others not. I sang quietly beside Grant, who was not ashamed to sing out. He seemed taken away by the music and was comfortable to praise God his way.

I was surprised to learn that time can move quickly in church when a speaker is dynamic and excited about what he believes. The pastor spoke about the goodness of God and His forgiveness that morning, and it brought my thoughts to my mother and how we were seeming to restore our relationship, which had seen many years of broken communication and hard feelings. Then the pastor spoke about forgiving ourselves, saying that often we beat ourselves up for things we don't even need forgiveness for. I squirmed a few times, thinking he was talking directly to me.

Grant smiled down at me a couple of times while the preacher spoke, and when he ended with "If God forgives you, how do you dare not forgive yourself?" Grant put his hand over mine and squeezed it.

The sermon was thought-provoking, and at times I felt uncomfortable, but I wasn't ready for him to end when he did. The half hour had gone by so quickly, I hadn't noticed my stomach growling once.

I was quiet as we got up to leave. I didn't recognize myself as I stopped Grant with my hand on his arm. "You were wrong about the band being the centre of attention," I said as he waited. "I think God was."

Grant looked down at me with the piercing stare I was getting a little more used to and smiled. "I didn't mean the band," he whispered as I blushed.

I waited in the back foyer while he went to get Kylie. I smiled at a few people as they walked by to exit, and a few shook my hand, as is usual in many churches.

"Okay. Wanna go out for lunch?" Grant asked, joining me by the back doors with Kylie in her car seat.

"Sure," I agreed, nodding.

"Do you want it to be just us, or do you want to join a group? Usually a bunch of us go out after church, but if that's too much, that's okay too," he asked.

"I don't care. I'm good with anything you want," I lied. I would've preferred just he and I and Kylie, but this was his turf, and it might be nice to see him with his friends, although large crowds weren't usually my favourite thing.

"Just come with us in my truck and we'll pick up your car later."

I nodded and we left.

Kylie fell asleep in her car seat on the way to the restaurant, so we tried not to disturb her as we sat in a group of eight people along a long table in the middle of the establishment. His friends seemed nice, although one of them was heavily pregnant with her first baby and not in the best of moods. When she learned of my occupation, however, she had a lot of questions for me and seemed relieved with some of my answers.

"Do you have kids?" she asked near the end of our conversation.

"No, not yet," I answered, shaking my head.

She seemed more aloof after that, as if the validity of my answers would be subject to question, since I hadn't the appropriate experience to possibly know as much as I seemed to.

The lunch was good. There was a lot of laughing and fun, and I felt quite at ease by the end of the hour or so we spent there. Grant was comfortable with these people. He was funny and I could see he was well-liked. One woman flirted with him a bit and I instantly felt envious, which surprised me. I tried to ignore it but somehow couldn't, leaving me to berate myself. I had no business feeling that way.

Kylie woke up just as the food arrived. No one seemed bothered by that. Rather, she was handed around the table among a few people, especially the woman who seemed to like Grant. She gushed a lot over her. He put Kylie in a highchair, and she ate happily from her "child's plate" of mashed potatoes and carrots.

When people started to leave, Grant wiped Kylie's face and wrinkled his nose as he lifted her from the chair.

"I don't think I can leave her like this until we get home. I'll just go and change her and then we'll leave," he said, looking apologetically to me.

"Oh no," gushed Tamara, the woman who very clearly had a huge crush on Grant. "I'll do that, little lady," she added, charging in and grabbing Kylie from her father's arms.

Kylie didn't seem to care and off she was carted by the beautiful blonde woman with high-heels and a tight navy dress. I couldn't help but look down at my flat black comfortable shoes, briefly thinking how boring they looked.

Grant glanced at me and shrugged. "Tamara's okay. She works in the church nursery a lot. Kylie likes her. She babysits sometimes for me when my mom can't."

"Oh," I managed, trying for nonchalance.

He looked over my shoulder suddenly and stopped short. Before I could say anything, he excused himself, leaving me standing beside the empty highchair. He walked to the very back of the restaurant. I peered at the table of his destination and could see Sandy sitting with a man I didn't remember meeting. I couldn't hear what they were saying, but by what I could see, Grant looked tense and serious. He shook hands with the man but soon came back to where I stood. He was quiet but smiled at me slightly with no comment.

Tamara returned with a happy Kylie, and Grant thanked her graciously for changing his daughter's dirty diaper. Tamara seemed very excited about doing that for him. I hadn't even changed Kylie's foul nappy, but I found myself nauseated. Thankfully, we then said our goodbyes to Tamara as we exited the restaurant.

"You okay?" I asked as we pulled away. I noticed Grant's demeanour had changed somewhat since seeing his mother.

"Sure," he answered, a little too quietly. "Apparently I just met my mom's new boyfriend." He didn't sound happy.

I didn't say anything more but suddenly found myself wishing I'd taken my Rav to the restaurant.

As we drove, Grant talked a little about some of the people I'd met at lunch, but he didn't touch on Tamara or his mom's friend again.

"Thanks so much for inviting me." I smiled genuinely as I reached for the handle of the truck before Grant could come to a complete stop in the church parking lot.

"Wait," he said. "I'll come to that side and get your door."

"No need," I said as I opened the door and, too quickly, tried to hop out. As luck would have it, in my haste I tripped, as is typical of me on a good day, and fell to my knees, skinning the right one like a six-year-old who falls off a bike.

"Oh no!" Grant yelled, running around to my side as fast as he could.

"I'm fine. I'm fine!" I said, too abruptly, as I scrambled up and started dusting myself off. Drat the shorter skirt I was wearing. Although my left knee also appeared scuffed, it wasn't bleeding like the right one was. A stream was trickling down the front of my lower right leg. I unzipped my purse and hunted for a tissue. After finding a used one, I dabbed at the scrape and tried to wipe off the worst of the blood.

"I have a First Aid kit in the truck," he said, starting to open the back door.

"Please, no!" I begged, trying to smile. I limped the few steps to my car as fast as possible, eyes tearing from the pain coming from my knees. I had one goal—to get home and away from this yet another embarrassing situation.

I heard him stop behind me. I honestly didn't know what he could possibly be thinking of me now, and I kept my eyes on the Rav as I got my reddened face and knees inside. I slammed my door shut and started the engine, but suddenly he was there knocking on my window. I opened it, my eyes staring straight ahead.

"Thanks for coming to church with us," he said. Something in his tone made me turn to look up at him, and when I saw the small smirk, I couldn't help but smile myself.

"Grace isn't my middle name," I whispered.

He burst out laughing and said, "Clearly."

"Oh!" I replied, playfully hitting his arm with the back of my hand and feeling just a twinge of hurt.

"You don't stop surprising me," he smiled, looking through me again.

"You surprise me too," I replied, hearing Kylie protest loudly in the back of his truck. "You better go. Your girl needs you."

"I think you're right," he agreed more seriously, looking down into my eyes again. He waited with the arm I'd hit still resting on my door.

Years ago when I was in high school, I had a young teacher who was very charming. He was always appropriate toward every student, including myself, but many of us young girls were enamoured with him. One day while he was leaning over my desk to help me with some equation I have absolutely no recollection of now, I looked up and stared into his face. His brow was slightly wrinkled in concentration, and I could smell his musky cologne. His face was close enough that I could see every detail. As I glanced at his mouth, I had an overwhelmingly and sudden urge to kiss him. Thankfully, I didn't act on it, but it is seared in my memory. It was the first time I'd ever wanted to kiss someone. I had felt that same compulsion after I'd met Grant at the restaurant, and now I felt it again but even more so. I exercised self-control and didn't act on it, but this time I felt more than a twinge of longing.

I thanked him again for inviting me to his church and for lunch, and my heart skipped a few beats as I pulled away. I went home to wash and bandage my sore knees.

# Chapter Nineteen

THE PHONE RANG, STARTLING ME.

"He's got it!" exclaimed my mother before I could say hello. "But I can't come into the city until next week, Trish. Could you possibly pick up the information from Boss Agency?"

I put the phone on speaker and continued making the grilled cheese sandwich I was busy with.

"I can, Mom," I answered, "but is that okay with Mr. Boss? I don't know if he'll give me the information, since I'm not the one requesting it."

"Of course he will," she said, as though I was simple-minded. "You were with me at his office the last time. He knows who you are."

"Okay then," I agreed. "Tell him I'll come tomorrow after I sleep. In the afternoon sometime."

"Thanks so much, Trish. I really appreciate it," she said.

We talked for a few more minutes and then hung up. She sounded excited—a big difference from a few months ago. I, however, had many reservations about how it would turn out, but after praying at length about it, I decided to let God do the worrying. After all, He apparently knew the big picture.

Grant and I had talked on the phone and texted more and more as of late, and he was big on "letting go and letting God." Somehow, I was becoming more convinced. I wanted to believe that as well. After all, since

God created me, why not trust Him? The pastor had spoken about that the last Sunday I'd gone back to church with Grant.

I still hadn't told my mom or dad about him. When my mother asked me what I was doing some nights, I always remained vague and said something like "nothing special," but that seemed more like a lie as time passed.

• • •

We'd gone out a few times when Sandy or Tamara was able to babysit. I hadn't been invited to his place yet, and sometimes I wondered why. He'd only ever dropped me off at my place, but he never asked me to come up. I felt comfortable with him but hadn't shared a lot of my history yet. I was, however, getting to know who he was, and when he was with his daughter my heart squeezed tightly watching how much he loved her. I thought of Stacy more than occasionally, and how blessed she'd been to have him for a husband. In my mind, she must have been pretty close to perfection. They probably had been the perfect couple.

We had gone to one other movie before this one—an action film. He told me he liked action and comedies best. I liked romance, but he wasn't as keen about those.

"It's not realistic," he said one night. He'd stomached a "chick flick" with me one evening, but as we watched I knew by the way he sighed and squirmed that it was something he was doing as a huge favour to me. I decided I wouldn't ask that of him again any time soon.

"And a car chase where a hundred cars are totalled in a one-minute clip and the hero gets out unscathed is realistic?" I laughed, walking beside him. "You just don't like the mushy stuff."

"Oh, I like mushy stuff," he smiled, speaking more quietly. "Just not so much on the big screen."

We were walking hand in hand, and his grip squeezed a little tighter. My stomach did a flop and my breath caught. I decided quickly on a different approach than the one I wanted to act on—the one where I stopped, grabbed his face, and kissed him.

"I think the only mushy stuff you're into right now is mashing stuff up for Kylie to eat," I said, as lightly as I could manage.

We'd reached his truck, and the parking lot was dark and quiet. He'd come to my side of the vehicle, as he did most often, to open the door for me. I wondered sometimes if he did it because of what had previously happened to my knees, but I opted to believe that he was being a gentleman. He didn't open the door when we reached the truck this time but slowly turned me and pushed me back gently against the door.

"Like I said," he breathed, close to my face and looking deep into my eyes, "I like mushy stuff."

He kissed me then. It was soft and gentle, kind of like a whisper. He stopped after a few long seconds and backed away, just a little, to look at me. His face was serious. He couldn't see me blush, but he saw the smile and came close again. This time the kiss was long and lush, and I could tell as it deepened and our breathing quickened that he was holding back.

Our kiss broke after some time, both of us breathing more heavily.

"Wow," we both said and then smiled.

"I better take you home, young lady," he said, shaking his head but still smiling, "before I do something we'll both regret."

In the moment I couldn't help but think I wouldn't regret it, but I knew he was right.

When he pulled up in front of my apartment, he came to open the passenger door for me. As I swung my legs as if to jump down, I paused. Looking straight at him, I asked, "Are we dating?"

He looked up at me, dumbfounded. "What?"

I felt foolish and didn't want to ask again, but so many times he'd introduced me as his friend, and we hadn't known each other for all that long, so I just wasn't sure of my footing. With the kiss tonight, however, I was pretty sure he considered me more than a friend, but I felt it should be clarified.

"Well," I stammered, "I feel like I don't know where I stand sometimes."

"Where you stand?" he repeated.

He was looking so incredulous that I became defensive and debated swinging my legs back into the truck to stare straight ahead instead of at him. I realized I was sort of stuck when he came closer toward me and stood with his body blocking my exit.

"Never mind," I managed, feeling increasingly embarrassed. "Thank you for the movie and popcorn."

"No," he said, firmly. "No. You do this. You start something and then you shut down. I was just surprised by your question. Ask me anything. I wanna talk."

"Well … now I don't want to talk. It's fine," I managed, looking away.

"You just feel silly because you asked," he accused.

I looked back at him, straight in the eye. "I do not," I replied loudly. "It's just that I honestly don't know where I stand. It may seem clear to you, but not to me." I suddenly didn't know where to look as I continued, so I looked everywhere but into his stare. "I mean, we're going out and having a good time. I think. I am, at least. But then I see you at church with Tamara, and I don't get it. She's beautiful. She's smart and … well, not very funny … but she's nice, and she's got legs that don't quit. She's clearly into you and would do anything for you, and she loves Kylie. And then there's Stacy. I know she's not here anymore, but I know you loved her so much, and she was pretty, and she must've been pretty perfect, and, Grant, I honestly don't know what you see in me. I don't. I'm none of those things, and why don't you see that? I don't get—"

"Trish," he interrupted loudly, stopping me from talking. I'd jumped a little and couldn't help but stare at him.

His face was so close to mine I could feel his breath. I suddenly thought of the veterinarian who had blown in his wife's face in labour and, like so many times when I'm nervous, I let out a giggle.

"What is going on with you?" he asked, looking mildly confused.

I had told him, with no confidentialities divulged, about the veterinarian in the delivery room when I'd lost my professionalism and laughed. "I'm sorry," I said now, trying to stop laughing and be more serious. "When you raised your voice, it reminded me of the vet blowing in his wife's face to get her to stop losing it."

"Yeah, well," he said, more seriously than I, "sometimes a guy's gotta do what he's gotta do, I guess. You know I didn't mean—"

"I know," I interrupted him now. "You didn't. It's fine. You didn't do anything wrong. I was getting carried away. I'm so sorry."

We both paused in our own thoughts.

"We're both tired, I think," he stated, "so I'm going to make this short, if that's okay. You asked if we're dating? The answer is absolutely yes. I thought we started the first time we met at Alfred's."

"Where I cried all night?" I exclaimed.

"I don't remember it that way, but, yes, a few tears were shed."

"A few tears." I rolled my eyes.

I was still sitting in the truck, and now he placed both hands on the seat on either side of my hips.

"Listen," he said, staring at me seriously, "I don't care about Tamara that way. She's nice and all, but she's certainly not my type. I think she knows that, but if not, I can make that real clear to her. Nothing's going to happen between her and I."

I nodded, seeing how serious he'd become.

"And as far as Stacy is concerned "—he straightened, taking a few deep breaths and shaking his head slowly before looking at me again— "she was my wife," he said, more quietly now. "That's always going to be. And, yes, she was a fantastic person, Trish, but she wasn't perfect. We had our ups and downs like everybody else. When someone dies, we think only of the good times, but I know more than anybody how we had to work on our relationship sometimes. Everybody does. She had hang-ups too. She came from a rough background, and when she became a Christian, all that didn't just go away. It was often a battle, but we worked on it ... together." He took a deep breath and finished. "I will always love her ... always ... but she's gone, and I have to move on. I want to move on."

I nodded again, saying nothing.

"I want to move on with you, Trish," Grant paused, suddenly looking away. He seemed deep in thought before he looked intently back into my eyes and simply said, "I love you."

I couldn't speak for a long time and then found my voice, but it came out in a nervous laugh.

"You can't be serious, Grant. You don't even know me," I answered, not able to tear myself from his gaze.

"I know enough," he came back with, but looked a little disappointed.

"How?" I asked. "How can you know that already?"

"I just do," he said simply and shrugged.

"You and I have been out quite a few times, but we're just getting to know each other. We still don't know much at all," I began, knowing as I was saying it that I had thought the exact opposite many times. When he looked at me, I felt like he knew me better than I knew myself. Although I'd learned a lot about him, time was an excuse for me now, and I just couldn't understand how anything this wonderful could ever happen this quickly, so I continued trying to make my point. "You and I haven't even seen each other's places, Grant," I grasped.

That made him smile and shake his head again. "Don't you think I'd love to take you up to your apartment?" he asked with a sheepish grin. "I would. I really would, but—"

"But what?" I pushed, confused.

"Well, honey, if that kiss was any indication of what's to come, I may not be able to keep my hands off you if we go up to your apartment."

I blushed the deepest red I could ever have blushed and tried to push him back. I was mortified. I had to leave now, and if he didn't move, I'd be forced to climb over the console and exit out the driver's door.

"Hey!" he exclaimed. "You wanted clear communication, so there you have it. I'm just telling you the truth."

I stilled then and slowly he backed away, grinning, letting me slip off the seat to place my feet on the ground. My legs were wobbly, and I hoped I could hold myself up. I tried to maintain some shred of dignity as he kept grinning but couldn't help myself.

"Honestly, Grant Evans, I think you enjoy embarrassing me," I accused.

"Of course I do," he countered back, now laughing, "and it's so easy."

"Well," I huffed, "I'm not!"

I tore myself from his grasp and tried to walk away. He grabbed my arm and pulled me in close.

"Good to know," he whispered as he kissed me quickly and then let go. I could feel him smile as I walked away.

*Chapter Twenty*

"THANK YOU FOR COMING WITH ME," I SAID AFTER GRANT GOT INTO THE passenger's seat of my SUV. We'd met at my place after work, and since I knew where the party was, we decided that I would drive. "I kind of forgot about the staff barbecue, but I wasn't sure you'd want to come anyway."

Grant smiled and adjusted his seat so he could stretch out a little more. "Of course I'll come. Meeting some of your work friends sounds like a good idea to me."

We chatted comfortably as I drove. I'd been nervous about seeing him again, but we didn't speak about his professed love from a few nights prior, and how uncomfortable that last conversation had been for me. He was at ease and teased me a little about my heavy foot, but I explained how I'd been created more for speed than keeping to the posted speed limit. He smiled and shook his head at that but said no more about it.

The gathering was out of town at Shauna's place. She rented a cute country house with a few other nurses. It was a beautiful little acreage with pine and poplar trees surrounding a large old house. Picnic tables dressed with cheerful cloths were lined up outside. I added the chips and dip I brought to the dishes of delicious looking foods. Shauna's boyfriend, Parker, and a few other men were flipping meat on the two barbecues set up near the house.

"Trish!" welcomed Shauna, coming toward us.

We introduced Grant to some of our colleagues and then to a few of the guys I recognized. He soon stood and visited with some of the men near the barbecue.

Shauna pulled me aside. I had told her a few days before about meeting Grant again, and she'd been intrigued by the man whose wife had passed away and was now with us at the party.

"When I told my mom I was going into nursing, she said she was so happy about that because maybe I'd meet a guy at the hospital," Shauna laughed. "I think she wanted him to be a doctor, but then she said that maybe I'd take care of a handsome man who would fall head over heels in love with me and ask me to marry him. I told her she'd read too many romance novels. When I told her I wanted to work maternity, she said, 'Shauna, that's such a poor choice! What are you thinking? You'll never meet a man there—unless you want to be a homewrecker!'"

Shauna paused and shook her head. "I've gotta tell her about this."

"How does your mom feel about pastors?" I asked, hinting for more information about her and Parker, the new pastor at our church.

Shauna blushed. "I haven't told her yet. I'm thinking if things progress, she won't be impressed."

"Why not? He's nice. Are things progressing?" I couldn't stop myself from asking.

"Hmm," she smiled back. "I'll let you know as soon as I know. I'm trying to get him to commit."

I laughed then, picturing poor Parker cornered in an interrogation room with his hand on a Bible.

As I visited with Shauna, a few other colleagues joined us, but my eye couldn't help but wander to Grant. He appeared to be at ease with everyone around him. He laughed easily and didn't seem to mind being with people who were strangers to him. I wondered if he just looked that way or if he really felt comfortable. I knew I could put on a good act sometimes, but often I didn't feel as self-assured as I tried to look.

The food was great and the company friendly. The time flew by, and everyone seemed to be having a good time.

"Okay," said Natasha, swaying a bit later that evening. She loved to party, and often was the "life" of them. "Lets all go around in a circle and introduce ourselves."

A few of us were visiting around the campfire, but some were milling in the yard. Natasha had been drinking a lot, as a few others had, and things were getting louder. Natasha and one of the other girls were flirting quite shamelessly with some of the new people—mostly interns and doctors.

"We already introduced everybody, Natasha," Shauna chimed in, laughing. "Just visit."

"But I want to get to know ev-er-y-bo-dy," she slurred. "Especially yoooou," she added, coming closer to the fire where we stood. She was looking and pointing straight at Grant and moved in closer to him.

"I think I know you," she added, squinting at him. "Have we met before?"

She was about to throw her arm around him when he stepped away. She tripped slightly, but he caught her. As soon as she stood straighter, he stepped away again.

"Aw, c'mon," pleaded Natasha. "Where do I know you from?"

Grant said nothing but looked uncomfortable.

Natasha wouldn't let it go. "I really think we've met before."

He shook his head. "No, I don't think so," he said evasively, looking away from her.

Natasha had never been my favourite person, but we worked together fairly well. I felt sorry for her most of the time. She wasn't happy. I could tell that she was making him uncomfortable, so I finally said, "Hey! He's with me!" I moved to stand between her and Grant.

Everyone quieted suddenly. Perhaps I'd sounded too aggressive, but I hadn't thought so. I stood my ground and stayed between my boyfriend and my colleague.

Not long after, I was helping Shauna clean things up when she said, "You know, Trish, you better take that man home. Poor guy. Natasha won't give up."

She was nodding toward something behind me. I turned to see Natasha falling all over Grant again and him trying to hold her off but having a challenge doing it. I sighed, thanked Shauna, and briskly walked toward my car.

"Grant, let's go," I said with a firmness in my voice that was meant for Natasha.

Natasha jeered at me but fell back and turned her attention to another guy who was walking past.

"Wow," Grant said as we pulled away. "She's ... intense."

"She's something else for sure," I agreed. "She was pretty sure she knew you."

Grant looked out the passenger window and didn't answer right away.

"Grant?" I asked, puzzled and feeling nervous by his evasion.

He sighed and looked at me as I turned my Rav onto the highway from the dirt road that led away from Shauna's house.

"I have met her, Trish, but it was a long time ago. A really long time. She hung out with someone I knew years ago. It wasn't a good scene, but it was short-lived."

I had so many questions, but Grant didn't continue. I couldn't stand it.

"Was there anything between you and Natasha?" I blurted out.

Grant looked stunned. "No!" he responded.

I must've looked doubtful when I glanced at him, because he insisted. "Trish, nothing has ever happened with me and that woman. She was just a friend of someone else I knew."

I nodded and smiled. "Okay," I said, "I believe you."

He smiled back. "Good."

I did believe him. He was a good man, and I'd never known him to lie to me, but still, in the back of my mind, I wondered what circumstance had brought Natasha into his life in any way.

# Chapter Twenty-One

GRANT SAT AT THE KITCHEN TABLE WITH HIS MOM. IT HAD BEEN A WHILE SINCE he'd met the man his mom had been with at the restaurant. Grant hadn't been around her place except to drop off Kylie, and he felt a bit guilty about that, since she'd been asking him to do some things for her. He knew he'd been avoiding her, so he finally decided to drop in and speak to her about her boyfriend. Their conversation had started with niceties but now turned serious.

"Mom," Grant said, trying to be patient, "the guy just started coming to church a few months ago. He's covered in tattoos and, quite frankly, looks really rough."

His mother sighed. "As I've told you, Grant, he hasn't had the same opportunities or background as us, but believe me, he's a nice guy who says God changed him, and I believe it."

"I don't know, Mom. I'm just worried."

"That may be, my son," said Sandy, now getting impatient, "but if anyone is going to be judgemental and tell me they're nervous about who I'm dating, it should *not* be you! And you know why."

Sandy stopped, and she and Grant stared at each other. Grant was unable to speak.

Sandy suddenly broke the silence. "We've been talking about this for twenty minutes, and I'm just going to tell you to leave it alone. I'm a grown woman and—"

"Who hasn't dated in a long time," interrupted Grant, shaking his head and looking down.

"Enough!" stated Sandy, standing up. "We're done with this conversation. Bottom line, Grant—I've prayed about it, and this is between Jack and me!"

She turned her attention to Kylie, who was pulling herself up on the chair next to her.

Even though Grant felt chastised, perhaps appropriately, he still had questions about the man his mother was involved with. She had only shared a few things she knew about Jack. He was about the same age as herself, had never been married, and had no children. He'd been involved with some bad stuff and had spent a short time incarcerated, but Sandy hadn't told Grant why. It was when his mom had divulged that tidbit of information that his radar really started chiming in, and so had he.

Sandy looked at Grant, suddenly softer.

"I know you're concerned for me," she started, "but after getting to know him, I'm really convinced that he's a good man."

Grant looked away, still not convinced.

"I'm going to ask you a question that you asked me a few years ago, Grant. If God forgives us," Sandy finished, "who are we not to forgive?"

"Sure," Grant nodded, unconvinced and a bit irked that his mother would throw his own voice at him. He was tired of the whole conversation and decided to give up on it for now. He got up, gathered Kylie, and left.

# Chapter Twenty-Two

"HI!" GREETED THE SONOGRAPHY TECHNICIAN, SLIDING THE DOOR CLOSED behind her. "My name is Whitney. I'll be doing your ultrasound today. Which pregnancy is this for you?"

Melissa and Trent glanced at each other and both answered in unison, "First."

They laughed, and the ultrasound tech smiled too. "Exciting, huh?" she asked.

"Yes. Very," exclaimed Melissa. "Except maybe for the nausea. That's not so fun."

"Oh, I know it," the technician said. "I have four kids. Been there."

They continued conversing, with Melissa asking about the age of Whitney's children and what her pregnancies had been like. Trent sat in the chair beside the bed. He was nervous and excited.

From the first day of her last period, Melissa was supposed to be around nine weeks pregnant, the opportune time for a dating ultrasound. Everything had seemed okay except for the spotting she'd had for the last two days. That concerned Trent, but Melissa had felt no cramping, which was comforting.

"This should be warm," Whitney said, squirting some ultrasound gel onto Melissa's lower belly. "I'm just going to take a look this way, and if I can see everything clearly, we don't have to move to the vaginal scan."

"Okay," Melissa nodded.

As the ultrasound technician began, she chatted cheerfully. A TV screen was on the wall across from Melissa and Trent so that they could see what Whitney saw. She measured some structures and then lifted the probe from Melissa's belly.

"If you don't mind, I think we'll check things out vaginally, Melissa," she said, matter-of-factly. "I'll just be able to see everything a lot more clearly that way."

Trent smiled at his wife as she went to the bathroom to change, but now he felt more nervous. He had to admit that he didn't know much about ultrasound, so he was hoping they'd see the tiny heartbeat, as expected, with the vaginal scan.

"Everything all right?" Trent asked Whitney.

She smiled and replied, "I just want to see things more clearly this way."

Being a nurse, Trent knew when someone in the health profession was avoiding a question, and Whitney seemed to be. Something in her tone had changed ever so slightly, and he recognized it as a subtle warning.

*Oh God*, he prayed silently, *please let everything be all right, and let us see a heartbeat.*

Whitney instructed Melissa how to lie on the bed and placed the tip of the thin ultrasound probe gently into Melissa's vagina.

"The ultrasound is clearer if we're closer to your uterus, Melissa, so I should see things better this way," she said, looking at her patient.

"That's fine," Melissa said cheerfully, unaware of Trent's concern.

Whitney measured some structures, but this time she seemed to concentrate more intensely on what was on the screen in front of her.

Trent moved closer to Melissa and took her hand. Melissa smiled at him, oblivious to his tension.

It seemed to take a long time, but when Whitney removed the bloodied probe, she was quiet.

"I'll just go speak to the doctor and I'll be right back," she said, smiling at them.

Melissa looked at the man she loved and saw the worry on his face. "Something's wrong, isn't it, Trent?"

"Oh Mel," he answered, not knowing what to say. "I don't think she saw a heartbeat."

"Maybe you're wrong?" she asked, hoping it was so.

"Maybe." He paused and tried to smile. "They'll tell us what's going on." He held her hand fast as they waited.

It seemed like an eternity before Whitney returned, but when she did, she told Melissa to change back into her own clothes and that the doctor would see them.

It was a few minutes before the doctor came in. "Hello, you two," he greeted. He recognized Trent from the hospital and shook his hand. "Hey … Trent." He paused. "Unfortunately, I have some bad news." He looked at Melissa. "What you're having is an early miscarriage, Melissa. It happens in many pregnancies, and we don't usually know why."

He scrolled through some of the many pictures taken by the technician and began explaining them.

Melissa didn't have medical knowledge like her husband. All she'd heard was the word miscarriage, and all she could do was stare straight ahead, not seeing the screen or hearing the doctor any longer. The ache in her heart was sudden and strong. Her baby wasn't alive. She had a dead baby. Her baby had died.

"Do you see here?" the doctor said, addressing Trent. He had let go of Melissa's hand and had moved to stand next to the doctor as he explained. The doctor gave him the sad news, not only about the loss of their baby but of the other strongly suspected findings.

Trent was in shock and felt like the floor had been pulled away and he was sinking, but suddenly he remembered Melissa and moved quickly to her side again.

Melissa was on the stretcher, racked with sorrow. Tears fell down her face. Trent moved in close and held her in his arms, rocking her back and forth.

"It's okay," he soothed. "It'll be okay."

Melissa shook her head. "It's not okay. Our baby's gone," she cried.

The doctor felt it best that he perform a procedure to take out the "products of conception." Melissa hated hearing that. It sounded so cold and like there had never been a baby at all.

"Won't it come out on its own," she asked quietly, "if we just wait?"

The doctor was kind as he explained. "In this case, Melissa, I think it's the best thing to do. Then I can also do an examination and take a really good look inside as well."

She was confused but nodded. She signed the consent, and the procedure was booked for later that day.

"Don't eat or drink anything from now until your surgery," instructed the receptionist before they left the clinic. "Be at the hospital at 3:00 p.m."

Melissa nodded numbly, walking as if in a dream. She suddenly felt so tired and overwhelmed, she just wanted to go home and lie in a dark room—hopefully to wake up later after the nightmare had passed.

Melissa and Trent walked hand in hand to their car, each saying nothing. Trent wished they could turn back time. He was worried about Melissa and was mourning the loss himself. He had been involved with telling people this news in the ER many times, but he hadn't realized just how devastating it was, until now. His child, the one he had dreamed about and talked about with his wife, was gone, and there probably would never be another.

● ● ●

The news from the doctor after the examination was not good. He told them that not only did Melissa miscarry, but a baby probably hadn't developed at all because of Melissa's abnormal uterus. Then the most devastating news—the doctor said it would be impossible to successfully carry a child with that sort of rare uterine anomaly.

Melissa had fallen into a deep depression, and a month later was still unable to cope well. She hadn't been back to work as a daycare worker, which she had loved prior to their loss, and she took no interest in anything around her. Trent talked to one of the psychiatrists at work, but Melissa flatly refused the offer of help.

Trent was in mourning too but was more worried about his wife than anything else.

"I don't know what to do, Trish," Trent's sad voice echoed over the phone. "Melissa is heartbroken, and I'm not even sure if she's grasped the whole diagnosis."

"I'm so sorry, Trent," I breathed. "This is awful."

"Yeah," he said.

We both fell silent for a moment, not knowing what to say.

"Do you want me to come? I could maybe help out?"

Trent thought about it. "No, no yet," he said. "I'll let you know though. Thanks."

"Any time. I'm serious," I said, feeling helpless. "I'll keep praying for both of you, Trent."

I meant that, and I prayed many times over the following days.

# Chapter Twenty-Three

SHAUNA AND I WERE CHANGING OUT OF OUR SCRUBS WHEN I GLANCED AT MY phone. My heart skipped a beat.

Grant: *Pick you up at six?*

Me: *Please*

We'd texted many times, but it had been a few weeks since I'd seen Grant, and I missed him a lot—more than I wanted to admit. I suspected that I did love him but couldn't recognize it. The whole thing was confusing, and I couldn't get the short timeline out of my head. In my thinking, it was ludicrous to think you loved someone so quickly after meeting them.

"By the smile on your face, I'm guessing that's from Grant," Shauna said with eyebrows raised.

I nodded. "Yep."

"Oh, that guy's crazy about you, Trish, and you are for him too. I'm so happy for you," she said.

"I don't know …" I paused. "I like him, for sure, but …"

Shauna laughed. "Well, maybe you can't see it because you're the centre of the affection, but at the barbecue … wow! Even when he was hanging out with the guys, he was watching you. And …" She paused. "You watched him too."

She laughed again and added, "The icing on the cake was when you almost pushed Natasha over and said he belonged to you."

"I never said that!" I denied.

"Maybe not in those exact words, but that's what you meant. You love him, Trish, whether you see it or not."

I didn't know what to say. I sat down in the chair to lace my Sketchers and mostly to appear busy with that.

"Can't recognize it, huh?" Shauna asked.

I shook my head. "I don't know."

Shauna stood to leave as she piped out, "You should, my friend."

That's what I liked about her. She didn't mince words and said it the way she saw it. Although, in this case, I wasn't convinced that she was right.

# Chapter Twenty-Four

GRANT CAME TO GET ME FIVE MINUTES EARLY. THIS TIME, HE CAME UP TO MY apartment. I was caught off guard a little, since he would usually text when he arrived, and I'd just run down. Then I thought of what he'd said the night he kissed me, and my heart stilled.

When the buzzer to the intercom went off, I jumped.

"It's me," he said.

"I'll buzz you in." I tried to sound nonchalant. I'd been feeling more apprehensive about our relationship, and now he'd see my apartment. I wasn't sure how comfortable I was with that.

I opened the door just as he got to it.

"I'm ready," I said.

"Great," he smiled. "Wanna show me your place first?"

"Oh," I took a step back. "Okay."

He leaned in close to my ear and whispered, "It's all right. Nothing bad will happen. I'll try to be good."

I blushed and rolled my eyes as I moved to welcome him inside.

One thing about a small apartment is that it takes only a minute or two to show someone around, and soon we were in his truck and on our way.

"I like your lack of colour scheme," he said, smiling as we drove.

"Well, yes, so do I," I agreed proudly. "I'm renting, so I can't paint or do anything exciting, so the more important question is, did you appreciate my eclectic decorating style?"

"Uh huh," he said, furrowing his brow. Then he shook his head and laughed. "Honestly, I don't know what that means, Trish."

I smiled. "I think people just say that when they can't afford to match everything perfectly, so that's me. Anything and everything goes," I returned, trying to defend my lack of decorating expertise.

"Then I like it," he nodded. "I like relaxed … not pretentious."

"Me too," I agreed, feeling thankful for that.

"I liked the picture over the couch," he said more seriously. "Was that painted by anyone in particular? It's really pretty."

He was referring to a landscape I had fallen in love with years before. It was painted in muted blues, teals, and beiges, and when I looked at it, I felt a certain calm and could imagine being there on the sand beside the ocean.

"Walmart," I smiled and laughed. "I bought it at Walmart, Grant. I have no idea who painted it or anything. I just liked it, and it was on sale."

He laughed. "Love it!"

"I'm a pretty basic girl," I said. "Now you know."

He didn't comment but simply took my hand.

We drove in relaxed silence for a while until we reached a park just on the outskirts of the city. On the way, we talked about Trent and Melissa and how sorry we felt for them. We both wished we could do something to help them but knew we had no course of action.

"Pray," Grant said. "We pray and hope they come to terms with what is or pray for a miracle. Either way, we pray for God's will."

I nodded in agreement but didn't think it was that simple. I'd been with couples trying to cope with the incredible grief of losing a baby, but then I remembered Trevor.

"Is that what you did after losing your son?" I asked quietly.

We had never really talked about the loss of their baby boy, and I didn't understand how, after all the loss this man had suffered, he could be so faithful to God and still see God's goodness.

We had just parked, and Grant became quiet, staring at a spot somewhere above the steering wheel. I was suddenly sorry for asking the question.

"When we lost Trevor, Stacy and I went through some real trouble. It was painful and awful. I'm not going to say it was easy, because it wasn't. Stacy blamed herself, saying that God was punishing her for what she'd done before she knew Him. It was really hard," he said, looking down. "Then we started to pray. Not just say a few words, but really ... pray. Together. Finally, it got easier, and God sent us peace, but it took time. Then Stacy got pregnant again, and all we could do was hold our breath, hope, and keep praying."

There had been a question on my mind since I'd learned about Trevor's inoperable heart condition, and although I knew it probably wasn't the best time, I thought I'd ask it anyway.

"Can I ask you something, Grant?" I said tentatively, unsure how he'd take it.

He looked at me and smiled gently. "Anything."

Now I paused, worried that I'd add to his pain, but I couldn't stop now.

"When you learned that Trevor's heart condition was ... well ... that he wouldn't live," I stumbled, "why didn't you end the pregnancy? Did you really think God would do a miracle?"

He waited before answering while I berated myself for pushing.

Then he slowly shook his head. "No," he breathed, with tears in his eyes. "Although we knew God could do it, we also knew that's not usually what happens."

I waited.

"We talked about it, but it was Stacy's decision. She said that even though she thought we probably wouldn't get the miracle of a healthy boy, she wanted to have all the time she possibly could with him. It was the only time we would have to hold him close."

He fought tears as mine fell.

He smiled in his pain. "I remember the kicks I felt, Trish. They were so strong, and we'd laugh. I tried to feel him every day. We dreamt of what he was like and who he'd grow up to be, just like every other baby. It's just ... he gets to do those things in heaven."

"I'm so sorry for all your loss, Grant. First your son and then Stacy. I don't know how to even tell you how sorry I am," I said, crying. I reached over and hugged him.

"Trish," he whispered into my hair, "it's okay. God knows the bigger plan."

He'd gone through so much pain and sorrow and here he was—strong and courageous with an unbound faith.

"I hope so," I answered, still unsure.

We pulled apart and I looked into his eyes. He wiped some tears off my cheek and smiled.

"I'm hungry," he stated, and I laughed.

He'd brought a cooler with him that contained some sandwiches, chips, and drinks. We ate at a picnic table under the setting sun.

"I want to tell you something, Grant, but it's going to sound weird," I started.

I'd been thinking of telling him about the search for my sister, and because he'd shared so much of himself with me, I felt even more compelled.

"You can tell me anything, Trish. I hope you know that," he said sincerely.

"Thanks," I said with a small smile. I hadn't thought of how I'd tell him, so I took a quick breath. "Well, my mom had a baby when she was really young and gave her up for adoption. Apparently, she tried to contact my mom years ago, but Mom wasn't comfortable with it, so she didn't reply. Now she wants to find her, and she hired a private investigator. He just gave her more information, so I'm going to find her. I have an address."

"Do you want me to go with you?" Grant asked.

I hadn't expected that offer, but my heart softened, and I smiled.

"I don't think so," I said, shaking my head. "I just thought you should know about this. My family's a little mixed up right now."

"Every family has stuff going on, Trish," he said with an encouraging smile.

Grant then told me about his worries about his mom and the man she was spending time with. I empathized greatly. When you love someone, you can't always see straight if you think they could be hurt in any way.

"I haven't known your mom for very long, but I think she's a wise woman, Grant. She won't do anything crazy. I know that for sure."

He smiled. "You're probably right, Trish."

We both were silent for a few minutes, watching as a few people strolled by.

"It's getting cool," he said suddenly. He stood to pack up the leftovers from our supper.

"This was so good, Grant. Better than fast food any day," I said, looking up at his handsome face. "Thank you so much. What a great way to end the day."

Even after the serious conversations we'd had, I felt more at ease with this man.

Together we finished packing everything and walked toward his truck, throwing away the garbage in the can on the way.

"I was serious, Trish," Grant said when we were back in the truck. "I can go with you to find your sister. It might be safer because you never know who you're going to find."

"I'll be fine, Grant," I said, smiling at him, "but you're sweet to offer."

"Well, think about it." He shrugged. "The offer's good anytime if you change your mind." He paused and then sighed. "Are we okay?" He had started the vehicle, but instead of putting it into drive, he turned to face me.

"I know I freaked you out the other night, but I can't apologize for saying I love you, because I do," he said, looking torn.

"I'm sorry I got mad," I replied, looking down at my lap.

"I didn't think you were mad. Maybe ... uh ... more in shock?" he asked with a hopeful look.

I glanced over at him and couldn't help but smile.

He smiled back and leaned toward me. I leaned in as well, and when our lips met, I felt like I was melting. He placed his hand on my cheek and deepened the kiss. When it broke, we both smiled.

"Someday you're going to realize you feel the same about me. I know it," he said smugly as we pulled out of the parking area.

I wanted to say it then, but something stopped me. Although I felt I was learning so much more about him, I still couldn't reconcile finding love in such a short time.

# Chapter Twenty-Five

I STARED AT THE ADDRESS WRITTEN ON THE PAPER IN MY HAND. I LOOKED UP AT the house again to be sure my GPS had brought me to the right place. My heartbeat quickened, and I nervously took a breath. The house was large and grand with beautiful landscaping. I suddenly felt intimidated and more nervous than I'd previously been.

I steeled myself, took another deep breath, and got out of the Rav, clutching the envelope as I walked to the front door. The bell chimed and I waited, nervously moving from one foot to the other. I thought I heard a small child's voice just before I almost gave up, so I moved closer to the large oak door. I leaned on it too hard and suddenly fell inside as someone yanked it open.

"Oh, I'm so sorry," I apologized as I stumbled forward, staring at the looming floor in front of me and trying to right myself but failing. As my knees hit the floor, I heard a voice I recognized.

"Oh my!" I felt a hand on my shoulder. "Are you all right?" she asked with grave concern.

I looked up into Sandy's eyes and gasped.

• • •

My hand shook as I took the coffee cup from Grant's mother. I didn't know where to start. I took a sip, put down the cup, and began.

"I don't know if Grant told you that I'm looking for my sister—the girl my mom gave up for adoption when she was fifteen. This is the address I was given by a private investigator. The last one he gave me was wrong too," I puzzled. "I'm a little confused because it shouldn't be that hard to find one person, especially since she did try to contact my mother years ago."

Sandy watched me in silence.

I smiled and apologized again, reaching for the coffee cup.

"You have a beautiful home, Sandy," I offered, before taking a sip. We sat in the gorgeous living room as Kylie crawled around and stopped to play with various toys on the floor.

"Thank you, Trish," she said quietly, looking somewhat strained, "but it's not my home."

"Oh?" I asked, even more puzzled.

Sandy sighed in resignation. "No," she began. "I'm just babysitting Kylie here today. This is Grant's place."

I must've looked confused, and I could see that Sandy was more uncomfortable now.

"What is it, Sandy?" I asked, feeling sorry for her obvious discomfort but not knowing why.

"May I see that information?" she asked, staring at the envelope I had laid beside me on the couch.

I looked surprised but nodded and handed it to her.

As she opened it, she sighed. She read some of the document and sighed again.

"Natalie Carr," she said, quietly. She looked up at me with tears in her eyes and told me what I'd been waiting to hear.

"She was a beautiful woman … so full of life and fun, but she wasn't always like that, Trish. She had a really rough upbringing … thrown around from foster home to foster home. Suffice it to say, she was in too many places at the wrong time and with the wrong people."

I was really confused but felt sudden hope that Sandy knew my sister.

"When I met her, Trish, I knew that only God could save her, and He did. She'd reached her lowest point, but God met her there. She came out of drug and alcohol addiction as well as other things, and she started a new life. Oh Trish"—Sandy leaned forward in earnest—"she changed more than night and day. She shone with the love of God as only someone with a new heart can."

"So you know my sister then?" I finally asked.

Sandy looked sad and nodded. "Yes, Trish," she said quietly, pausing before telling me. "But her name wasn't Natalie Carr anymore. She changed it when she got married."

I looked at her with sudden realization.

Then Sandy confirmed it with a nod. "Her name was Stacy Evans."

• • •

Every emotion blasted its way through my mind and body as I absorbed that information. It felt as if the blood had left my brain, and, in the shock, an overwhelming tiredness left me breathless. I could only think of one reaction, and this time it was not to laugh.

"I should go," I said simply, placing the cup I'd been holding gently on the coaster.

I could hear Kylie babble in the corner of my mind, and I wanted to say goodbye to her, but I was unable to focus so I stood up and started toward the door instead.

"Trish!" Sandy exclaimed, following me. "You can't leave now. You can't drive after finding out something like this. Please come back and sit down, honey."

I shook my head as I reached the front door. "No," I replied, not knowing what to feel or say but knowing I had to leave. I needed to be alone to sort out my thoughts.

I quickly swung open the front door and, in my haste, slammed into Grant, who had just arrived home. His briefcase flew to the side from the impact.

"Whoa," he laughed as I tried to get past him. "Hey?" he looked confused as he took in our expressions.

"I'm so sorry, Grant," his mother said, looking worried.

"Sorry?" he asked, looking at his mom but grabbing my arms and holding me in front of him.

"She was your wife," I whispered, tears falling from my eyes. I didn't know what else to say.

"What?"

Grant looked so confused, and I would have felt sorry for him if I hadn't been so overwhelmed.

"Come," Sandy said firmly to both of us. "You both come inside and sit down. We've got to talk and sort this all out."

Grant turned me toward the living room and ushered me onto the couch beside him.

Sandy sighed and handed him the papers from the envelope. "Read these, Grant," she said. "Trish came over this afternoon looking for her adopted sister. This explains it."

He took the papers and silently read them. When he read the name Natalie Carr, the realization hit him.

"Oh ... Trish." He closed his eyes and drove a hand through his hair. "What are the chances?"

Grant and his mom talked, and I was part of the conversation, but I couldn't speak. I couldn't believe that in the vastness of the earth and all people in it, his wife had been my sister. I had met her and hadn't known it. I'd rubbed her back in the throes of her labour, and I'd tried to help save her when she was about to die. I'd been there when she'd given birth to my niece.

With that sudden realization, I looked at Kylie and stood up. I went over to where she sat on the floor and sat beside her.

"Hey, baby girl," I said as she came into my lap. I held her as she clapped her hands together. At one point, she reached up with her tiny finger and caught a tear falling down my cheek. I felt an overwhelming love enter my heart and flood my soul.

When I looked up, Grant was staring at me with a mixed expression of sadness and love. Neither one of us spoke for a long time, but Sandy and I cried—maybe for Stacy, maybe for Kylie, maybe for what had passed or what was to come, but certainly for what was.

• • •

Over the next few hours I learned a lot more about my sister—some good and some not as much. She and Grant had met one night at a party thrown by a mutual friend. He was instantly interested but knew she was in a bad way on many levels. He said he couldn't stop thinking about her, and although he didn't want to be part of her way of life, God spoke to him about her often.

He'd met her again at a movie and offered to pick her up for church one Sunday. She'd scoffed at the idea but eventually called him and went. It took some time for her to accept the Lord as her Saviour, but after that, Grant knew he wanted to marry her.

Sandy hadn't initially been in favour of the marriage because of Natalie's background, and she was nervous for her son, but that hadn't stopped Grant. He was determined that she was the bride for him, so shortly after Stacy realized God's love for her, they married.

That's when Natalie changed her name. She told them that since she was changing her last name, she'd change the first one too to signify a totally new beginning. She'd been reading a novel at the time and had chosen the name of the heroine in that book. Stacy was a strong, loving woman who'd overcome many obstacles, and Natalie wanted to be that kind of woman.

Sandy had learned to love Stacy fiercely, and as their marriage became stronger, she knew that Stacy truly loved her son.

"Is that when you met Natasha?" I asked, remembering that at the barbecue Natasha thought she'd recognized Grant and he'd admitted to meeting her.

"It was," he answered. "I'm so sorry, but I just couldn't tell you about it the night of the party. Stacy and I agreed not to look back to the days when she struggled. Natasha was a close friend of Stacy's when we met for the first time. When Stacy turned her life around, Natasha was upset. She thought I'd taken Stacy away from her. I didn't know Natasha well, but Stacy said later she had to walk away from the friendship. She wasn't strong enough to continue because their relationship was so toxic. Natasha, apparently, didn't take that well, but Stacy didn't tell me how bad it got. She just said she had to walk away."

Later that evening I got into my SUV to drive home.

"You think you're okay to drive?" Grant asked with a concerned tone.

"Yeah, I think so," I answered, looking at him with a small smile. "Honestly, I started feeling better when your mom prayed for us, Grant."

"I still think I should drive you home," he offered. "This is so crazy, Trish."

"I know, right?" I whispered. "Unbelievable."

I shook my head as I started my car, assuring him again that I'd be fine.

I'd spent the last four hours at Grant's place. I would've left sooner, but Sandy had insisted we talk, eat, and pray together. Not only had the news been a huge shock for me but for them as well. When I told Grant that I was looking for my sister, I hadn't mentioned the name Natalie Carr. If I had, he would've known immediately that I was looking for Stacy.

Grant leaned into my driver's side window and whispered, "This doesn't change anything about us. I still love you." He brushed aside the lock of hair that had fallen out of my ponytail and kissed my cheek.

"Really?" I asked, turning my face to look at his.

"Really," he said with resolve.

I said nothing, but as I pulled away, I wondered how it couldn't change things.

# Chapter Twenty-Six

"OH, WHY DIDN'T I JUST REPLY TO THE AGENCY WHEN SHE TRIED TO CONTACT me years ago?" cried my mother.

I'd gone to my parents' place the next day, trading my shift with another nurse because I knew this couldn't wait. Both my parents were home for a change, and now they sat across from me as I shared the news about my half-sister—my mother's other daughter.

"I'm so sorry, Mom," I said, feeling so badly for her.

"It's okay, honey," soothed my father as he sat next to her, clasping her hand. "You didn't know."

She leaned into my father's arms, and as he held her, I could see only love and concern in his eyes.

The doorbell rang and I stood up to answer it.

"Trent!" I said in surprise as I swung the door open. "How are—"

"Trish ... what are you doing here?" he asked. He looked surprised, probably because I hadn't called to tell him or Melissa that I was in town, but he clearly had something else on his mind. "Sorry, I need your dad," he said quickly, pushing past me.

My father looked up into Trent's anxious eyes.

"What's going on, Trent?" he said, tensing, but not letting go of my mother.

"It's Melissa. She's ... well, she was in a bad way, and now I can't find her," he stammered.

I'd never seen Trent like this. He was agitated, anxious, and a ball of worry.

"Dr. Holmes," he said, "I thought the antidepressant was helping, but now I'm not so sure. She seemed better for a while, but for the last couple of days, she's been really despondent—distant, you know? I texted from work this morning, and she hasn't answered. I went home because I was worried, but she's not there and she hasn't answered any of my texts this afternoon either."

I began texting Melissa even before he stopped talking. Maybe she'd answer me.

"Did you try her family? Friends?" I asked.

"Yes." He nodded. "Her mom hasn't heard from her either, but they're in the city. I'm really worried."

"We'll fan out and look for her," said my dad, standing. My mother had stopped crying and stood up as well, straightening her skirt.

"I'll help too," she stated.

"Make a list of the places she goes to and we'll start looking," I said.

Trent told us a few of her favourite stops.

"Helen," my dad said, looking at my mother, "Are you okay to stay here and try calling people?"

He knew he was asking a lot after the news she'd just been given, but we didn't know Melissa's state of mind, and we needed to find her.

"Yes ... of course," she said, nodding. "You go. I'll be fine, Ted. I'll call you if I hear from anyone."

He gave her a quick hug and looked at Trent. "Give Helen any numbers of people you think she'd call. That way we do the driving and she'll do the calling."

"Good idea," I said as I grabbed my jacket.

Trent quickly texted some contact information for various family and friends to Helen. Then we left, ready to fan out to find Melissa.

"If she calls, I'll let you know," Trent said.

"Same," I replied, and my dad nodded.

We got into our vehicles, addresses in hand. Melissa had many friends and acquaintances. She could be anywhere. For over an hour we hunted but with no result. I could tell by Trent's texts that he was frustrated and worried.

I was at the last address Trent had given me to check out when I remembered what Grant had told me more than once: "Pray about everything. God is good and knows the whole picture."

I stopped the car and bowed my head. "Dear Lord," I prayed anxiously, "you know where Melissa is, and you know her state of mind. Please let us find her."

I sat for a few moments, staring at my phone and half-expecting someone to text me with good news. A memory pushed into my mind just then and I pulled my car out onto the road. Maybe it was a long shot, but still ...

Twenty minutes later, I drove onto the yard site of the ranch that belonged to Melissa's parents. I saw Melissa's parked Prius and breathed a short sigh of relief. I couldn't see Melissa or anyone else around, so I walked up the stairs in front of the house and banged on the door.

"No one's home, but can I help you?" asked a deep, raspy voice behind me.

I jumped, having not heard anyone approaching. I turned to see an older man dressed in overalls, a plaid shirt, and a cowboy hat looking up at me from the bottom of the veranda.

"Please," I said, starting to descend the stairs, "can you tell me if you've seen Melissa? Her car's here but—"

The friendly ranch-hand smiled and asked, "And you are?"

"Oh, I'm sorry," I apologized. "I should explain. I'm Trish Holmes, a friend of Melissa's. I'm looking for her. No one can find her, but she told me about a favourite spot here on the ranch. I thought I'd just check it out."

He told me his name was Brian and he'd worked for Melissa's parents for years. He'd known Melissa since she was a baby and had watched her grow up.

"You'd be talking about the swing by the water," he said, nodding knowingly.

Brian gave me the directions and asked if he should join me. I declined, but after I started out, I stopped for a minute to think. Trent had called numerous times over the last weeks and told me how depressed Melissa was. I knew that sometimes antidepressants worked the opposite way, and instead of feeling better, people could become suicidal. I debated going back to get Brian but decided to continue on my own.

I walked down a dirt road until I reached the large rock he said would be to my left. I then walked down a narrow path toward the creek. I heard the rush of water over rocks before I saw it.

And then I saw her.

Melissa was sitting—not on the swing she had told me about, but on the bank beside the stream. She stared across it as though in a trance, her feet dangling in the cold water. I watched as she kicked a toe up and the tiny spray from that small action dripped back into the moving water. I breathed a sigh of relief.

I didn't want to disturb her. She looked so serene and at peace. Instead, I backed away as quietly as I could and quickly texted Trent and my parents that I'd found her. Unfortunately, I'd forgotten to turn my phone to vibrate, so Trent's text soon sung out into the silence, and I abruptly dropped my phone.

Melissa turned, startled, as I scrambled to grab my phone off the ground.

I looked up to see her staring at me with a smile that almost reached laughter.

"I'm so sorry," I said, feeling foolish. "Just ... um ... continue with what you're doing," I stammered, embarrassed.

"Oh Trish," she said, standing up. "I was just thinking about you."

I must have looked befuddled, and she laughed out loud.

"What?" I asked, confused and still brushing dirt off my phone.

"I should probably be the one asking what," she said. "Like ... what are you doing here?"

Melissa wrapped her sweater a little tighter around herself.

"Oh yeah." I paused. "Looking for you. Trent came over to my folks' place and told us he couldn't find you anywhere. He's really worried."

"But Trent's at work," she said, now the one looking confused.

"He left work because he said you weren't answering your phone," I replied.

"Oh," she offered simply. "I guess I left my phone at home ... or maybe in my car."

"Are you all right?" I asked, trying to see into her face. I'd walked toward her and now could see her red-rimmed, puffy eyes.

"I guess so," she said, hugging herself with crossed arms. "It's been a tough time."

I just nodded, not knowing what to say. How could I possibly relate to what had happened to her and Trent? I had never lost a baby, and I'd certainly never been told I couldn't have one. How devastating for them.

"I'm so, so sorry Melissa," I said. I had texted her often over the last weeks and tried calling, but she'd been evasive.

She nodded now, turning away and walking back to the edge of the stream to sit again. I slipped off my shoes and joined her. We sat side by side in silence, circling our toes in the moving water.

"You know," Melissa said, quite a while later, "losing the baby was horrible enough, but knowing that I'll never carry one …well, I can't wrap my mind around that."

"I'm sure," I offered, unable to say anything else.

"My uterus isn't shaped right or something, I guess," she explained. "They say it's the worst they've seen and that women with this kind of septal defect can't carry babies because they won't grow properly … or something like that." She sighed. "Defect," she stated. "There's a word you don't hear every day about yourself, thank God. I know it's a medical term, but it's awful when you hear it about you." She teared up as she continued. "Just like products of conception," she gasped. "My baby wasn't that to me! It was a real baby, not just a product."

She cried then, leaning into my side like a child. I simply held her and somehow understood. Even if I'd never been through it, I'd had a taste through other people's grief, and it was always the same—completely heartbreaking.

After a while, she straightened and took a few deep breaths.

"I suppose Trent told you all this already."

I nodded, giving her a side-long glance, suddenly wondering if that bothered her. "That okay?"

"Sure," she answered immediately, shrugging. "I get it. You're not only close friends, but you're both nurses. You understand this stuff more than I do." She paused, in her own thoughts.

"Does that bother you, Melissa?" I asked. "That Trent and I talk sometimes?"

She gave me a side-long glance and a half smile. "It used to ... a little ... but now it doesn't." Her smile grew. "Besides, he doesn't talk to you, or about you, as often as he used to."

I smiled back.

"You know," I sighed, "I've known Trent for a long time, Melissa. I once wished I could love him in another way, like you do, but it never happened. I know why now."

Melissa waited for me to continue.

"God knew we weren't meant for each other like you and he are. Melissa, Trent loves you so much. I've known him his whole life, and he saw other girls, but he never, ever loved anyone. He is crazy about you, and clearly he was waiting for you. God knew you needed each other ... and He knows all about this baby thing too."

We were silent for a while longer, lifting our feet from the even cooler water as the late afternoon waned.

"Do you think they're right ... that I won't have children of my own?" she said, breaking the silence.

I sighed. "I'm really sorry, Melissa."

She nodded with tears forming again.

"Trent's really worried about you," I said softly.

"I know," she answered. "I tried some antidepressants, but nothing improved. I've been so sad all the time. I can't seem to get out of it. I thought I'd come here to get away and maybe get a different perspective." She looked at me as a few silent tears fell. "I needed to have it out with God too."

I put my arm around her, and she laid her head against my shoulder again.

We sat for a long while and then we talked ... about everything. We talked about loss and how it changes everything and everyone involved. I told her about Stacy and finding out that she had been my sister. She was shocked by that, and we talked for a long while about it. As our time together grew to a close, we discussed Trent and laughed more about his quirks. She shared a little about Grant's idiosyncrasies as well, and I found myself intrigued.

The sun was low in the sky, and even the mosquitoes had gone to bed because of the cool air before we walked back to the house together.

"I feel a little better," Melissa said. "You're a good listener."

"Hmm," I said, "so are you."

"At least we have good men," she returned. "I can't imagine going through this alone. As nuts as I've been lately, I don't know why he even puts up with me. And now that I can't have kids ..." She looked like she was going to melt down again.

I stopped walking and grabbed both of her shoulders.

"Listen!" I said firmly. "I know Trent, and I know he loves you more than anyone on the face of the earth. No matter what happens, Melissa, he loves you! Having children or no children will never change that."

She looked at me and slowly nodded. "That's what he said too. He said God let this happen for a reason, and we may not ever know why, but He knows the whole picture."

"He sounds like Grant," I said, smiling and letting go of her as we started walking again.

"Do you believe that Trish?" she asked simply.

I thought before answering. "I know that God is good, but I also know it doesn't always feel that way."

We walked in comfortable silence for a few minutes.

"What's happening with you and Grant anyway?" Melissa asked.

I rolled my eyes. "Well, things are ... more complicated now."

She looked at me as we reached the yard. "How so?" she asked.

"Because of what I just told you. My sister was his wife!"

"I'm not seeing the big problem, Trish," she said simply.

"And ... he told me he loves me," I added.

"What?" she exclaimed. "When?"

"A while ago, actually," I answered.

"Wow!" she said. "He doesn't waste any time."

"That's what I thought," I replied. "It's too fast. How could anyone possibly know that so soon?"

She opened her mouth and then closed it again.

"Well," she started eventually, "Trent told me he loved me after just a few dates. I know we knew each other years ago, but it blew my mind a little anyway. Honestly, though, I knew I loved him too." She shrugged her shoulders and continued. "I think when you know you just do, and when God's in it, it just happens the way it should."

"Hmm," I said. I'd have to think more about that.

Melissa and I hugged each other before we climbed into our vehicles.

"Hey, Trish," she said before I closed my door, "I'm sorry I took you away from being with your folks right now. You're all going through a lot."

"No," I told her emphatically. "It's fine. We were all more worried about you. I'm just glad I found you."

She held up the phone she'd found on her passenger seat, shrugged, and smiled sheepishly.

I smiled as I drove away, relieved and thanking God that she was safe.

# Chapter Twenty-Seven

"HEY, MOM," I SAID, KNOCKING SOFTLY ON HER BEDROOM DOOR.

"Come in," she answered.

She was sitting in front of her dresser brushing her hair and staring into the bevel-edged mirror. She turned to face me when I entered the room. I could see she had been crying, and sympathy filled my heart.

"Are you okay?" I asked, coming to sit on the edge of her bed.

She tried to smile. "I will be. I think I'm just … overwhelmed today."

I sighed. "It's been one of those days. Really overwhelming."

She nodded numbly.

"I'm glad you found Melissa, Trish. I don't know her well, but I'm glad she's safe," she said vacantly.

"I'm really sorry, Mom," I said, genuinely concerned for her. "I'm so sorry that Stacy was your daughter and you never got to meet her or know her."

She looked down at the carpet as if lost in thought. She nodded.

"You know, Mom, I didn't get to know Stacy well, but I did take care of her. She was really nice, I think."

I didn't feel it was necessary to mention the little I knew about her life before Grant. What would be the point of breaking my mother's heart again? After all, Stacy had changed and had lived a great life with Grant in the last few years. That's what I wanted my mother to know.

"Do you think she had a good life, Trish?" she then asked, making me wonder if she'd just read my mind.

"I know that Grant loved her very much, Mom. I know she was happy when I met her," I answered. It wasn't a lie but just a little evasion, I reconciled in my mind.

She accepted that and replied, "Well, that's good at least."

My mother stood up then and came to sit beside me on the bed. She asked again about Melissa, and I told her a little of our conversation.

"That poor girl," she said, shaking her head. "That's devastating news. And here I've had children and the first one I didn't keep."

She started to cry again, and I hugged her.

"Mom, that wasn't your fault," I assured her. "You were fifteen-years-old. You had to do what your mom wanted. You can't blame yourself. Please."

She nodded, unconvinced.

"It'll take time, Mom. You need to give this a lot of time," I said, still holding her.

We held each other for a while until we heard my father coming up the stairs.

"I'll be all right," she said, patting my arm and standing.

"Hey, my ladies," sang out my father as he swung their bedroom door open fully. "How are you both doing?"

He had gone back to the hospital for some emergency after I'd texted that I had found Melissa. It had been a few hours, but now he was home again.

"We're fine," my mother and I both chorused.

All three of us looked at each other and smiled.

"We will be," I said, looking up at my mom. She looked down and nodded.

"Well, I'm hitting the shower and then early to bed," said my dad, crossing the room and giving my mom a gentle kiss on her cheek.

My mom smiled, and her eyes followed my father as he went into their en suite. She sighed. "Yes, we will be."

I stood up, gave her another hug, and said goodbye.

"Why don't you stay the night, Trish? It's late to drive back," she said.

"It's not that late, Mom, and it's only a two-hour drive. I start a string of night shifts tomorrow, so I'd like a long night's sleep in my own bed tonight. That way I can sleep in as long as I want tomorrow."

"Well, honey, can I make you coffee first?" she asked, forever the hostess.

"No, Mom," I said, "but thanks. I'll pick up something on my way out. Just have a good evening, and don't worry."

She nodded.

Before I left her room, she stopped me with one last request.

"Trish?" She paused.

"Yeah, Mom?"

"When you're done working your nights, and when it works for you, I'd like to meet my granddaughter."

•  •  •

I stopped at a drive-thru to grab a coffee and cheeseburger before leaving town and was on the highway by 8:00 p.m. I turned the radio on and listened to some old rock and pop songs, turning up the volume to keep from getting sleepy. After an hour or so, I played with the instrumentation options and found the Christian radio station I liked.

I was just getting into the last hour when my Bluetooth indicated a call.

"Hi," I answered.

"Hi," said Grant on the other side. "What are you up to?"

I explained that I had decided to drive to my parents' place with the news about Stacy and then added a little information about Melissa.

"She was in a better frame of mind when I called her just after leaving my parents' place," I told him. "Trent sounded better too. They were on speaker together."

"I feel really bad for them," Grant said.

"Me too. I can't even imagine that."

"How are you doing, Trish? You haven't had an easy time of it either," he stated.

"Well," I said, "that's life. I'll get over the shock soon, but I'm not so sure about my mom."

"It's got to be tough for her," he said.

Our conversation was a bit halted, but what could either of us say?

Before we ended the call, I had to ask: "My mom wants to see Kylie. Would you be okay with that?"

"Of course. She'll want to see her and get to know her too. Of course that's okay. When?" he asked.

"I need to get this set of nights over with and then we'll arrange something, if that's all right?"

"For sure," he answered. "Just let me know when it works for you."

"Thanks, Grant," I said, smiling a little and suddenly wondering what my mother would be like as a grandma.

"You be careful driving, okay?" he said.

"Well, I don't know," I snickered. "I thought of getting in my car tonight and not driving carefully, but since you told me too—"

"Hey! Don't forget—I know how fast you drive."

I smiled at how he sounded when he laughed, and it felt good to laugh with him.

"When will I see you again?" he asked more seriously.

"After my nights?" I queried.

"How many?" he queried back.

"Six, with one off in between. I had to make a trade to make this trip work, so now I'll be paying for it," I answered.

"Apparently we'll all be paying for it if I only get to see you in week," he stated sarcastically.

"I guess so," I said, suddenly wishing I could see him. "I'm sorry. I wish it could be sooner."

"Me too," he said.

We said our goodbyes, and I promised to text when I got home. I don't know if it was because I heard his voice just then, or if it had been the incredibly emotion-filled couple of days, but when I clicked the button to end the call, my eyes filled with tears and I had to stop the car.

I pulled over to the closest approach I could find on the side of the road, placed my car in park, and cried in the dark. I cried for everyone.

I cried for my mom, who had lost a baby all those years ago and then lost her again before knowing her.

I cried for Grant, who had lost a son and then a wife he adored and had been left to raise a daughter alone.

I cried for Stacy, who would never know the sweet little girl she had given birth to, or how well she and Grant were doing.

I cried for Melissa and Trent, who not only lost their hopes and dreams in a failed pregnancy but now had to live in a future with no children of their own.

As I cried, I prayed for them all— that God would keep all the people I loved safe and that I would be a help to all of them. I confessed my lack of faith and asked for wisdom in my life choices, especially involving Grant.

I cried and asked that I would know the goodness of God and really believe it, every day and in every circumstance.

The song "He Knows" by Jeremy Camp was playing, and as I listened to the words, I thanked God. For the first time in my life, I really believed that God truly knew what was happening in our lives—mine, Grant's, everyone I loved, and everyone else.

Like the song said, God knew every tear I cried and every hurt I'd felt.

I'd run from so many things, but still God was there, always knowing and showing me His unconditional love, even when I didn't see it. As a child, teen, and now as a young woman, nothing had ever separated me from Him. Nothing.

As I pulled out to begin the last half hour of my drive, I suddenly knew on that quiet, dark highway what Grant had said so many times—that God *is* good, and He is good *all the time,* even and maybe more so during the worst times. Especially when I couldn't see it.

"Thank you," I breathed over and over as I cried again. "Thank you for loving me—no matter what."

# Chapter Twenty-Eight

MELISSA HAD APOLOGIZED PROFUSELY FOR WORRYING TRENT AFTER SHE'D returned home, and Trent, as always, had tried to understand. He had gone back to finish his shift once he received Trish's text and had worked the next few days as well.

"Just … please tell me where you're going from now on," Trent said, holding Melissa as they lay in bed a few nights later.

"I told you. I needed some time alone to sort some things out," she said quietly. "I always think better on the ranch, in that place. When I was a kid, I went there when things got tough, and I guess I just needed to go back to think things through, but I'm sorry I didn't tell you."

"We're in this together, Melissa. I wish you'd believe that." He sighed.

She nodded, her head on his shoulder. "I know you say that, Trent, but I also know you really wanted kids, and I just can't imagine why you'd stay with someone who can't give them to you." Her tears were threatening. "It's not what you signed up for. I'd understand if it's a deal breaker."

With that, Trent moved up on his elbows, pushing Melissa abruptly over to her side of the bed. She looked surprised, but he looked at her with exasperation.

"Do you not know me at all by now? I've told you this over and over. I made a promise for better or worse, and maybe this isn't the better part, but a promise is a promise, and I'm keeping mine! What do you take me for?" he said angrily. He'd stood up and was now pacing around the room.

He was clearly hurt and had had enough. Over the last long weeks, he had tried to tell Melissa, in a gentle and thoughtful manner, how much he loved her. He had held her, consoled her, felt overwhelmingly sorry for her, and had tried to understand. Why couldn't she understand that he loved her no matter what happened? As many times as he had told her, she still didn't believe him. Now the stressful weeks had caught up with him.

"I've tried to be patient, Mel. I have. I've tried to make you understand! If you think my heart hasn't been ripped apart too, well … you'd be wrong. I wanted our own children too, but"—his voice broke and became softer—"if that can't happen, then that's going to have to be okay. We have to be okay. Somehow we have to get through this and then get on with our lives—together."

Melissa stared at her husband and said nothing for a few seconds. She'd never seen him angry before. He'd always been so gentle and soft-spoken. She watched him now as he walked back and forth, upset, and pushing his hands through his thick, blond hair. She loved the way he moved and the deep resonance of his voice.

"Okay," she finally breathed, tearing up. "I believe you, Trent, and I love you more than I could ever tell you."

He stopped suddenly and then slowly came toward her to sit on her side of the bed. He placed his hand on her cheek and rubbed her temple gently with his thumb.

"I love you, Melissa, with my whole heart. Nothing will ever change that."

"I love you too, Trent, forever, and I'm so sorry," she whispered as he lowered his head close to hers.

Before she could say any more, he kissed her—softly at first but then with a passion that only two people who are the other half of each other have.

Much later, after they were both breathing easily again, Melissa ran her hand along Trent's back. She stared at her husband as he slept.

There were still so many things she didn't know about him, but she couldn't wait to find out.

# Chapter Twenty-Nine

MY SIX NIGHT SHIFTS BEGAN WITH AN INCREDIBLE BURST OF BEAUTIFUL BABIES. We literally ran for the first three nights, and I slept most of the day and next night out of sheer exhaustion.

It was during my fifth night out of the six that I cared for a patient with a history much like Stacy's. This patient had also had a previous caesarian section and was trying for a vaginal delivery. I did a lot of praying as I watched her closely in labour and thanked God when things turned out well. Unfortunately, it got me thinking again of the night Stacy died, and I woke up the next day having hardly slept.

I entered the Labour unit feeling tired and somewhat grumpy on my sixth, and last, night. Thankfully, Shauna and I were working together. She'd been off for a week, so she bounced into work bubbling over with enthusiasm.

"I am so not up to your energy level," I said as she chattered on.

The night looked promisingly "quiet" (a word nurses never breathe out loud when working their shift). As is usual, babies come in fits and starts. I've always said, "it's all or nothing" and more than often, that's the case. Well, we'd had our "storm," and now we only had one person in labour, who I was not assigned to care for.

Shauna and I had just done two hours worth of stocking cupboards, which were badly depleted, and doing "checks" on the things that needed updating. We were now sitting in the break room.

"What's up, buttercup?" Shauna cheerfully inquired as she placed her feet on the chair across from her.

I smiled. "With what?"

"Oh, don't play dumb with me. The man!"

I looked up from my phone, which I noticed held a recent text from Grant, and replied, "He's good."

"That's not saying enough," she said dryly.

"He's great, actually," I smiled. "It's all the other stuff that's over-whelming."

I shared some of the details of the days preceding my string of night shifts. Because we were alone in the break room, I told Shauna about Stacy being my half-sister. As I spoke, I was surprised that it didn't seem to bother me as much as it had. Maybe it would be all right. Maybe God, in some wonderfully strange way, had planned it this way.

"Wow," Shauna said. "That's a lot to take in, Trish. Really. Wow."

"Right?" I said, shaking my head.

Shauna cleared her throat. "Have you told him you love him yet?"

I didn't answer, and she could tell that I hadn't admitted it to him.

"I just think, maybe, this might make a difference," I said lamely.

"Even you don't believe that, Trish," she said, standing up and walking to the sink to wash her hands before returning to work. "Don't be a chicken. He loves you, and you clearly love him. Take a leap of faith, girl."

Instead of replying, I looked down at the vibrating phone in my hand.

Grant: *Wanna do supper tomorrow after you sleep?*

Me: *Since it's my last night shift, would breakfast work before I sleep?*

Grant: *Even better to see you sooner. Wanna come here?*

Me: *Sure, but I get off at 7. You up that early?*

Grant: *Remember I have a small child?*

I smiled then and sent him a happy face emoji. I stood up, seeing that a woman had just walked onto the unit who looked like she was probably in active labour.

"Let's have another baby," I said, knowing our break was over.

"That's what we're here for," exclaimed Shauna, throwing the paper towel she'd used to dry her hands into the garbage.

The couple, Ryan and Allison, were having their second baby, and she was coming fast. Shauna and I asked questions about Allison's prenatal history as fast as we could between her contractions.

"We have a two-year-old boy at home," Ryan shared excitedly as he paced beside Allison, who was breathing hard during a strong pain. "This is a girl, and we're super pumped."

"I have to poop," Allison said, grunting, as Shauna and I quickly peeled her clothes off.

"I'll get you to lie down real quick first and check your cervix. That sensation might just be the baby's head ready to come out," I instructed.

"Okay," groaned Allison, "but hurry, please."

"I will. I promise," I said while donning a sterile glove.

She lay down between contractions that were coming more often.

"You're doing great!" I said as I felt for dilation, thinning, and the position of the baby's head. "You're nine centimetres; the head is low and in a perfect face down position, Allison. It won't be long."

"I feel so much pressure!" she wailed again, grunting. "I gotta go to the bathroom!"

"Allison," I said, calmly, "that's the baby's head you're feeling. I know you feel like you need to go, but I can't let you up to the bathroom. You'd have the baby in the toilet. You'll soon push, and all that pressure will be gone once the baby's out."

"I want an epidural!" she yelled.

"Well, I don't think we'll have time for that, Allison. The baby will be here before we'll even arrange for it."

That piece of news did not impress my patient but made her wail even louder. She grunted and screamed through the next contraction as I felt the rest of her cervix disappear from under my fingers.

"Call the doc, please," I said to Shauna, keeping my gloves on before even prepping her. This baby wasn't going to wait for us to get the bed apart for the birth.

"Done," said Shauna moments later.

I could hear Shauna busy behind me getting instruments, Oxytocin, and other things ready, but it all faded into the background as I concentrated on Allison.

"Look at me," I said softly to Allison.

As she glanced up, I caught her eye and, with a smile, calmly said, "Your baby's head is right here. You give a push with the next contraction and the head will be born. It will burn like crazy, but if you can push past that you'll be holding your baby. Okay?"

She nodded, breathing rapidly.

I could feel the baby's head start to rotate and said, "Allison, your contraction is starting. Take a few deep breaths."

She did.

"Now hold your breath and push," I said, looking down as the not-so-small head with thick, black hair came toward me.

"Now stop and pant," I said quickly. The baby's entire head slowly emerged.

"And now just breathe," I added while quickly feeling for a cord around the baby's neck. I found one loose loop and quickly slipped it over the head.

"Okay," I continued, looking up again at Allison. "The rest of the baby's ready to be born. Are you ready to push again, or do you want to wait for another contraction?"

"I can't wait!" she said, grunting loudly while holding her breath to push.

The anterior and then posterior shoulder came easily. The rest of the baby's body came with a large splash of clear amniotic fluid, and I lifted her onto her mother's stomach. The baby screamed immediately, and everyone laughed.

"She's not impressed," I smiled, feeling warm after the excitement of delivering her.

I looked up at her parents, who were beaming with delight as they touched and got to know their new daughter in those early moments that people treasure to memory. Ryan's tears brimmed over, and as has happened many times before when watching fathers with their new babies, my eyes teared as well.

"I'm sorry I missed it," said the young doctor who'd been paged for the birth. He ran, breathless, into the room just as the cord stopped pulsing between my fingers.

"That's okay," said Ryan, glancing at the doctor. "I think we were in good hands."

Ryan looked at me and mouthed "thank you" as I moved aside so the doctor could continue with cutting the cord and delivering the placenta.

I smiled as I did vital signs and assessed Allison. Shauna attended to the baby and put identification bands on her and her mother.

"Everything looks great," said the doctor, sounding impressed, after examining Allison's perineum and placenta. "You don't even need stitches."

"Thanks!" said Allison. "I had so many stitches with our first baby. It was ridiculous!"

"Well, not this time," piped up Shauna. "That's probably because Trish delivered you. She's pretty good at it."

"I think it was because you had great control at the end, Allison," I said sincerely. A patient who has control does themselves a huge favour sometimes.

"Well, thank you anyway," Allison said, beaming up at me. "I'm glad you didn't let me go to the bathroom. You were right. She would've been born in the toilet."

Ryan laughed and said, "But then I could've called her my porcelain doll."

We all laughed, enjoying the emotional high that comes with a beautiful birth experience. I was glad that Allison and Ryan could always consider this a wonderful memory.

I'd thought of that often since Stacy's death. I had attended many births that weren't as easy and where things were unexpected and didn't go as "planned," and I'd come to one conclusion: In the end, a healthy mother and baby always meant a good birth experience to me.

After Allison was moved to the postpartum area, our unit was without any labour patients. The other patient who had been there at the start of the shift had been sent home, deemed to be in false labour. It was a rarity not to have any patients on our usually busy unit, but we knew it wouldn't last long, so we all enjoyed the lull.

I'd been sitting on our break room couch for a few minutes, which I had often said was the one I should have at home, since it was much more comfortable. The other nurses understood how tired I was, as they'd also experienced working long stretches. They were either very quiet or had left the room. The next thing I knew …

"Wakey wakey," whispered Shauna, a distant voice in my ear.

"Wh ...what?" I asked, opening my eyes gradually. "What time is it?"

"Time to go home," she said, smiling down at me. "I thought I'd wake you up before the day staff come in and find you sleeping."

"Oh no!" I exclaimed. "I'm *so* sorry!"

I looked at my watch. It was 6:00 a.m. I'd been asleep for almost three hours.

"How could you leave me here?" I asked, feeling distressed and ashamed.

"Listen," she answered. "Nothing's going on. No one else came in. We're just admitting one of the inductions for today. She just got here and is fine. Why shouldn't one or two of us get some rest when nothing's happening? We didn't need you, Trish. Relax."

That made me feel better, but although I knew others had done it, I had never slept on my shift before, and I felt guilty about it. I thanked Shauna and the other nurses for letting me rest but told them I wouldn't let it happen again.

I drove to Grant's place feeling anything but tired.

# Chapter Thirty

"I TALKED TO MELISSA," GRANT SAID, FLIPPING A PANCAKE OVER IN A FRYING PAN on the stove. "She and Trent are thinking about going to some adoption agencies to get on the list for a baby."

"Wow," I said, bouncing Kylie up and down on my lap by the kitchen table. "That's fast."

"Mel's been in such a depression since the miscarriage. Now that she's coming out of it, she'll be determined to do something about the problem. She's a problem-solver. I know that. If she wants a baby, she'll get one. It's probably good," he answered.

"Hmm, hopefully," I said. "Adoption isn't as easy as it was years ago. There aren't a lot of people giving up babies anymore."

"Well," Grant said as he brought a freshly made pancake to the table, "God knows, and if He has a baby for them, they'll get one."

I smiled as I tore up a pancake in tiny pieces for Kylie. I blew on a small piece, but before I could finish, she pulled it from my fingers and ate it.

"Okay, missy," I grinned, bopping her gently on the nose. "If you're going to be like that, you're going into your highchair. I won't get any if you're not going to share." She giggled as I lifted her into the chair and placed the tray in front of her.

"You'll want her in there anyway, Trish." Grant nodded toward the highchair as I got her settled. "She's a really messy eater, and she'll have you covered in no time," he added, walking back to the stove.

She squealed for more food. Now that the pancake was cooler, I placed some pieces of it in front of her.

As I watched Grant at the stove, I asked, "Can I help you with anything?"

"You are, by feeding her," he said, working with the contents of the frying pan again.

"Do you like cooking?"

"I do," he said, glancing toward me and then back at the pancake on the flipper. "I'm average, I guess, but I really enjoy it. It's cathartic sometimes."

"I'm not a good cook. I guess I should tell you ... I don't even like it that much," I admitted. "My mom is the kitchen queen. She's always been a great cook, but she didn't really teach me. That's something she said she regrets now, since I'm pretty pathetic, and she knows it."

Grant laughed.

I continued. "She told me she did a great disservice to the man I'd marry and that he certainly won't be marrying me for my culinary skills. She told me once to be honest from the get-go that I can't cook well. If that's a problem for him, he should know right off the bat, she said."

I'd been busy watching Kylie scarf down the pancake and small sausage pieces that Grant had prepared for her, so when I was done nattering, I didn't really notice he'd been quiet. When I glanced his way, he was looking at me with a smirk, and I blushed.

"What?" I asked. "I'm telling you the truth. I can't cook. There. Now you know."

"Well," he smiled, "I was wondering about that, since you've never invited us over for a meal or anything."

"Oh, you can come for a meal anytime," I said simply, smiling back. "Just maybe bring your own food."

He laughed again and said, "Stacy was pretty good, but I kinda taught her some stuff, so I can teach you too, if you want."

I turned my attention back to Kylie, unsure of what to say. He noticed my silence but said nothing more about cooking.

We talked about everyday things and how my night shifts had gone. It was comfortable and relaxing, and we enjoyed laughing at Kylie and how much she enjoyed eating.

"This breakfast is amazing. Thank you," I said as I looked at the fruit and whipped cream he'd put out to top the pancakes. "Kylie doesn't really seem to enjoy the whipped cream so much."

"No," he smiled. "She's not a real sweet-tooth, actually."

I looked at her and made a face, saying, "You don't know what you're missing, kiddo."

She laughed at my scrunched face and stuffed a plain piece of pancake in her mouth.

Kylie finished her breakfast quickly and was soon playing on the floor with some toys while Grant and I finished eating.

"She really is the cutest baby," I said, glancing down at her.

"She is pretty cute," he agreed, smiling at me. "She looks like her mother, and a little bit like her aunt."

"Really?"

"Yeah," Grant replied. "Her smile reminds me of yours a little. Stacy had that same one too—the way your mouth moves up, a little more on the right side than the left. Kylie does that too when she smiles."

"I didn't think Stacy and I looked at all like each other," I said slowly. Grant, his mom, and I had looked at pictures and done some comparisons, but neither Grant nor Sandy had said anything then.

He stared at me before he spoke again. "Just in that one way. I actually noticed the night Kylie was born," he continued, pausing for a beat. "When you introduced yourself to us, I thought, *Hey, she's got that same crooked thing goin' on*, but it just went through my mind for a second."

"Crooked thing?" I asked. "What?"

The word "crooked" somehow didn't feel complimentary. I got up and excused myself, asking where the bathroom was. He laughed and gave me directions.

Once in the bathroom I smiled into the mirror. I hadn't thought my smile was crooked, but he was right. The right side was slightly higher than the left. No one had ever mentioned that to me before, and suddenly I wanted to go home and take a look through my old pictures to see what I'd missed all these years.

While in the bathroom, I took in the beautiful decorating. Everything went well together. Even the blue towels were perfect. I sighed. Maybe my smile was the same as my sister's, but that's where the similarities stopped. I didn't like cooking, and I certainly didn't care to decorate.

When I returned to help clean up what was left of the breakfast mess, Grant had already done most of it. I went to the sink, wet the kitchen rag, and proceeded to the table.

"You're getting quiet on me again," he said, turning from the dishwasher where he'd just placed the last plate. "If it's about your smile, you should know I love—"

"It's not! It's nothing," I interrupted as I glanced at him.

"Don't do this, Trish," he said, closing the dishwasher door and coming to stand next to me. I continued wiping the table rather furiously. He stopped my hand and made me look at him. I could hear Kylie banging a toy in the corner of the kitchen and tried to turn his attention onto his daughter.

"She's fine," he said firmly. "I know what's bothering you, and you don't have to worry." His voice softened as he came even closer to me and grabbed both my hands, making me let go of the cloth.

"I don't think of Stacy every time I look at you. I know it's you, Trish."

I looked down, shaking my head. "That's not all I'm worried about," I admitted, taking one step back.

He wanted me to be straight with him, so I decided I would be.

"Stacy was probably a good cook, and I'm not. She was also a great decorator. I mean, look at this place!" I let go of his hands and gestured with mine, indicating the entire house. "Your home looks amazing. It's perfect! I mean, even the bathroom would impress my mother. She's like that too—all perfect, and everything looking perfect, and perfect stuff and—"

Grant interrupted my speech with a laugh so large it made me jump.

"You kill me, Trish," he said, smiling. "For one thing, this house wasn't decorated by Stacy. I moved in with Kylie after Stacy died. We've only lived here for a few months. We bought the house before Stacy passed away, but she was never here. It was decorated by someone I don't even know. If you'd known Stacy, you'd know she wasn't perfect, and I loved her for who she was. And I love you for who you are too."

There it was again, but this time, all the questions and concerns that had run through my head halted. I didn't want to overthink or doubt anymore. I loved this man. I knew it, and now I wanted him to know it. The many revelations I'd had on the drive home, nights before, came to the forefront of my heart and mind, and there was nothing more to say except ...

I grasped his hand again and looked into his eyes. "I love you too."

Grant stopped moving as we both held our breath. Kylie was still jabbering to herself in the corner, but I could hardly hear her.

"Finally," he said before our lips met. The kiss was long and held a promise of so much more that I didn't want it to end.

When we pulled away, he breathed as he held me. "I'd ask you to stay and sleep here, but maybe that's not the best idea. Are you too tired from working all night to drive home, though?"

I smiled, feeling a flush on my face from the kiss. "It's not that far a drive, Grant," I managed, "and besides, I did have that nap at work." I looked at him and had to say it. "You actually look more tired than I feel. Kylie up at night?"

He shook his head. "No, just a dream, and I couldn't get back to sleep. No big deal."

He smiled and reached for the sweater I'd placed on the back of the chair. As he helped me into it, I could feel it before I heard him laugh.

"What?" I asked, bewildered. "Why are you laughing?"

"Joy," he smiled. "It's just ... joy."

He gave me another hug and then walked me to the door. "I'll ask my mom if she can take Kylie tonight if you want to go out for supper."

"Hmm ..." I paused. "Or you could come to my place? I could whip up some Kraft Dinner."

The look on his face fell somewhere between disgust and concern, and I knew he was thinking of how to reply without hurting my feelings.

It was my turn to laugh. "Kidding," I said. "You talk about honesty, but you don't live it, Grant Evans. If you don't like KD, just tell me."

"I don't like KD," he said without missing a beat.

"Well then," I continued, "I guess you'll have no choice but teach me how to cook, or better yet, you'll have to do all the cooking, cuz macaroni is about all I know how to do. Except cans of soup. I do those too."

"Please stop talking before I change my mind." He smiled and hugged me. "We're going out. Seriously. I'll call my mom and see if she can watch Kylie."

Kylie had crawled to the door, and I reached for her, giving her a huge hug and kiss before leaving.

# Chapter Thirty-One

"I'M SORRY, SWEETIE, BUT I JUST WON'T BE ABLE TO TONIGHT," SANDY SAID over the phone. She didn't like texting all that much, so Grant had phoned her as soon as Trish left. "Another time would work, though."

"I kind of need you tonight, Mom," Grant said, hoping she'd change her mind. She didn't often have plans, he thought.

"Like I said, Grant, another time would work for me but not tonight. Jack and I have plans."

Grant had tried not to think too much about his mother dating. He was sure it wasn't the dating in general but rather whom she had chosen to spend her time with that bothered him.

"Still the same guy, huh?" he asked, sounding displeased.

"Yes," she said simply. "I've invited you over several times, but you haven't come. If you would get to know him, I think you'd like him, Grant. I really do."

"Well, another time then, Mom. Gotta go," he said hurriedly. He knew he wasn't being fair to his mother, and when he'd prayed about it, he felt guilty. But this guy bothered him.

"Don't be like this, Grant. Come over next week and have a visit with us, okay? You and Kylie can come for supper one night."

Grant thought about it. He owed her at least the consideration of getting to know him a little. If he spent time with Jack, at the least he could try to find out his true motives. Grant agreed and his mom sounded pleased. They decided what night would work for them. His mom then said she would ask Jack to confirm.

"If it works for her, would it be all right if I brought Trish along?" asked Grant before ending the conversation.

"Of course," answered Sandy. "I'd love to see her again."

"I'll ask her then. Later, Mom."

He hung up as Sandy was saying goodbye.

Sandy sighed as she clicked the end button on her phone.

● ● ●

"Trouble?" asked Jack, coming into the kitchen from outside on the deck. He'd come over early and they'd been visiting before Sandy excused herself to take the call.

"Oh," said Sandy, startled as she turned to face him. "Not really, Jack. It was Grant."

"I know he's worried about you," he said in his low, bass voice as he came to stand next to her. "He probably has a right to be."

"No," she said firmly, looking up at the very tall man beside her. "He has no right to judge you when he doesn't even know who you are. Unfortunately, he had to be the man of the house when he was way too young, so he worries about me, but he has his own life to live, and I have mine."

"Yes, you do," said Jack.

"Yes, I do," echoed Sandy, smiling up at him.

## Chapter Thirty-Two

I COULDN'T SLEEP WHEN I GOT HOME FROM GRANT'S THAT MORNING, AND after the excitement of declaring that I loved him, all I could think to do was text Melissa and Shauna and tell them about it. I knew Shauna would be sleeping and wouldn't get back to me until later, but Melissa was thrilled with the news. She texted back—so much more like herself—with exclamation marks and smiling emojis.

As circumstances sometimes dictate, though, Grant couldn't find a babysitter for our planned evening together, so since I was tired and needed to catch up on more sleep anyway, we decided to postpone until later that week when it would work well for both of us. Unfortunately, Kylie picked up a stomach flu of some kind the very afternoon of our next planned date, and Grant cancelled because he thought he shouldn't leave his little girl with anyone else. He asked my opinion about her symptoms, and I told him he should watch her temperature and give her clear fluids after her stomach settled but not to force food or drink on her if she didn't want any. If it lasted longer than a day, perhaps she should be seen by her doctor.

My mother called later in the afternoon the next day and wanted to arrange a time to meet Kylie. She said she'd be glad to come to the city, but Grant and I discussed it and arranged to drive out together the next weekend.

By the time the weekend rolled around, I was missing Grant more than I would ever want to admit. When he pulled up for the drive, I was waiting at my window and almost ran to his vehicle.

"Hi!" I exclaimed, throwing my bag in the back next to Kylie's car seat before Grant could race around to open the door for me.

"Hello," said Grant, grabbing me around the waist and kissing me.

"Mmmm," I said as the kiss ended. "Nice greeting."

"I missed you," he said softly, resting his forehead against mine.

Kylie squealed and I laughed.

"She missed you too," he said with a wink and a smile.

We got into the truck and headed out of town.

"I talked to my parents. They want to know if you'd like to stay at their place instead of going out to the ranch house with your aunt and uncle."

"I guess we could," said Grant, "but the ranch house is set up well for kids, since they have grandchildren. Mel's folks have a crib and stuff, although I did bring Kylie's playpen. We could do that."

"Please do," I begged, talking in a rush. "That way my dad can meet Kylie too, and I'd like you to meet him as well. He might be on call so he might not be there the whole time. If you stay, it's more likely that you'll meet him, if that's okay with you. If not, though, it's whatever you want. I'm good with—"

"It's fine," laughed Grant, cutting me off. "Really, Trish. I'm fine with it."

I smiled at his profile as he drove. He was so handsome, and his hair had grown longer over the last months, which only made him more striking. I liked his longer, dark hair and the way he'd brush it over his forehead with his hand.

"Kylie's all better?" I asked.

"It didn't last long," he said as he raced by a car going slower than us.

"Good," I said. "So you didn't have to take her in?"

"Nope, stayed home and prayed," he answered, glancing at me.

"You pray about everything, don't you?"

"I hope so," he said. "It sure helps when I do."

Kylie started fussing, and I tried to hand her a toy, which was difficult from the front seat.

"What do you do when she needs something back there and you're the only one here?" I asked.

"Well, either I let her cry it out or I pull over if it gets too bad," he answered, concentrating on the road. "She usually falls asleep pretty quick if she's fussing, so the crying's short-lived."

"Seriously?" I asked.

"Seriously," he answered, glancing at my inquisitive face. "What did you think parents do when their kid cries? I can't constantly be pulling over. We'd never get home."

"I guess," I pondered and glanced at Kylie.

Sure enough, her eyelids were getting heavy. Soon she'd be asleep.

"She's a pretty good baby," Grant smiled. "I don't like the crying, but she's usually good in the car. She saves it for evening, usually, if she's going to have a meltdown, and by then we're usually home."

I smiled at how relaxed he was around Kylie. He enjoyed her so much and was proud of his daughter. Suddenly I thought of him at her delivery and how his eyes had lit up at his first glimpse of her. Then I quickly caught myself wondering if I'd ever see that look on his face as he gazed at a child he and I might have.

I shook myself out of the daydream when Grant asked, "Hey! Did I lose you there for a minute?"

I laughed a little and answered, "Maybe for a minute. I'm good now."

"It's okay if it was a good dream," he said softly, taking my hand.

"It was," I said, looking at him again but saying nothing more.

We reached my parents' home right before supper. When we walked in, both of my parents were in the kitchen and came to greet us. I didn't know how they'd react to meeting Kylie and Grant, but for some reason I hadn't expected as much excitement.

"Mom, Dad, this is Grant Evans. You may have met him at Trent and Melissa's wedding."

My dad grabbed Grant's hand with a hearty shake. "I think we did meet you, but fleetingly," he said, smiling. "I'm Ted."

"Dr. Holmes," replied Grant, "I think we were introduced at the wedding too, but there were a lot of people. I'm sorry if I don't remember."

"That's certainly fine," interrupted my mother, taking his hand in hers after the men were done. "I'm Helen. Please call me Helen, and it's not Dr. Holmes to most people. Call him Ted."

"All right," Grant replied, nodding.

We all turned our attention to Kylie as Grant introduced her. "This is Kylie. I think she's the one you really want to meet."

Grant took off her pink sweater and set Kylie down in the large entrance, where she stood tentatively and looked around. She had just started taking a few steps but now opted to fall to her knees and crawl. She went toward my mom, and my mother, whom I'd never seen play on a floor, went to her knees as well. Her eyes teared as she watched Kylie.

I glanced at Grant, who seemed mesmerized by his daughter as she stared at her newfound grandmother with large blue eyes.

Kylie had been "making strange" with new people lately, and we didn't know how she'd respond to my parents. We watched as my mother talked to her softly, still on her knees.

When Kylie crawled closer and stopped to sit in front of her, we all waited. She looked up at my mother as if assessing the situation. Kylie's dark curly hair was wet at the nape of her neck, probably due to being too warm in the car. She suddenly stuck a chubby fist into her mouth and drooled. My mother laughed but kept talking in her usual voice, telling Kylie that she was her grandmother and that she loved her already. As soon as that was said, Kylie crawled into my mother's lap and cuddled into her. It was one of the sweetest, most precious moments I've ever had with my own mother, and it didn't even involve me.

At that moment, I saw her in a different light. Suddenly, I vaguely remembered a time when she had comforted me when I was young. Why had I forgotten that? Maybe I'd been the one who had moved away from her. Maybe it had never been her fault at all, but mine.

I shook my head from the memory when I heard my dad say, "Lets all go into the kitchen. Supper's almost ready. I barbecued. Hope that's okay."

"Perfect, Dad," I said, smiling at him.

My mother gathered Kylie up in her arms and we all walked into the kitchen.

"When did you get a highchair?" I asked, almost stumbling over it.

My mom and dad looked at each other.

"Well," my dad started, looking at me like I was a bit daft, "if we're going to have grandchildren, they need a place to sit, Trish."

"And we bought a crib as well," added my mom excitedly. "We hope you'll stay here sometimes, Grant, or let us take care of Kylie if you need a break?"

Was this even my mother?

I must've looked confused, because my parents glanced at me but then spoke to Grant.

They both talked quickly and at once, saying that in no way did they want to step on toes or be too pushy or anything, but they were thrilled to welcome Kylie into the family, and they were more than willing to do anything for her.

Grant laughed.

"Did you get all that?" I smiled at him.

"I think I got the gist," he said to me and then addressed my parents. "I really appreciate this, Ted and Helen. Kylie can never have too many people who love her, and clearly you do already. If you promise to take her, even when she's melting down, it's a deal."

"I think we can even handle that," said my mom, beaming.

"You haven't seen her meltdown yet," Grant joked.

We all sat, and my dad said grace. He thanked the Lord for bringing Grant and Kylie into their lives. As he prayed, I thought of what a wonderful man he was to love and accept a granddaughter who wasn't his biologically. My heart swelled with the love I saw around the table. I hadn't felt that for a very long time.

Later that night after Kylie was tucked into her new crib in the guest room, where Grant would stay, we found ourselves alone on the patio. Grant had grabbed a drink from the fridge and came to join me on the outside patio by the pool.

"Hey, where are your folks?" he asked.

"They turned in already. Dad was up late last night, and Mom was tired too," I answered.

"Want something?" Grant asked, indicating the drink in his hand. "I can probably grab it for you if it's in the fridge. This kitchen is massive. Not sure I'll find it if it's not in the fridge."

"No, I'm good," I said, smiling up at him. "Sit and relax."

"It's getting colder," he noted, grabbing a blanket off one of the deck chairs and sitting down.

I cuddled into the blanket I had around me already and agreed.

"How did Kylie go down?" I asked.

"Easy," he answered. "It's like she knows she belongs here."

"That's great," I smiled, closing my eyes. "Could've gone so many ways. This is good."

We sat in silence, enjoying the sounds of nature for a few minutes.

"Can I ask you something?" Grant said, breaking the silence.

"Sure." I looked across at him.

"Your mom ..." He paused. "You've told me about her before, but—"

"I know what you're going to say," I interrupted, "but believe me, that's not the woman who raised me. I wanted to ask her tonight who she was and where she put my real mom."

He laughed. "I'm just spit-balling here, but maybe you aren't the best gauge of your mother's character. Sometimes when we're too close it's hard to see things the way they really are."

I sat up straighter, my eyes never leaving him. "Wise words from a man who can't even mention his mother's boyfriend."

"Hey," he said defensively, "that's not the same at all. I don't even know the guy."

Grant hadn't told me a lot about Jack, but when he had spoken about him, he'd usually become uncomfortable and changed the subject quickly.

"So ... don't you think you should at least give him a chance?" I asked.

"Now you're sounding like my mom," he said, pausing. "I know it's inevitable, Trish. I just don't want to think about it."

"You're someone who talks about loving others—and don't get me wrong, you show it every day—but I don't know why this is different, Grant. Don't you want your mom to be happy? She's a smart lady. She won't do anything stupid. You need to trust her."

"Okay, okay!" he said, throwing up his hands. "As you know, we're going there this week, and I'm sure I'll get to know him a little better."

We looked at each other and waited. I was the first to smile and raise my eyebrows.

"Woman ... you're beautiful," he said softly.

I wasn't expecting that and blushed immediately.

"Wanna take a swim?" he asked, moving his eyebrows up and down.

"Too cold," I replied, feigning a shiver. "Swing?" I suggested, looking over at the loveseat that hung low under the deck overhang.

He didn't answer but stood and took my hand. His kiss was warm and inviting. We moved over to the swing and sat for a long time, discussing everything and anything we wanted to.

• • •

"Please come back soon," crooned my mother, regretfully letting go of Kylie after our weekend visit was over. "Ooo, I will miss you, baby girl," she said as Grant buckled his daughter into her car seat.

"She'll miss you too, Grandma Helen," said Grant, smiling.

As Grant and I had previously decided, he told my mother a little about his years with Stacy but left out the worst details of the life she'd led before they'd found each other. He had told me her previous life didn't matter; rather, her new life did. Although they'd had their hardships, their life together had been good. I also learned more about Stacy, which endeared Grant to me even more. While he talked, I thought that it must be difficult for him to share so many special moments, but he would look sad for only brief seconds before continuing.

Although there were tears for Stacy, Kylie more than made up for them by giving us many more moments of laughter. I stood back, feeling overwhelming happiness for my mother and the little granddaughter she'd been so blessed to find.

"Trish," she said as she hugged me goodbye, "thank you."

"For what?" I asked.

"For finding them and bringing my granddaughter to me," she said sincerely, holding my shoulders with tears in her eyes.

I glanced at Grant and saw him smiling.

My mom turned to him and thanked him again, rather profusely, before adding, "I'm sorry Ted couldn't be here to say goodbye. He thought he might get back before you had to leave, but you know how it goes." She turned and looked at me.

"I know, Mom," I smiled, feeling a twinge of disappointment. "No biggie."

My mom thanked Grant again, and then it was time to leave. As we travelled home, I thanked him also, mimicking my mother and laughing.

"Oh Grant," I said as I stroked his shoulder in mock adoration, "you're just the best. I mean, I can't thank you enough, and I just want to go on record as saying ... thank you. Thank you a million times over. Thank you, thank you—"

"This is not a good look on you, Trish," he said laughing and moving my hands back to my lap. "Stop it. Your mom is clearly thrilled to have found Kylie." He looked at me more seriously and continued. "I, for one, am glad I could be a part of this for her. She's a nice lady. She went through a lot and now, maybe, she'll be able to put it behind her. Something, or I guess someone, good came out of it."

"Okay, okay," I replied. "Sorry. I was just kidding. I am glad for her, and I'm super happy that my folks really like you."

"Ya think?" he said with a hopeful tone.

"Oh man," I said, rolling my eyes. "They love you!"

Grant paused, thinking. "It's good to know they're quicker than you are."

I glanced at him.

"I mean ... smarter," he said simply.

"Whaaat?" I asked, bewildered.

"It only took two days for them to fall in love with me. I told you—when you know, you know, but you wouldn't listen to me, so you waited and waited," he said, shaking his head as if very disappointed.

"Funny guy," I mumbled, looking out the passenger window to my right. "Ha ha," I said, drolly, looking back at him.

The grin on his face was huge, and I punched his arm.

"Hey! No need for violence, lady," he said, rubbing his arm as if it hurt.

"So now I'm a lady?" I whispered.

"Yeah, baby," he said, reaching over and grabbing me for a quick kiss.

I broke from the kiss, laughing, and said, "Watch the road! I want to live to see my wedding day!"

Both of us stopped instantly and I couldn't breathe. What was I saying? What was I thinking? What was wrong with me?

He said nothing but pulled over at the closest vacant approach on the side of the road.

I suddenly felt nervous as he got out and opened the door next to Kylie's car seat. I looked back and he smiled at me, whispering, "She's asleep."

I could hear him rummaging around for a few seconds. Then he came around to open my door. He took my hand and helped me out of the truck to stand next to it.

I remember it was a cool day with the fall leaves turning beautiful shades of orange and yellow. A soft breeze blew threw our hair as he looked into my eyes and kissed me. Then, in a sudden but smooth movement, he was on one knee with my left hand in his. My head swam.

"I want you and I to live to see our wedding day, Trish," he said simply. "Would you like to plan for that with me?"

As was usual, many questions ran through my head, but only one answer came quickly to my lips.

"Yes," I nodded and laughed. "I do. I really want to plan for that!"

He stood up, threw his head back, and yelled to the heavens, "Yes!"

Then we hugged and kissed and hugged some more, and the little box he'd presented to me while on his knee was opened. Inside was the most beautiful ring I'd ever seen.

I must have stopped breathing for a while because when he broke the silence, I let the breath go that I didn't know I'd been holding.

"Well?" he asked, sounding a little nervous.

I was gazing at the ring but now I looked up into his eyes.

"What?" I asked smiling, feeling dazed.

"Do you like it?" he ventured.

"Oh!" I said, pausing. "I don't like it. I love it!"

He breathed again in relief and then said, "And you've only known it for a minute and you already love it? That doesn't sound like you." He was teasing me again, and I laughed.

"I guess I'll never live that down," I said.

"Nope," he smiled as he pulled the ring from it's velvet covered box.

As he placed it on my finger, my eyes teared. I gazed at the beautiful diamond solitaire with many tiny stones seated into the rose-gold band.

"I know it's really easy to say right now," I said, stammering slightly from the tears, "but God seems even more good today."

Grant laughed and held me in a tight hug. There, beside the highway, with cars and trucks blasting past, we promised ourselves to each other. It may not have seemed like the most romantic place for a proposal, but in those short minutes, it couldn't have been better.

"I'm sorry. I couldn't wait," he said when he dropped me off at my place that evening. He'd come around to my side of the truck, as was his routine, and now we were standing beside it on the sidewalk. "I got the ring the day you told me you loved me. It's been burning a hole in my pocket ever since. I wanted to ask you that night, but then my mom couldn't babysit, and Kylie got sick when we planned the next date. I wanted to arrange a romantic dinner when we got home but—"

"Grant," I interrupted, putting my hand on his shoulder, "this was perfect ... perfect. I just want to marry you." I looked deep into his eyes and he returned a hungry look.

"And I want to marry you," he smiled. "Tomorrow would be great."

I grinned and we kissed goodbye.

As I turned to walk away, I said in a practical tone, "I have to get a dress first." He laughed.

## Chapter Thirty-Three

TELLING FRIENDS AND FAMILY OF THE HAPPY EVENTS IN OUR LIVES ARE SOME OF the moments that make life worth living. Graduations, upcoming nuptials, expected babies, and other joyous and life-changing announcements are what treasured memories are made of. Although graduating with my nursing degree had been the highlight of my life up until that time, it didn't compare to the exhilaration of planning to wed the man I'd fallen in love with.

On our way home the afternoon of the proposal, Grant and I had called my parents immediately with the news. They were ecstatic and, although they didn't know Grant well, they said they trusted my judgement and that if I was good with it, so were they. Although I wanted to call his mother, since we were going there for supper in a couple of days, we decided we'd tell her then. I felt like bursting and just couldn't resist telling someone, so I called the person who had always been there for me through thick and thin.

"Trent!" I said excitedly as soon as he picked up the phone. "Grant and I got engaged," I blurted before he could even get a word out.

"What?" Trent exclaimed. "I'm putting you on speaker."

I could hear Melissa in the background and suddenly I thought of Grant, realizing that I probably should have waited to announce this when we were all together. Oh well! Too late now.

"What happened?" she asked, coming near the phone and sounding strangely excited already.

I could hear Trent, and before I could stop him, he exclaimed, "Trish and Grant are engaged!"

Melissa squealed, "Oh yay! Trent, I told you it would happen."

Trent replied, "I know, honey. You told me. I just wasn't sure she'd say yes."

"Of course she'd say yes, Trent. I could see Trish loved him a long time ago. She just wouldn't admit it," replied Melissa.

"Well, you do have a gift for seeing into people," he told his wife.

I'm sure the conversation between them would've gone on had I not cleared my throat.

"Oh, sorry," said Melissa. "We're *so* happy for you guys. Do you have a date set?"

"No," I laughed, "and now I feel bad about not waiting for Grant. I should have waited until we were all together."

"Don't be silly," returned Melissa, pausing. "He actually ... already told me."

"What?" both Trent and I chorused.

"Oops," Melissa said. "I was just supposed to act surprised, because Grant really felt bad. I called to ask him something else and then he told me your news. I'm really sorry."

I smiled. It was good to know Grant was excited too.

"But why didn't you tell me?" asked Trent, talking to Melissa again.

"Because, sweetie," she answered him, "I knew Trish would want to tell you herself."

"Are there other secrets you're keeping from me?" asked Trent, sounding amused.

Silence from the other end ensued but then Melissa said, "Hmm ... I'm thinking."

I could hear scuffling and Melissa laughing. "No! Okay! Stop! I haven't got anymore secrets!"

"Hey you two," I interrupted. "Get a room."

I could hear them both laughing.

When Melissa stopped, she said, "Honest, Trish, I'm sorry Grant told me. I shouldn't have let on."

"It's fine. Now everyone closest to us knows, except his mom. Grant wants to tell her in person when we see her in a couple of days," I said. "Please don't tell her if you talk to her, okay?"

"Mums the word, Trish. No problem," promised Melissa. She paused. "Trent! We should tell her!"

"Sure," he replied.

Melissa gushed. "We put our names in with two adoption agencies in the city. We're super excited and praying like crazy that a baby will come our way. We have some red-tape stuff to get through, but the lady at the agency thinks it will all go smoothly. They say it may be a long wait, but we're going to hope not too long."

"Oh Mel," I said, "that's great news! I'll pray. I promise."

"Well, if we can't have babies of our own, we certainly have enough love to share with ones we don't make ourselves. Right, hon?" Melissa asked Trent.

Trent replied with love in his voice. "Absolutely."

"I'm so happy for you guys," I said. "I know the perfect little one is out there for you. I know it."

"Thanks, Trish," they both said.

We talked for a while longer, and although Melissa was unimpressed with what she considered a "pathetic proposal" on Grant's part, she was happy about our engagement.

"Mom and I are going to look for gowns soon. Wanna come?" I asked Melissa.

"Do you have to ask?" she said, wanting to know when.

I told her I'd text her as soon as I knew the date, and as I pressed the button to end our call, I couldn't help but smile.

I was so relieved that Melissa sounded like herself again. She'd risen above their terrible news and had a fresh new attitude and a new goal. I prayed that God would bless them with a baby sooner rather than later.

Then I called my mom to arrange a date and time to begin planning for our wedding.

# Chapter Thirty-Four

"WHAT'S WRONG?" I ASKED FINALLY, CONCERNED WITH GRANT'S SEEMING LACK of enthusiasm and stony silence.

"Nothing," he said, looking seriously at the road as he drove towards his mom's place.

"You wouldn't let me get away with that so I'm not letting you either, Grant. You've been fidgety and kind of … well … persnickety since you picked me up, and I want to know why," I said firmly.

He smiled. "Persnickety, you say?" he asked, mocking me in a fake British accent.

"Don't make me laugh. Tell me what's up with you before we get to your mom's," I insisted.

He looked serious again and said, "In hindsight, I think we should've told her about our engagement without Jack being there."

"Why?" I asked, not knowing what possible reason he'd have for that kind of reasoning.

"He's not family," he answered. "This is a family thing."

"No, it's not just a family thing. We've shared our news with a lot of friends. And anyway," I continued with reason, "your mom may be getting serious about this guy. They've known each other for a while. Who knows? He may be family someday."

I could feel his tension increase immediately in the quick breath he took. He opened his mouth as if to say something but then quickly shut it.

I felt sorry for him. He wanted to give Jack a chance but was having such a hard time with it. I just couldn't figure it out. Grant was so loving and thoughtful to everyone else, but when it came to this guy, he struggled so much. Was it just because it involved his mother? Was he so close to her that he didn't want another man in the picture? That might make some sort of sense, since his mom had been widowed when her boys were so young. Grant was the oldest and had needed to step in and be responsible for many things a young boy normally wouldn't have been. He and his mom hadn't seemed unusually close when I'd seen them together, but what did I know? I decided then that I would closely observe everyone tonight and maybe be able to figure some of it out.

"Grant and Trish!" greeted Sandy as we entered her small home. "Come in! And there's my baby girl," she said, turning her attention to her granddaughter. She lifted Kylie from my arms.

"Supper's ready," she said cheerfully as she took Kylie's jacket off.

"You've met Jack," Sandy said, looking at Grant and giving a nod toward the kitchen.

When Grant said nothing, she looked at me and smiled.

Sandy walked toward the kitchen with me following.

"Trish, this is Jack," she said, making a hand gesture toward the man on the opposite side of the counter, who was tossing a salad. "And Jack, this is Grant's girlfriend, Trish."

I came closer and smiled upwards at the man in the apron. I'd had a glimpse of him those many months before in the restaurant where Grant first met him, but he'd been far from my sight, and my mind had been on other things that day. Tonight, in the bright light of Sandy's kitchen, he was nothing like I expected at all, and I found myself taken aback. Grant had told me "he looks rough," but in my wildest dreams I wouldn't have imagined this. In that moment I knew why Grant felt hesitant. If I'd brought a man like this home to my parents, they probably would've kicked him out. And me as well.

Jack was very tall with a muscular build. His arms were covered with tattoos. It was impossible to guess where they ended because they ran up past the ends of the sleeves of his T-shirt. He looked to be in his late forties or early fifties, maybe a little younger than Sandy, and he had dark, almost black, hair that ran down to the middle of his back. He wore a blue bandanna across his forehead and had a scar, about two inches long, on his right cheek. It was hard to miss, but it didn't seem to detract from his rugged features.

I stood back as I observed him, but because the apron didn't seem to fit the picture, I couldn't help myself. I started laughing.

"I'm sorry," I finally gasped, "but that apron just doesn't match the rest of you at all."

What was wrong with me? What was I thinking? Sandy better be right about this guy being nice, because he looked like he could snap me like a twig if he chose to.

Everyone was quiet and stared as I tried to control my laughter, with little success.

Suddenly, a smile spread over Jack's dark features and he broke into a low, deep laugh. It was the sound of thunder or horse's hooves running, or some such beautiful sound that only God can make.

"Hi there," he said, holding out his hand to me and shaking it.

"Again, my apologies," I said, having gained some element of decorum. "It's so very nice to meet you."

"You as well," he said smoothly in his low, bass rumble.

I stepped back and looked at Grant and Sandy. She had a smirk on her face, but Grant's expression was impossible to read. If I had to guess, unfettered disdain would come to mind.

I didn't make that better when I blurted out, "The Rock!" and snapped my fingers, pointing at Jack. "That's who you remind me of! The Rock! With hair, though," I added, admiring his long, wavy hair.

Everyone looked at me with wide eyes, but I wasn't finished. "Or ... Roman Reigns? Is that his name, Grant? He's another WWE fighter, right?"

I stopped as everyone gaped at me. Why couldn't I shut up? I steeled myself by remembering that I'd promised to observe everyone tonight and not do the talking. Now I'd be lucky if they didn't think me a complete idiot.

Thankfully, Jack laughed again as Sandy smiled, adding, "I can see it." She was looking at Jack pretty intensely, as if assessing him in a new light.

The subject was dropped as Sandy showed us to our seats at the table.

I looked over to Grant as we sat, and I mouthed "I'm sorry" with a shrug.

He gave me a questioning look and shrugged as well. He didn't smile.

The conversation revolved around Kylie after Sandy asked Grant to say grace and we started eating. When there's tension between people, if there's a child around, it's safe ground to talk to the baby, so Sandy and I did that for a few minutes.

"Have you decided how we're going to celebrate Kylie's first birthday, Grant?" asked Sandy, handing him the casserole she'd made. "I know it's a few months away, but the time will fly by, and we could talk about it, just for fun."

"I don't know yet," he answered, seeming very intent with the food on his plate.

"Well," she said, "I've been thinking about it. I'm sure a lot of people would come. After all, many people were involved with her care when she was first born, and they love you and her to bits. It wouldn't have to be huge or anything, though. That's your call." She paused as Grant kept eating.

She looked at me and added, "Trish, your parents should come too."

"Oh, that would be nice! I'm sure they'd love to get to know Kylie's other grandma!" I said enthusiastically.

Grant looked irritated and stopped eating, putting his fork down. "It won't mean anything to her. She's too young."

Sandy and I looked at him in surprise as Kylie destroyed the food on her highchair tray, oblivious to the tension around the table.

"It's not just for her, son. It's for all of us—to remember not only when she was born but to celebrate her life," Sandy said softly, and I got the feeling that she and Grant had discussed this before.

"It would be great for all of us to get together, Grant. And really fun to watch her enjoy her first birthday cake. C'mon," I said, smiling, "Every kid deserves a great first birthday party."

He was sitting to my left and I put my hand on his arm. I felt him tense, but he didn't move his arm away.

I was waiting for Grant to speak, feeling confused about what seemed a non-issue to me, when Jack spoke.

"Maybe the memory will hurt too much," he said succinctly, looking directly at Grant.

You know the saying "Nobody moves. Nobody gets hurt"? That's exactly how it felt in the silent moments after Jack spoke.

The sound of Grant pushing his chair back and standing broke the silence, and he glared at Jack before leaving the room.

The three of us looked at each other and sat for a few moments, not knowing what to say. Noticing her daddy had left, Kylie started fussing and reached toward Sandy, who turned her attention to the baby.

I got up and started toward the back door where Grant had stormed out, but Jack's voice stopped me.

"I got this, Trish," he said calmly, rising from his chair.

My mind raced. Grant was in a bad mood, and I certainly didn't think Jack was the right candidate to calm him down, but what did I really know? I'd never seen this side of Grant before. I was certain, however, that he hadn't come here liking Jack, and no scenario I could play out in my mind between them would help that.

"No," I disagreed, shaking my head. "I better go. Believe me ... this is better." I paused, not convinced of what I'd just said.

"Even you don't look convinced of that," smiled Jack, reading my mind. "It's time, anyway."

When I looked over at Sandy's face, she looked anxious but nodded at me and gave a shrug. "Maybe he's right, Trish. The guys should talk."

I hesitated before nodding slowly, going back to the chair I'd vacated.

Jack left with a calm but serious look on his face.

Sandy and I looked at Kylie and spoke to her again, both of us uncomfortable with what had just happened. I felt concern for Grant, but I also felt irked by his behaviour.

Then I thought of what Jack had said. Maybe there was truth to his statement. Of course there would be. As happy a moment as it had been when Kylie was born, the sadness of that day would overshadow the joy as well. Grant had suffered a huge loss. As much as he loved his daughter, perhaps the memory of his heavy grief was still too much to bear.

I looked toward the back door where the men had exited and listened for voices. The sun had gone down, and the faintest hint of dusk remained. I couldn't see anything outside.

"Don't worry," Sandy said, watching my anxious expression. "They won't kill each other. They've needed to talk for a long time now. The volcano's got to erupt sometime, and Jack's a big boy. He can take it."

"What?" I said, confused. I'd been more worried for Grant. He wasn't a small man but certainly smaller than Jack.

"Honey," she continued, "I love that son of mine more than my own life, but he does this sometimes—not as often as he did when he was a small boy or, Lord have mercy, a teenager—but still once in a blue moon. He'll stew and stew about something, and it builds up in him until he explodes. After that, things get a lot better."

I had never seen that part of Grant. She undoubtedly saw the horrified look on my face because she quickly added, "Oh sweetie, he's never hurt anyone or anything like that. He just needs to spill it all out sometimes. He used to go to the ranch and muck stalls or sling hay bales. For a while in high school, he took boxing so he could punch stuff. It's usually something physical he needs to do to get all that negative energy out. Then he deflates and comes to his senses."

She waited, expecting me to say something. I'd never seen Grant this way and was a little blown away by what she was telling me.

"Trish," she confessed, "I have to admit, Grant is a lot like me. I blow hot and cold also. It's not a trait I'm proud of, but there it is. I've had to work on controlling my temper, and I had to teach him that anger is sometimes okay, but it's what you do with it that matters." She paused, looking a little embarrassed, and then asked, "What did your family teach you to do when you're upset?"

I thought it a strange question, especially for two people who were just getting to know one another. Where were the normal questions, like "Where are you from? What are your hobbies? What do your parents do for a living?" Even "Do you really love my son?" would be a better question than this.

"Uh," I said, unable to think straight. "I guess we keep it more inside and take more blood pressure pills when we need them."

Sandy smiled but didn't let my attempt at humour sway her. She waited for me to say more. With the intensity of her stare, I felt like a deer in the headlights, but I finally blurted out the truth.

"I try to get away. Run away, I mean. I think that's sort of what my dad has always done when Mom gets to be a bit too much. He's a doctor, though, so he's really busy with his practice and being on call a lot, but I guess I run ... maybe like him," I feebly admitted. I turned my face down and played with the hands in my lap. I felt my eyes tear and told myself to smarten up. I felt like running away then. It was all it took for me not to flee the kitchen, run out the front door, and drive home.

Sandy seemed to take in stride what I'd just admitted. "That's what Grant seemed to do right now, but he's not. He'll be looking for a physical way to deal with his anger about me dating Jack. I just hope he doesn't think he can take Jack down. I'd fear for my son."

With that I looked up suddenly, anxiety etched on every part of my face. What was she saying?

The silence broke with Sandy's sudden laughter.

"Glad you're paying attention," she said, smiling. Apparently, Sandy had a similar humour as her son.

"Trish," she said calmly, "everyone has their own way of dealing with the stresses of life, but I've learned that you have to have a plan for how you're going to deal with them. I could ask you all kinds of frivolous questions, like "What kind of cooking do you like to do." Don't get me wrong, I want to get to know those things about you too." She paused. "But since I see that ring on your finger, I'm guessing you're going to be my daughter-in-law soon, so I feel there are more important questions to ask."

I blushed and looked at the beautiful ring on my left hand.

Sandy continued in such a loving and caring tone that I couldn't help but feel even more fondness for her.

"I need to know that you'll have a plan when you feel like running away because, honey, in marriage, you will feel like that at some point."

I looked at her and she looked deep into my eyes again and smiled gently.

"My son needs to know that you won't run from him or Kylie. You saw him tonight. He's not perfect, Trish, but I can see that he brims over with love for you. If he makes the vow to cherish you until death, he'll keep it. I know it, and I hope you feel the same way too."

I might have felt threatened had Sandy not been so kind in the way she expressed the wisdom in her heart. Grant had been through so much, not only with the past grief he'd suffered but also with what had been in Stacy's past. Although he hadn't given me all the details, I knew it hadn't been easy for them.

I didn't know what to say, but Sandy broke the silence.

"Now let me see that ring," she chimed cheerfully, taking my hand when I offered it. "That is beautiful, Trish. Did he choose it himself or did you go together to pick it out?"

"No," I smiled, feeling proud of Grant. "All him."

"Hmm ... he does have good taste," she added and then winked. "Another thing I taught him well."

We both laughed as Sandy got up to start clearing dishes.

As I began cleaning up the left-over food on Kylie's highchair, Sandy asked, "So do you have any hobbies?"

• • •

Grant felt even angrier when he reached the shed in his mom's back yard.

The raised garden beds that she had asked him to make before summer were overflowing with produce. He immediately knew who had finished them and it added to his ire.

He sat for a few minutes on the edge of the one nearest the shed. He noticed the nice handiwork and the sturdiness of the structure and felt guilty that he hadn't finished them for his mom when she'd asked him.

*Nice of him to step up*, Grant thought bitterly.

Why was he so angry? He'd asked himself that so many times since meeting Jack.

Whenever Grant had spoken to him, Jack seemed to have an uncanny way to unnerve him without ever saying much. It was like he could see right through him, and now the comment tonight. Well, that was enough.

Even with all the excitement of the engagement to Trish, who he was positive was the woman God wanted him to spend the rest of his life with, Grant had been thinking a lot more about Stacy. As the date approached, marking a year since her death, Grant hadn't told anyone, but he'd become more and more anxious. He had felt overwhelmed with the news of her being Trish's half-sister, but he'd tried to concentrate more on how Trish felt and how it impacted her. He'd been worried about Kylie and meeting new grandparents and how that would play out. All the while, his mom's relationship with this man played heavily on his mind. He had distanced himself from his mother because of it.

Oh God, he prayed silently now, please keep me focused and strong with what I need to be and what I need to do.

With that, he sprang up and went into the garage to find something to take his stress out on. The frame around one of the windows in the garage was rotted out due to age, a poor seal, and wet weather. It needed replacing, and Grant had previously done a bit of work on it. It wasn't a big job, but at least he'd be able to do something. All the wood had been cut out for the new frame, so it was just a matter of nailing it on.

He had just found a hammer and some appropriate nails when he heard someone enter the garage behind him.

"Trish?" He paused, not turning around. "Could we talk when I'm done out here? I just need to fix this window for my mom."

When no answer was forthcoming, he turned and was disturbed to find Jack staring at him. He stood straight and tall in the doorway to the garage.

"Oh," said Grant. "Thought you were Trish."

"I don't think I'm as pretty," said Jack with a quick half smile.

"You got that right," agreed Grant, looking back at the hammer in his hand.

"I think we need to talk," offered Jack.

He waited to give Grant a chance to start. After he'd waited a minute or so, he took a deep breath. "You know, Grant, your mom is an amazing lady, and I think you need to know that there's nothing on earth that would make me want to hurt her."

Grant turned to face him. "I'm sure you think that's true, but sometimes, even if we don't want to hurt someone, we do it anyway."

Jack crossed his arms and leaned onto one side of the garage's door frame before softly replying. "Like Stacy hurt you?"

It was like a kick to the gut for Grant, and he turned his face quickly away from Jack's stare.

"I don't know what you're talking about," Grant said, anger and confusion in his tone. "Stacy didn't hurt me. She died."

"She left you," Jack said simply. "It hurts when people leave, even if they don't want to or it's not their fault. It still hurts the ones left behind."

Grant didn't know what to say. To make things worse, Jack continued.

"First your dad and then a son and then Stacy. That's a lot of hurt for one man ... even a strong man with good values."

Grant wanted to leave the garage, but even more overwhelming was his urge to punch something. He looked at the hammer in his hand and the nail in the other, picked up a piece of the wood for the window frame, aligned it with the window, and started beating nails into it. He hammered a few and then looked up, hoping Jack had left. He hadn't. Grant paused as Jack waited.

"Hey," Grant started, "if my mom wants you in her life, that's her business, not mine, but don't come in here and try to give me advice and pretend to know what we've been through. You don't know the half of it."

He began hammering again with a vengeance.

Jack had to speak loudly to be heard, but he wouldn't stop now.

"You're right, Grant, but your mom has told me enough. I think you're the strongest type-a-guy. You help others through their tough stuff and don't think it hurts you. I mean, look at your life, man. Your dad dies when you're just a kid, making you the man of the house whether you like it or not. Your wife's an addict, but you see her through that and then, when you're finally happy, you lose a baby and then she dies! I mean, I had a rough life, and I lived rough because of it. I don't know which is worse. Your life is one trauma after the next, but you keep standin' and telling yourself you can't fall because you've got Jesus. Honestly, I think that's why I bother you so much. I think I'm your last straw."

As much as Jack's voice had elevated in volume due to Grant's overzealous hammering, Grant's anger had increased as well.

"I'm fine!" Grant yelled as he suddenly stopped what he was doing. "I have God, and He is my strength!"

They both looked at each other as Grant gasped.

"Says the man standing there pounding the heck out of an innocent window," said Jack, just loud enough for Grant to hear.

Grant stared at the broken glass around him. As Jack spoke truths that Grant had never verbalized, or perhaps even realized before, he hadn't noticed that he'd hammered the frame so hard that the window had shattered. Now he stared at his bloodied hand and suddenly felt overwhelmingly tired.

"You're right, Grant. God is our strength ... no doubt about that. He's proven it to me over and over, and I've put Him through hell to prove it, but He also understands that we're human," Jack said calmly, "and He's okay with that too. He doesn't expect us to be perfect and strong all of the time."

Grant said nothing but looked over at Jack as he continued.

"I don't know how you've survived what you have, and if you have to take some of the anger and blame out on me that's okay, but understand one thing—I'm stickin' around. Your mom is the wisest woman I've ever met, and she lives what she believes. No hypocrisy. I respect her like no one else, and I plan to treat her right."

With that firm declaration Jack turned and left the garage.

As he walked away, Grant stared at the back of the man his mother had grown so fond of. Jack had said some things that no one had ever acknowledged before, and although hard to hear, Grant appreciated, at least in a small way, that Jack had noticed all of it. He was right. Grant hadn't dealt with his anger. Sometimes he did feel angry at God for everything that had happened.

Grant knew he should clean up the mess he'd made with the window, but instead he got on his knees and started praying ... but not like he usually did. This time he told his creator what he really thought of a lot of the things that had happened in the past, and most of it wasn't what you'd hear in a Sunday morning church service.

● ● ●

"Oh my gosh!" I exclaimed when I saw Grant's cut-up hands. "What did you do to yourself?" I glanced at him and Jack as well, wondering if he'd had anything to do with this. I wasn't impressed.

Jack had come back into the house more than an hour before and again suggested I not go outside to talk to Grant. He simply told me, "I think your man needs some time to himself." I had listened and left him to himself. But now, seeing his hands, I chastised myself inwardly for listening to Jack.

"It's nothing," Grant said, looking mildly embarrassed.

"Nothing more than a few paper cuts," Jack threw in softly, smiling.

Grant looked toward him and gave a quick nod.

Sandy and I looked at each other questioningly and shrugged. She mouthed "men" for only me to see, and I tried not to laugh. Whatever had happened out there in the back yard seemed to improve both their moods, and the tension was gone. Suddenly I was sorry the evening was coming to an end.

Grant excused himself to the bathroom to clean up his "paper cuts" and then we got ready to leave.

"Congratulations, Grant and Trish, on your engagement," exclaimed Sandy as she hugged us in the front entrance before we left.

"Oh, yeah," Grant said in surprise. He looked at me and added, "We were going to tell them together."

"What could I do?" I asked innocently, throwing my hands up. "You left and Sandy saw the ring."

"And I'm thrilled about it," Sandy said, hugging her son again.

"Congratulations, you guys," added Jack, who had been holding Kylie and was watching us say our goodbyes.

Grant shook the hand Jack offered. "Thanks," he said quietly.

Jack nodded and then enveloped me in a big hug. I took Kylie from him and we promised we'd see them again soon.

Grant held my hand tightly as we walked to the car.

We didn't talk much on the drive home, and he didn't tell me about his conversation with Jack in the garage, but the tension in his body and voice were gone.

It may sound strange, but there was a feeling of absolution in the final kiss we shared that night.

# Chapter Thirty-Five

"THAT'S THE DRESS, TRISH! IT'S PERFECT!" EXCLAIMED MY MOTHER.

I exited the dressing room for what felt like the hundredth time that day. She came to stand alongside me as I stood by the large three-way mirror.

"It's breathtaking," agreed Sandy, who had been sitting and smiling throughout the whole afternoon.

"It is nice," agreed Melissa thoughtfully, tapping a finger on her lips as she slowly walked around me to view every angle.

When I'd asked her to be my matron of honour, she had cried with happiness, saying she was sure I'd choose Trent. I told her that since my mother seemed a bit old-fashioned when it came to these decisions, we'd be going the traditional route, and besides, I'd grown to love her as much as I did Trent. She had taken her new role very seriously since then.

"Uh huh," Melissa said after a thorough investigation, "It's wonderful. Perfection, really."

I laughed at her serious expression.

"Don't laugh," she said. "This is a very important decision. Grant has to be blown away by your beauty as you walk down that aisle!" She smiled now and clapped her hands. "And in this dress, I know he will be."

"They're right," agreed Shauna, who had agreed to be a bridesmaid. "You look gorgeous, Trish."

She and Sandy sat and grinned at each other, nodding in agreement.

As beautiful as I felt, I wasn't sure if I was simply more relieved that we'd all made the final decision or that I really preferred this dress over the many others I'd tried. I turned around and smiled, happy to agree.

The dress was made of the whitest material my mother could find at the bridal shop. She hadn't agreed with my initial preference for a softer off-white at all. In fact, the look on her face when I made the suggestion was nothing short of horror. She had been correct in thinking the whiter white would look better on me with my darker colouring, though, so it was a win for both of us in the end.

I had to admit that I felt very pretty gazing at my reflection in the long mirrors, and I couldn't help but smile. The A-line dress was simple but elegant. A small amount of lace adorned the bodice and chapel train.

I sighed, moving away from the mirrors and going back to the dressing room. I'd slowly gotten used to being gawked at as the afternoon progressed, but I was glad it was over. I hurriedly changed, with the attendant's help, and went to join the others.

"Oh, this is wonderful for you!" said Sabina, the bridal shop owner, in a heavy Romanian accent. "Not only is it lovely on you, but it fits perfectly. That hardly ever happens."

"You will order her own for her, yes?" asked my mother, in more of a statement than a question. She turned her full attention to Sabina.

Rarely did my mother buy anything off the rack, and she certainly wouldn't dream of it for her daughter's wedding day. We hadn't lived together for a long while, and she didn't know my personal preference for consignment stores.

"Of course we can do that," nodded Sabina. "When is the wedding date? It will take six months for it to arrive."

I gasped and stopped their conversation with, "I'll take this one. I like it, and I'm happy with it."

Sabina and my mother both turned to look at me. Sabina looked at my mother's expression of dismay and then at me again.

"Well, it will cost you much less if you take this one," she admitted, taking a step further away from my mother.

"Perfect," I agreed, smiling cheerfully. "Wrap it up."

I purposely didn't look at my mother's face, because I suspected that her eyes were boring into me in a rather unfavourable way.

Sabina laughed, "Oh no, dear. That's not how it works. First, we look at every detail to be sure it's perfect, and then you return for one more fitting, just to be sure. It is ... what you call ... a process."

"Oh," I said, simply. I had learned in the past week that I was not well-versed in wedding etiquette of any kind, and this clearly included the purchase of a wedding gown.

"All right," I smiled, nodding.

I then bravely faced my mother, who had been busy sighing her displeasure as Sabina and I had been talking. I walked the short distance between us and tried to explain.

"Mom," I said, softly, "there's no need for spending more money than necessary. This dress is perfect. You said it yourself. I don't care that other people may have tried it on. I'm really happy with this one."

She tried to smile but finally just nodded.

"Daughter, we are alike in some ways, but in others ..." She sighed again.

She stood back again to stare at the dress Sabina held. The wedding shop owner held it up as my mother searched for the fatal flaw that would force me to order one not touched by any hands, other than the ones that crafted it.

I smiled and shrugged to the other women in our party, who were watching us. No one said a word as my mother continued her inspection.

"It is beautiful," she finally conceded. "I suppose if they check it very carefully and make sure all is fine, I'll have to be happy with it."

I smiled, looked at Sabina, and said, "I'll take it."

• • •

I'd been involved a little with Melissa and Trent's plans for their special day, but I still had no real idea just how much work went into organizing a wedding celebration.

I was feeling a little overwhelmed that evening after Melissa showed me the pages of checklists that would need completing, along with the suggested months to prepare. Grant and I hadn't decided on a specific date, but most of the women close to me insisted that they needed months to complete everything.

"You're exhausted," said Grant that evening.

"I am," I nodded, leaning on his shoulder as we sat on the couch in his living room. We'd chosen a movie to watch after Kylie had settled to sleep, but I couldn't help dozing off.

I lifted my head and glanced at him.

"Honestly, this wedding planning is crazy, Grant. I guess I knew it would be a lot of work, but you should see all the decisions we have to make. There are more to-do lists than I could've ever imagined."

He smiled, taking my hand.

"I sort of remember," he said and furrowed his brow a little.

"Yeah … I guess you know," I smiled. "You've done this before."

"Well, I didn't do a whole lot of it," he said sheepishly.

"What?" I asked, curious now and looking up at him.

He admitted it then. "Stacy and I eloped."

"What?" I exclaimed, sitting straight up. "Is that an option?" I added quizzically and more to myself.

"Yeah," he smiled, ignoring my comment. "She was so over her head, and it kind of got outta hand, so one day we'd just had enough. We arranged the Justice of the Peace, went to the courthouse, and did it."

"Was your mom there? What about your brother?" I asked, shocked.

"Of course my mom was there, Trish, but my family isn't like yours," Grant explained. "Joe was somewhere far away and probably wouldn't have come anyway. Stacy didn't really have any family, so it wasn't the big deal it is for your family. Besides, as my mom told us, 'It's the marriage that counts—not the wedding. That's just one day.'"

I leaned back on the couch, still looking at him. "Sandy's pretty wise."

I fleetingly wondered what she had thought as she watched it take an entire day for us to decide on one wedding gown.

"I think my parents would excommunicate me from my family if we eloped." Feigning disappointment, I continued. "Here I thought you could deal with most of the stuff on the lists, since you've had experience."

"If that's who you think you're marrying, you've got a lot to learn, baby," he said, laughing. "I've got no talent for the girly stuff."

"Girly stuff, huh?" I said, trying to look serious. "You mean you seriously won't decide on decorations and flowers with me?"

"Sure," he agreed. "I'm good with no decorations, and dandelions are fine. Now that that's decided "—he paused to move closer to me—"I just wanna marry you and then make love to you."

I blushed and looked down at my lap. He lifted my chin, so I had to look at him.

"I'm serious—about both of those things—but in that order." He kissed me softly.

I pulled out of the kiss quickly and said, "I don't want to elope, but I don't want to wait months and months either."

"Let's plan it for as soon as our schedules work then," he stated simply.

"Wh ...what?" I stammered.

He grinned at first and then shrugged. "You told me the other night that you needed a dress, and you've got one."

I couldn't help but smile and shake my head. "You know it takes more than that to plan a wedding, Grant."

"Look," he said, sitting up straighter and looking at me more seriously. "We've been having trouble setting a date because of work schedules and trying to make everyone happy. Let's just pick a date and make it work."

The doubtful but curious look on my face compelled him to continue.

"I'm serious. The most important people in our lives will make it a priority, and if anyone can't come ... well, that's usual for every wedding, whether it's going to be in two weeks or in a year."

My mind spun. I felt I had to reason with him, but now I felt conflicted.

"Melissa and Trent planned theirs in three months, and everyone thought that was ridiculous. Ours will be even larger. Melissa said she thinks that because my parents know just about everyone, we'll need at least six months to plan. The wedding books say it takes a year, and my mom just said she'd like at least that long. But ..." I stopped, feeling breathless.

"But what?" he said softly, leaning back on the couch and smiling at me.

"I don't want to wait either. I want to be with you too ... in every way."

"You've got a calendar," he said, grabbing my phone off the coffee table and handing it to me. He then got up and grabbed his own from the kitchen. "Let's commit. Then we'll call the most important people who should be there and, unless they can't attend because of a life-or-death situation, we'll set it up."

We perused our calendars and decided a month from that very night would be our goal.

Melissa, having had the experience of planning a wedding before, offered to take over the bulk of the work, and I was thrilled to accept her offer.

"If I can plan mine in three months, we can do yours in one. It'll be a challenge, and you may not get everything you want, but it'll be beautiful, I promise," she assured me.

"I don't even know what I want." I laughed on the other end of the phone. "Grant says dandelions are good enough for flowers, if that helps."

Grant looked at me and whispered, "Sure! Throw me under the bus."

Melissa paused before speaking. "Well ... you tell that man that you will not be having dandelions as your wedding flower. Not only is it a weed, but they're not in season."

Grant and I both laughed. "That's sort of a relief, actually. Yellow is probably the only colour I'd rather not have."

"What's wrong with yellow?" asked Grant with a twinkle in his eye as I gestured for him to keep quiet while I was talking to Melissa.

She and I made a date to seriously plan, and my heart beat fast in anticipation as I pressed the END key on my phone.

We called the most important people in our lives. Although I suspect my mother passed out when we told her, the date was set and the majority of the closest people to us seemed avid to come.

"Feel good about it?" Grant asked after hanging up from the last call he had to make.

"Nervous," I answered, not able to keep the smile off my face. "It's more of a reality now."

"A good reality?" he asked, stroking my cheek and playing with a stray hair that had fallen from the ponytail I'd stuck it in earlier.

"Hmm," I breathed, sighing. "Yes."

We shared a long, deep kiss and were both out of breath when, suddenly, he broke away and stood up.

"Okay, it's late," he said tightly. "You better go."

I felt a little hurt but slowly stood and straightened my shirt.

"I hope you're not upset," he said, apologetically. "I'm just stopping before it gets out of hand."

"I know," I agreed, looking down but feeling conflicted. "I know we believe sex after marriage is the right way to go, but I thought that maybe, since we're getting married in a month anyway ..." I looked up at him, trying to look charming, and saw him smile.

He came closer to me, and my breath caught as he drew me into a warm hug.

"That's a really great offer," he said softly, "and you have no idea how much I'd love to take you up on it, but..." He paused. "I know you're worth the wait, Trish. You haven't been with anyone before, and I want it to be really special for us. We'll be sorry if we don't wait, and I don't want to start our marriage that way."

I felt incredibly treasured in that moment, and I left his place that night feeling undeniably loved and loving him even more.

# Chapter Thirty-Six

MELISSA STRAIGHTENED THE LAMP SHADE ONE MORE TIME AND LOOKED around their small living room area with a critical eye. She ran to the hall mirror and checked her makeup. She went back to the living room and re-stacked the wedding magazines, placing the planning binder neatly on top. She stared at them and then decisively carried them all to the bedroom, where she placed them on the dresser instead. Then she went to the kitchen to be sure she'd covered the cookies she'd made with enough cellophane so they wouldn't dry out.

All the while she fussed, Trent sat on the couch with his laptop, trying to concentrate on an article he'd found on a medical website regarding the most common paediatric emergencies. His mind wasn't completely invested, however, since he couldn't ignore his wife's nervous energy.

"You know," he said as he looked up, "they're not coming here to judge every little detail of our lives, Mel."

"Oh, right!" she said, looking at him like he'd lost his mind. "That's totally what they're coming here for, and we have to make the best impression!"

"Honey," he said, putting the laptop down on the coffee table and standing up, "as I told you with the last agency, I know these are important interviews, but I don't think they'll care about the carpets or the cookies."

Melissa took a deep breath, as if trying to gain patience with this man who she felt didn't clearly understand the gravity of the situation.

Thankfully, the doorbell rang then. Melissa jumped to grab Trent's laptop and place it neatly on the desk, where it usually sat. Then she joined Trent at the door to welcome the two people from the adoption agency, who Melissa knew could determine their entire future.

They were nearing the end of the visit, and Melissa hoped it had been going well, when one of the interviewers asked, "Have you thought seriously about adopting a child with special needs or a health issue?"

Melissa glanced at Trent and he at her. They had discussed it at length. They both nodded as Melissa turned to the interviewer and replied, "We've discussed it and we feel that it would be an option, of course. Although I don't have a medical background, my husband does, so we think we'd be okay with that. Well ... Trent would be awesome, of course. I don't know so much about me, but I'd try hard."

Melissa looked at her husband with the panicked gaze that Trent recognized as "save me." Trent smiled, nodded at the interviewer, and added, "We'd be fine with that. If we could have our own biological child, we'd love that child no matter what issues came up, and that's the way we feel about an adopted child as well. That boy or girl will be our own, and we will love him or her no matter what."

Melissa's heart welled with pride for her husband, and with that said, the interview soon ended.

As Melissa closed the door behind the two people from the agency, she breathed a sigh of relief.

"I don't think I breathed the whole time," she said as she turned to face Trent. "How do you think it went?" she asked, a bit anxiously.

"Fine," said Trent, coming to her and wrapping his arms around her waist. "You were great."

"Oh Trent," said Melissa as she hugged him. "I hope so. I don't think I was so impressive, but I know you were. You knew just what to say and how to say it."

"You think I was making my answers up?" he asked, lifting one eyebrow as he pulled back to look at her.

She smiled at him and shook her head slowly. "No. That's just it. You always know the right thing to say, while I let my nerves get the better of me and ramble on. I know you made a good impression. I just hope I did."

He laughed and hugged her again. "Don't worry, honey. You made a perfect impression. You were yourself, and that's who I love and that's who you're going to be as a mother, so that makes it perfect."

"You always know what to say to make me feel better," Melissa said. "I love you so much."

They kissed slowly and then Trent whispered, "Now we pray for a baby."

# Chapter Thirty-Seven

THE NEXT FEW WEEKS WENT BY IN A BLUR. IN THE MIDST OF THE CRAZINESS OF working and planning, I thought more than once that we might have made the wrong decision about expediting the date, but then I'd see Grant and immediately knew we'd made the right one.

Although a drill sergeant at times, Melissa was the best wedding planner a girl could have. She'd taken over and knew the ins and outs of what was needed and the right people to contact. She definitely knew how to prioritize, and she worked so hard that I felt guilty. Eventually I asked her if more of it should be my responsibility.

"Of course not," she assured me a week into it. "I love this, and our interviews with the agencies are over, so now we pray for the baby while we work. Besides, I took more time off from the daycare right now, so I have all the time in the world for this."

"Thank you," I said, feeling so blessed for having her in my life. "Grant and I talked about it, and we're going to pay you for all the work you're doing. After all, you really are doing a wedding planner's job, so you should be compensated for it."

"Absolutely not!" she insisted. "I'm your maid of honour. It's my job."

I laughed and replied, "Maid?"

She glanced at me then and rolled her eyes. "Nicer sounding. Matron makes it sound like I'll need a walker to get up the aisle."

We both laughed and I agreed.

I'd asked Trent previously how he felt about Melissa spending so much time on our wedding plans, but he assured me that Melissa was in her element and needed something to focus on. He'd been working his full-time rotation but also overtime as of late. I suspected he was trying to keep his mind off all things adoption as well.

"Mmmm," Melissa groaned softly after we tasted the first bite of a moist vanilla raspberry butter cake. "This is lovely, don't you think?" she asked, looking at me with great expectation.

"It's great," I stated, wiping my mouth with the small napkin provided. "It really is good. We'll get it."

Melissa laughed and looked at the bakery owner. "She's never done this before. She doesn't know the drill." The baker nodded knowingly, with a smile.

"What?" I asked, oblivious to what they were smiling about.

"You should try at least a few different kinds to compare," stated the baker, handing me another sweet confection.

My mind travelled back to the many wedding dresses I'd tried on and I sighed. That day not only my opinion mattered, but four others did as well. Today it was just Melissa and I, and I wanted to fast-track the decision. In all honesty, I didn't care much about which kind of cake we ordered. I love all cakes without judgement, but for this decision, I just wanted something pretty on the table for tradition's sake.

In the end, it was the first one I liked that Melissa agreed with as well, and I felt we could have saved time if she'd just listened to me in the first place. I had the good sense, for a change, not to verbalize this. I didn't want to ruin what was clearly glorious for her.

It was much like that with the many details and decisions over the next few weeks. Melissa would tell me what I needed, and I'd nod, tell her what I liked, and she would approve or disapprove of my decision.

My mother gave her own approval and disapproval as well, which made it even more fun. She made many trips to the city to be sure things were appropriate and sensical. She wanted no expense spared and offered to pay for most of it, but, in turn, she also knew she had the right to give her huge opinions. As much as we'd grown in our relationship, this tested it occasionally, but most times when disagreeing we would take a few moments to step away from one another to breathe. One such "moment" occurred when deciding on the venue. This happened the very day after Grant and I had decided on the date of the wedding. Apparently, my mother had "come to" from the swoon she had fallen into the night before.

"You cannot expect a whole town of people to travel over two hours to the city for your nuptials," she expressed rather forcefully. "I've already spoken to Pastor Edward. He is perfectly happy to marry you on the date you've chosen, and thankfully the church is available. It's really a miracle, and you should be thanking me for arranging it, and God for allowing it, on such short notice. Also, I've checked with Elise at the town hall. That really is our only option for the reception, so it will have to do. I suppose we must be thankful that the hall is even available. That's probably because it's not the season for weddings right now. If your wedding were in warmer weather, there would be more options, but since this is what you want—"

"This is what we want," I interrupted before taking another deep breath. "Mom, thank you for all you're doing. I appreciate it, believe me. I want a nice wedding, but it doesn't have to be fancy. Really. I don't need that."

"You say that now, but when you think back on it, you'll be grateful that I helped make it the day you'll remember for the rest of our lives."

Don't get me wrong. On one hand, I was impressed that my mother had gotten over her initial shock so quickly. We hadn't given her a lot of time, which, in hindsight, was perhaps a bit thoughtless on our part. I appreciated that she hadn't wasted much energy trying to change my mind about the date, but I didn't miss the digs she sometimes threw into the conversation. I was even a bit impressed that she had risen to the challenge of making plans so quickly, even without regard to my opinion.

I quickly decided another plan of action would be more effective if the next month was to be remotely tolerable.

I dumped her on Melissa.

"Mom," I said gently, "Melissa offered to help plan the wedding, so all decisions should be discussed with her. Is that all right?"

Silence can mean many things. I love it when it comes as a calm, still quiet that envelopes you in warmth and wonder … like a hug.

This was not that kind of silence.

"I see," she said with a familiar terseness in her tone. "Well, who needs me then?"

It wasn't a question, really, but rather a statement.

"Oh Mom," I said, feeling immediate guilt. "I need you, Mom. I really do. You're amazing at planning and organizing. You've always done so much of that, but you're the mother of the bride. I don't want you to do all the hard work, and Melissa is excited to do it. I want you to enjoy this wedding without all the stress."

"Trish," she replied, "I want to do this for you. You're my only daughter."

The guilt and shame I felt in the moment of silence following that statement was profound, and I prayed sincerely for forgiveness as she continued.

"I love this sort of thing too, and I'm good at it. At the least I'd like to speak to Melissa and offer her my help. I insist. Please." She paused. "Of course, you'd have to be okay with that."

I breathed. She was trying.

"Mom, I know that between you and Melissa, I'll have the most wonderful wedding a girl could ever have," I said with sincerity.

We said our goodbyes shortly after I'd given her Melissa's contact information. I then texted Melissa nervously, to warn her.

I apologized to her, but Melissa assured me that there was no need for that, and of course my mother should be greatly involved. Why would I ever think otherwise?

I felt appropriately chastised, but I also left the conversation feeling that what I'd said was true—I would have the most beautiful wedding possible, and it would be because of the two gifted women in my life who would make that happen.

Then I had to pray, again, to ask forgiveness for an uncharitable heart.

## Chapter Thirty-Eight

MELISSA AND MY MOTHER WORKED SO WELL TOGETHER THAT IN RARE moments over the next four weeks, I felt the tiniest amount of envy at how much fun they were having together. It was easy to overcome, however, because the result of that duo's work was nothing less than amazing.

As the day approached the emailed invitations were sent—another huge disappointment for my mother, by the way, who had wanted hand-scripted invitations. Nonetheless, it all got done. The Ts were crossed and the Is dotted on the all-important documents, the flowers vased, the cakes decorated, the caterers readied, the musicians practised, the decorations bought and some made, the dresses and suits fitted, and the rings polished.

Exhaustion was on the menu, as I imagine it is with most weddings, but excitement's presence far exceeded how tired we were as the day neared.

Thankfully, I was able to work at the hospital a little less during the few weeks leading up to the wedding, due to wonderful colleagues who were willing to step in. One thing about most nurses—we help each other in times of need. I appreciated my colleagues like never before.

The great group of friends I worked with even threw a surprise "breakfast" bridal shower for me one morning when I came to work. Shift change, as we'd found before, was an opportune time for celebration, as the night staff and day staff would all have a better chance to attend, at least for a few minutes. Some of the staff who weren't on shift had come early and brought breakfast foods for everyone to enjoy. Shauna, who had arranged most of it, was off shift, so she'd come early to decorate the break room. Thankfully, the labour ward wasn't too busy, and my colleagues on the day shift took turns to bring their well-wishes too. I was moved by their generosity and kindness, but I blushed a lot opening the gifts that morning.

"We decided we'd go with a boudoir theme," piped up Shauna as I lifted the first piece of lingerie from a bright-pink gift bag. "After all, people having sex is a necessity if we all want to keep our jobs."

She had a point. There would be no labour and delivery nurses without that.

"We are the 'produce' department of the store," laughed Jane, a seasoned older nurse who was soon retiring. I had learned so much from her and would miss her incredibly when she left.

"True that," laughed a few other nurses around the break room table.

I received beautiful gifts of not only lingerie but oils, soaps, and some things I suspected I may need instruction for. I didn't want to seem naïve, so I nodded and laughed along with the others as I unwrapped those few items, thinking I'd later check with Grant, or maybe Melissa, to see if they were any wiser.

"Thank you so much, Shauna," I said as I helped her straighten up the room two hours later.

"I'm just glad it wasn't too crazy here this morning. That was an answer to my prayers, I'll tell you. I was taking a chance with you working today, but Anne said if it was busy, she and the others would try to cover for you until you could go, so it would've worked out anyway."

She stepped down off the chair she'd been standing on to pull down the few balloons she'd hung.

"You go and I'll finish up here," she said, shooing me out of the break room. "You shouldn't have to clean up after your own shower, Trish."

"Well ... thank you for arranging it, Shauna. Really. You and the others mean a lot to me," I said, dumping the disposable tablecloth into the garbage.

I turned toward the door and saw an ambulance stretcher coming down the hall.

Shauna looked at me and said, "Trish, you mean a lot to a lot of people too. You just maybe don't know it."

I hugged her before running to find out which room was vacant for our new patient, who sounded suspiciously close to delivering. She did less than an hour later.

As it turned out, the day that had started in celebration continued that way for many other people. Ten babies were born during the rest of my shift, and most were celebrated by elated parents and would hold special memories for years to come.

The woman who had come on the stretcher that morning, however, struggled with addictions that seemed too many to count. When her baby was born, he immediately showed signs of distress and withdrawal. The NICU team whisked the tiny boy away even more quickly when his mother looked at us and, in her drug-induced high, slurred, "I don't want it anyway! I have too many kids already."

After the next two twelve-hour days, which continued to be very much like the first, I was finally off work and would continue to be until our short honeymoon was over. I was exhausted physically and emotionally, but I couldn't wait to resume helping Melissa and my mother with the last-minute preparations before our wedding day.

Melissa and I had burned the midnight oil at my parents' place finishing up the last few details, and we had just folded the last bulletin. My mother had retired to bed an hour earlier when we assured her that we were both perfectly capable of folding paper without her supervision. When she'd said goodnight, I noticed that she didn't look nearly as tired as we two younger women did. She had been right. She was good at organizing and preparing for events, and although she'd always done things like this, I hadn't seen just how gifted she was at it.

"That's it," sighed Melissa, brushing a lock of hair from her face to tuck it behind her ear. "The last detail. Done."

She grinned as she looked across the kitchen table at me. "Just the final touches of decorating the church and the hall tomorrow, the rehearsal in the evening, and then you get to relax and just enjoy your wedding day."

"Maybe I will," I said, looking at my tired friend, "but what about you? I'm worried about you."

"Oh! Don't be!" she exclaimed. "Your wedding day is the day I've been waiting for. I love weddings, and to boss everyone around on yours? Well, that'll be all fun for me." She laughed. "Seriously, I can't wait to see how all our plans come together, Trish. This is going to be the best day of your life!"

The guys had pitched in with whatever Melissa assigned them.

"It's safest just to do what we're told right now," Trent had said to Grant earlier that day.

Grant had nodded as they pumped fists in agreement.

Grant's brother, Joe, had surprised everyone by calling a week earlier to say he would attend. The brothers hadn't seen each other in years, and Grant was quite shocked to hear that he was coming. Grant had asked another friend to stand up for him earlier, but that friend had gladly given the honour to Joe when he heard he would be there.

Sandy, although disappointed that Jack wouldn't be able to attend, was very excited that her younger son would be coming, and she became very busy preparing for his stay at her house. She watched Kylie for us when we needed her to and spent time cooking meals so that she wouldn't have to spend a lot of time in the kitchen when Joe got there. We didn't visit as much with Sandy as I would've liked during those few short weeks, but when we did, she amazed me. She didn't always say much, but what she did say held wisdom and always left me thinking more deeply.

Pastor Ed offered us marriage counselling, but because we lived too far away to commit to biweekly sessions, he emailed us a program instead. Grant and I tried to get the lessons finished, but it was challenging due to time and schedule constraints. We failed to get them completed. I felt guilty about this, but I also thought that I had received much more wise advice from Sandy than from the few lessons we did read.

Before we knew it, the rehearsal dinner was over, and everyone dispersed. Melissa wouldn't allow me to see Grant any more before the wedding, so I found myself deep in thought about him. I was in my childhood bedroom and I'd flopped down on the bed and was staring up at the ceiling. My mind wandered to the last time we'd been alone. We had met a few nights before when we quickly grabbed supper at a fast-food place. We then went to my apartment to attempt finishing the last lesson of the marriage counselling program.

"Stop it!" I said with a smile as I batted his hand away from a threatened tickle. "Be serious, Grant. Pastor Ed may not agree to marry us if we don't at least finish reading the last lesson. We've skipped some already, so I think we should get this one done. You know ... for closure."

"Let me ask you a question," he said, his mind clearly not on the email glowing from the iPad I held. "Won't you still say 'I do' if we don't read that tonight? I know I will, with or without it."

I looked at him and shrugged, trying to maintain a serious expression. "Maybe not," I began. "I may miss a sudden revelation that will change my mind. Wouldn't you like to know tonight rather than, say, at the altar, if I want to dump you?"

"That's not even funny." He laughed and started tickling me. "If that's what's going to happen, close the email right now."

"Okay, okay, okay," I laughed, unable to catch my breath. "I give in!"

He stopped and sat back on the couch, looking at me intently. He took the iPad from my hand and placed it on the coffee table.

"Come here," he said. He leaned toward me and held my face with both hands before kissing me deeply. As he threaded his hands through my hair, I felt like I was melting.

We kissed for too long, and I knew it when I stood up, feeling off-balanced, a while later. I then tripped, stumbling over the corner of my own coffee table as I tried to reach the chair across the room.

He smiled as he observed my ungraceful movements.

"Swept you off your feet, huh?" he said softly.

I sat down across from him and answered in an indignant tone, "Absolutely not!"

He nodded and slowly smiled. "Oh ... but I will," he promised.

I blushed and a warm thrill ran through my entire body as I picked up the iPad, scrolled to the email again, and began reading out loud the last lesson in the marriage counselling program.

# Chapter Thirty-Nine

AS I LAY ALONE IN MY CHILDHOOD BEDROOM LATE THAT NIGHT BEFORE OUR wedding, I found myself smiling and dreaming about what would happen the next day.

I heard a soft knock on the door, glanced at the clock and smiled.

"Come in, Dad," I said, clearing my throat.

"Hey, punk," said my dad as he entered. He crossed the room to sit on the edge of the window seat as I sat up straighter in bed.

"Ready for this?" he asked with a small smile.

"Absolutely," I answered, smiling back.

"I think you're marrying a good man, Trish," he offered. "Knowing that will make it easier for me to walk you down the aisle tomorrow."

I looked at the clock again. "I think you mean today, Dad," I said.

He glanced at the clock and smiled again. "I guess it is late." His gaze became serious as he continued. "When Grant asked me if your mother and I would be all right with this, I was a little surprised, I admit, but pleasantly."

"What?" I interrupted. "He asked you?"

"Yes, he did," answered my father. "He asked us if we'd be okay with him marrying you."

I burst out laughing and said, "It's the twenty-first century and I'm a grown woman! That's crazy!" I felt suddenly a little put, and left, out.

"Whoa, Trish," my dad continued, putting a hand up as if to stop my rant. "I know what year we're in, but I think it says a lot about his character.

He wouldn't have had to do that, but from a father's perspective, I think it shows integrity and respect for all of us, including you. It's not like I really have a say anyway. Everyone knows you're old enough to make your own decisions, but it's a nice gesture, nonetheless. Besides, I think he wanted to get more of a feel for where you came from. We talked for a long time, actually, about a lot of things ... including what happened that night."

He didn't have to explain what night he was talking about.

He continued as I listened, looking at the man I'd always respected and loved so much.

"From what he told me about the night Stacy died, and then about meeting you again, well ... Trish, Grant sees you as a gift from God and that this relationship is something good that came out of something really bad."

I held my breath, unable to speak.

"That's how he feels, but can I ask you a question?" he continued.

I looked up into my father's deep brown eyes and nodded.

"Do you feel treasured by this man, honey? At least, say, 95 per cent of the time?"

It was a simple question but somehow felt so important.

I nodded again, forgetting my previous indignation. "Yes, Dad. I do."

"Good then," he said with a smile. "I've seen a lot of people in many different relationships, and I don't know much, but I know this for sure ... if you don't feel treasured before you get married, then that's not the person you should be promising to spend your future with."

I couldn't help myself. "Do you, Dad?" I asked, concern etched on my face.

"What?" he answered, his brow furrowing.

"Do you feel treasured?" I asked again.

He looked down. "Trish, your mother and I, well ... I made a promise to her in front of God and many witnesses years ago. Sometimes when you go through the hard times, you have to remember the words you said and hang on. It's always worth it—even if only because of the vows."

I couldn't speak until he looked at me and said, "I'm so glad you feel treasured, honey, and I can see that you treasure him too. That will make your vows so much easier to keep."

"I love you, Dad," I blurted, my eyes tearing and overflowing. He was the strong, loving man of integrity that I'd always thought him to be, and now I thanked God for him and what he'd told me about Grant.

After my father left the room, I texted my very soon-to-be husband. I hadn't learned all the details of the conversation between him and my dad, but it didn't matter to me anymore. What mattered was what my dad said about Grant and, more importantly, what I knew about him.

Me: *I can't wait to be your wife.*

Grant: *I can't wait either.*

Me: *Sleep well, knowing I love you and I'll be meaning my vows tomorrow, even if we didn't read all the lessons*

Grant: *Trish ... I will too.*

## Chapter Forty

THE WEDDING WAS THE STUFF OF DREAMS. ALTHOUGH I'D HELPED MELISSA and my mother with a majority of the decorations and knew the colours and how we'd fashioned things in the last few days, I still felt that I'd been dropped into a scene from a Hallmark movie when I entered the church.

Melissa couldn't contain her excitement, and although she was my "maid" of honour, she somehow managed to supervise everything as well.

I'd spoken with her many times regarding her dual responsibilities, and each time she'd simply say, "Everything will be planned out, Trish. I'll be standing beside you, and you and I will be the only ones who know what an amazing multi-tasker I am." Then she'd laugh and add, "I'm really just a great delegator, and so is your mom. Believe me, we didn't do it all by ourselves."

To this day, I have no idea of the many people I should still thank for making our day the wonderful day it was.

I probably would have cried as I walked toward Grant at the front of the church if it hadn't been for the concentration I needed to successfully get there without stumbling.

"Don't worry, honey," my dad whispered, knowing me well. "I'll catch you if you fall."

The fresh flowers, placed that morning by some of Melissa's "elves," lined the aisle and arched over the front of the church. The ridiculously many red and white roses, which my mother insisted on, filled the sanctuary with their fragrance as my father walked me successfully to the front. Reaching for a kiss, I looked up at my dad before he gave my hand to Grant.

Say what you want about a tux and tails. Maybe it's "old-fashioned" and not the "in thing" to do, but I found my mother correct about not only my white gown that day but the tuxedo too. Of course, the man in it didn't hurt my eyes either. He was breathtaking.

As we made our promises to each other, I didn't cry. I know that's unusual for me, but I can honestly say that I was truly lost in his eyes. In those few moments, time stood still.

I didn't hear much of what Pastor Edward said either. I know he said deep and meaningful things. Other people told me so later. Although I may feel a small amount of regret not remembering his words now, I openly admit that I don't regret anything about how I felt looking at Grant that day. We pledged ourselves to one another, wholeheartedly and without reserve, smiling and not taking our eyes off each other. Everyone else blurred as we placed the rings on each other's fingers. Suddenly, we were told to kiss as man and wife. We laughed as we pulled away from the short kiss and he grabbed my hand.

"Everyone!" Pastor Ed boomed. "Stand and put your hands together for Mr. and Mrs. Grant and Trish Evans!"

Our smiles were endless as we descended the steps and walked down the aisle to the song "Something Beautiful" by The Newsboys. I should mention that this song was not approved by my mother.

"Unless you can arrange to bring the original band here to perform it, that is not an option," she'd firmly said. "We will not have taped music at my daughter's wedding."

She and I had spent hours choosing the most beautiful, mostly traditional, music for the entire ceremony, which was played by a small orchestra of people she knew and most of whom I did not.

Knowing that both Grant and I loved the song "Something Beautiful," Melissa surprised everyone after the announcement when the first notes were heard, blasting from the church's sound system. With sudden realization, I looked at her beaming face and whispered, "thank you."

Then we danced down the aisle, completely joyful and thankful for this day and the many more we hoped and prayed for from that moment on.

• • •

The reception was a blur. As the toasts were said, we laughed, and I cried an embarrassing number of tears. Except for those, it was an evening of dreams.

My mother was in her element and accepted the accolades she deserved. When it was our turn to speak at the end of the program, Grant and I thanked her and Melissa profusely for all they had done.

Grant's younger brother, Joe, who had cut things very close that morning with his flight coming in late from Portugal, gave the toast to his brother. He was darker skinned, probably from being in the sun, and about the same height as Grant. His sun-bleached hair was shorter, and his build more muscular. He had a tougher persona than his brother, which I was curious about but had no time to dwell on that day. He was a charismatic speaker and had everyone's rapt attention when he told of some of their antics as young boys. I looked at Grant as he laughed and nodded in agreement with some of the things Joe said. There was much I didn't know about Grant, but I couldn't wait to find out more.

"Trish," said Joe near the end of his speech. He turned to look directly at me. "I wasn't sure about this whole thing when I first heard about it."

I could feel Grant tense beside me. I didn't know why, and I certainly didn't know why his brother would say that when he didn't know me at all. I felt as though the whole room held their collective breath.

Joe looked conflicted but then continued. "I don't know you, but I know this. If Grant loves you ...well, you and I can trust that. He's never let me down, and I know he won't let you down either. I'm glad tonight that I have the privilege to welcome you into our family, sister." He smiled, raising his glass, and said, "A toast to Grant and Trish ... my brother and sister!"

The room raised their glasses, and we all forgot the momentary tension. I'd cried enough in front of all these witnesses and now started to feel tears well up again, but this time Grant, knowing how I hated that, grabbed my hand and stood up. He brought me swiftly next to him, and when we were both standing, he grabbed my waist, dipped me, and planted a quick kiss. When we stood straight again, I was laughing instead.

When Joe returned to the head table, I saw Grant's serious expression as he mouthed "thank you" to him. As quickly as I wondered about it, though, the thought vanished, as it was time for Grant and me to say thank you to the many people who had helped make our day grand.

Sandy came toward us holding Kylie before we left for our hotel room much later.

"Trish," she began, "your parents have offered to take Kylie for some of the time you and Grant are away on your honeymoon. I hope that's all right with both of you." I looked at Grant, feeling that it wasn't my place to give permission for anything regarding his daughter.

"Well?" he asked, turning his gaze to me.

"Well what?" I replied, looking confused.

"Is it okay if our daughter stays with your parents?" he asked, smiling.

"Our daughter," I whispered, feeling my heart skip a beat with the realization.

"Yes," he added, looking at me more intensely. "Our daughter."

I slowly nodded, looking at him with a ridiculous smile on my face.

I turned to Sandy and nodded. "Yes … yes. That's fine. Of course. Whatever you grandmas decide is fine with"—I glanced at Grant—"with us. Right, Grant?"

"Absolutely," he grinned, looking from me to his mother.

"Great!" said Sandy, "I'll talk to Helen. Between the two of us, we'll be sure to take good care of this little one. You two have a fabulous honeymoon and don't worry about a thing."

Kylie had been dressed in a beautiful red satin and lace dress for the day but had recently been changed into a comfortable sleeper and was bundled for the cool weather. She now lay, sleeping, on Sandy's shoulder.

"Now to get this little party girl to bed," Sandy said, hugging us both goodbye.

"I'm amazed at how well she did," said Grant smiling, softly touching Kylie's cheek before letting his mom move away. "See you in a while, little one. Soon we celebrate you on your birthday."

"Oh!" Sandy remembered before turning to leave. "Jack texted tonight and sends his congratulations. He apologized, again, for not being able to make it for your wedding, but he hopes it was all you wanted it to be."

"It was! Please tell him that," I replied. "He's pretty much the only one close to us that it didn't work for. Please tell him again how sorry we are."

She smiled and nodded. "I will."

Grant and I stood together as she carried our daughter toward her car. She had been invited to stay at my parents' house with Kylie, which made it easier for both grandmas to get time with her, and Sandy didn't have to drive back to the city that late at night.

We stood looking as our daughter left with her grandmother. We were so blessed to have all the wonderful people in our lives who loved us and Kylie.

I sighed, feeling tired but so happy.

Grant turned me slowly to stand in front of him and looked down into my eyes. We looked at each other for a little while without speaking, but I felt there was something he needed to say. Finally, he spoke.

"I haven't told you this before, Trish, but ..." He paused, and I could tell it was difficult for him.

I reached up to touch his cheek in encouragement for him to continue.

"Before I watched Stacy be wheeled into the operating room that night, she said something that I didn't understand. I thought she was talking about Kylie, and that's why I wanted her with me so badly when we got back to the room she was born in."

I vaguely remembered that he had seemed almost desperate to hold his daughter after we had left Stacy, but that had seemed normal to me.

"But now," he continued, "I think she meant you, Trish. Somehow, in a weird way maybe, she knew something. Maybe God gave her the message. I don't know. But I think she meant ... you."

I stood back and waited. "What did she say?" I whispered, mesmerized in his serious stare.

He took a deeper breath, came as close to me as possible, and placed both of his strong hands on each side of my face. Then my breath caught when he breathed, "Promise me ... you'll find her."

I couldn't make sense of it, but when we kissed all I felt was ... him.

# Chapter Forty-One

MAUI IS A STUNNING PLACE TO VISIT. NEVER IN MY WILDEST DREAMS HAD I EVER thought I would go there. An aroma of humid, floral elegance envelopes you as soon as you step off the plane, and it doesn't leave until you fly away from the island. It's the natural scent of Hawaii, and if I could have bottled it and brought it back with me, I would have.

The ten days we spent enjoying the ocean, the tropical plantations, and the beautiful sites and sounds of the island will forever be etched into the deepest recesses of my mind. If I ever suffer from dementia, I truly hope the memories from that special time are the ones that loop over and over in my mind.

"Was it everything you thought it would be?" asked Sandy, sipping her coffee across from me at the kitchen table.

Sandy was caring for Kylie at Grant's house the day we returned so that she could see us as soon as we got home.

"It really was," I said, smiling. I held Kylie on my lap. The little girl had welcomed us both back with smiles and giggles. She seemed to have grown bolder and now was running circles around everything. She slid off my lap just as quickly as she'd climbed on.

I laughed and Sandy smiled.

"She's busier, I think," I said.

"She's busy, that's for sure," Sandy agreed. "I'll be honest ... I'm ready for a break. There's a time and season for raising little ones, and this grandma has had her day. Don't get me wrong," she continued, standing to refill her coffee cup, "I love caring for her. I just need a short break and then I'll be ready to rumble again."

The laugh that bubbled up from my throat was cut short by the crash we heard coming from the next room. I jumped up to investigate and found a smiling Kylie running toward me and away from the broken lamp in the living room.

When Grant and Jack returned from their errand, they found me on the floor, sweeping glass into a dustpan.

"Don't walk there," I said, pointing to an area I hadn't swept yet.

Jack chuckled softly. "Miss Kylie again, huh?"

Sandy smiled and nodded. "Yes."

"It's my fault," I quickly said as I cleaned. "I wasn't watching her closely enough."

"Trish," said Sandy, shaking her head, "it's just as much my fault. And you'll never be able to watch her enough. She's a going concern."

"Besides," observed Jack, "it just evens out the room."

Grant glanced toward the opposite side of the living-room and saw the empty space that had once held the twin to the ruined lamp.

He looked at me and shrugged.

"Too fancy anyway," he winked.

Grant had gone with Jack to pick up something from the hardware store as soon as we arrived. Jack was going to fix the leaky toilet in one of the bathrooms, so Grant had gone along. They seemed much more at ease with one another, and it made both Sandy and I glad.

We thanked Sandy and Jack profusely for the babysitting they'd done over the last ten days.

"We didn't have to worry about Kylie at all," Grant told them. "It was great to relax."

"Well, thank Helen and Ted as well. They did the first few days, actually. It worked out well. It gave me a chance to spend some time with your brother," Sandy said. "Joe thinks he might stick around awhile longer this time."

Grant raised one eyebrow, and his face held a more serious expression for a fleeting moment. Then he smiled slightly and said, "That's great, Mom."

I hugged Sandy and said, "We'll call my parents and thank them too."

"You sure you don't want me to fix the toilet before we go, Grant?" asked Jack in his bass tone. "I don't mind doing it."

"No," smiled Grant. "Time to get back to real life, I guess."

I smiled as Grant closed the door but then turned my attention to investigating the floor to be sure I hadn't missed any glass. I got down on my hands and knees for a more thorough look.

Kylie had scooted to her box of toys and was now banging a mallet on a very loud, brightly coloured xylophone.

I caught Grant staring at me. "I'll go fix the toilet. That okay?"

"Sort of a necessity, I think." I smiled up at him.

"Real life," he said, rolling his eyes.

Later that night, after Kylie was asleep and we'd unpacked the treasures we'd found in Maui, I came out of the en suite into the large master bedroom, which I now shared with Grant.

He was lying on the bed on his side, still in his jeans but no shirt.

We called my parents to thank them for all they'd done and tell them a lot about what we'd seen in Hawaii. They laughed, remembering some of the same places they'd been to a few years before.

"We told you you'd love it," said my mother. "It's really paradise on earth, isn't it?"

"Certainly beats the cold weather here," I agreed. "Remind me to go back again during another winter."

After pressing END on my phone, I looked over to Grant, who gave me a steamy look and said, "Come here and warm me up."

I smiled seductively and nodded as I walked slowly toward him.

"Let's pretend we're back in Maui."

# Chapter Forty-Two

WHEN WE HEARD KYLIE THE NEXT MORNING, GRANT GROANED AT THE SAME time as I did. We had gotten used to our late nights and late mornings on the honeymoon, so if it hadn't seemed like reality yesterday, it certainly was today.

My phone rang as Grant stumbled to Kylie's room and I answered it, smiling.

"Hi, Trent!" I said.

"Hey, Trish! Welcome back!"

"Thanks. It's … good to be back." I laid back on my pillow.

I could hear Melissa from a distance away at first and then louder as she said, "Hey! Put Grant on speaker too."

I scrambled from under the warm covers and wished for the flannel PJs I'd once worn, for practicality and comfort, instead of the flimsy lack of material I wore now. I fleetingly wondered who the first person was who invented lingerie and knew it couldn't have been a practical woman. Although I had to admit … it did serve a purpose. It just wasn't warm.

As I came into Kylie's room where Grant was changing her diaper, Melissa squealed, "We're getting a baby!"

"Wh … what?" I asked, surprised by the news.

"Wow!" exclaimed Grant. "That's awesome!!"

He plopped Kylie gently on the floor and disposed of the wet diaper. He took a clean baby wipe, used it to clean his hands, and then came closer to me and the phone.

"Yeah," said Trent, sounding surprised but happy too.

"When?" I asked.

"In a week or so. Hopefully before Kylie's birthday party. Then the baby can come to the party with us if that's okay," said Melissa.

Grant and I both laughed as we said, "Of course!" together.

"That was super fast," I commented later as Grant, Kylie, and I ate breakfast.

"What are you thinking?" he said, looking at me seriously.

"Oh ... nothing," I said slowly, playing with my eggs.

"That isn't a nothing expression, Trish," he stated as he drank his coffee.

"Well, on one hand I'm thinking that we all prayed for this baby and that it's a wonderful surprise that we should just thank God for," I started.

"And on the other hand?" asked Grant, putting his cup down.

"It's really fast, Grant. I ... well ... I just hope the baby's okay. Sometimes with kids that have issues it's faster to adopt, and I know they told the agencies they'd be willing to take a baby that's not perfect ..." I looked up at him.

Grant got up and came over to me, interrupting the sentence I didn't want to finish anyway. As he helped me to stand in front of him, I shook my head. "I'm sorry. I'm not saying that it would be a bad thing to adopt a baby with special needs, Grant. I didn't mean that at all. It just looks really hard to me, and I love Trent and Melissa so much and—"

His kiss stopped my rambling, and when we moved apart, he smiled softly.

"I knew what you meant," he said, "but God's got this. We've all prayed for this child, and He'll help them care for him, or her, no matter what."

"You're so wise," I sighed, "and you always seem to know what to say."

"Not always," he smiled. "You'll find that out yet."

"Good! I'd like to know you're not perfect." I rolled my eyes and quickly kissed him again. "Now go to work and leave us girls to clean up this mess."

We both looked at Kylie, who was smiling up at us with food all over her face and tray. The floor hadn't missed out either.

"Hmm," I said, my eyes widening. "Let me rephrase that. She'll make the mess, and I'll clean it up."

He laughed. Before leaving the house, he suggested, "Try to nap when she does this afternoon. I'll miss you tonight."

My looming night shifts were on his mind and I sighed, nodding.

"Real life," I said under my breath as I grabbed a rag to begin cleaning.

# Chapter Forty-Three

GRANT, SANDY, JACK, AND I PLANNED KYLIE'S PARTY FOR THE EXACT DATE OF her birthday. Joe attended the party planning but mostly played with his niece that evening. He couldn't seem to sit still long enough to concentrate, but Kylie loved him more than ever for it. I'd never heard her laugh as much as she did that night.

The party would be on a Saturday, which worked well for most family invited. My dad would be the only person unable to attend. He had to fly overseas for a medical conference he was speaking at and couldn't change his plans.

The initial list of invited people had grown by leaps and bounds. Grant felt that many of his—and now our—church family had to be invited. Many of them had rallied around him after Stacy's death to help with meals and babysitting when Sandy couldn't. He had appreciated it beyond words and now wanted to share a celebration with them. Between those people, Grant's employees, and the nurses from work who were closest to me, our list was long by the time we finalized it.

My mother had been thrilled when I phoned her, and she asked if she could be in charge of the food and decorations. Knowing how she loved Kylie and had a gift for event planning, we were more than happy, and thankful, to let her run with it. I could hear papers shuffling while still on the phone, and I had no doubt that she'd started making lists before we'd even said goodbye.

The party would be at our home because it was the best option for space. Because of the larger crowd, we had to arrange eating places in all the rooms on the main floor and the larger one on the second story as well.

Sandy agreed to take more responsibility for Kylie during the meal, making it possible for Grant and me to mingle, fill drinks, and help my mother as well.

The decorations were hung in the morning, transforming our home into a colourful array of glittering pink and gold.

"It looks like a unicorn threw up in here," said Joe, walking into the house an hour before the party was to start.

Unfortunately, my mother, who had been instrumental in making our home appear that way, heard his comment. Without speaking, she turned on her heel and headed back to the kitchen from where she'd come.

"Thanks," I said, rolling my eyes toward Joe. "A lot."

Joe laughed. "Just sayin' it like I see it."

"For your information, she's put a lot of work into this," I stated. "Go apologize." I tried not to smile as I stared him down.

He took a step toward me and stopped when he saw my eyes narrow.

"What makes you think you can tell me what to do?" he started.

"I'm your sister. You have to listen," I answered, shrugging my shoulders.

"Sure," he said softly as he moved past me. "Pull that card."

I saw him smile as I sang out, "Uh huuuh."

I ran upstairs to use the bathroom and made a quick stop to check my hair and makeup. By the time I bounced downstairs again, my mother was laughing at something Joe had said to her. I shook my head. By what I'd observed over the last weeks, I thought he'd probably be able to charm the horn off a unicorn.

"I think it looks great," said Grant, wrapping his arms around me from behind. "I think we're ready."

"Mmm," I said, "I didn't hear you there. More of this," I encouraged, referring to the hug and taking a deep breath of him. He always smelled so nice.

"Later, babe," he whispered in my ear and let go.

"Hey! Joe!" he said loudly. "We might have time for a game of pool. Upstairs?"

I walked into the kitchen where my mother was busy supervising and looking completely at ease. Although Sandy and I had told her we'd help make the food, she'd hired a local caterer instead, insisting that she wanted us to enjoy ourselves and it was her gift to us.

I suspected my mother had a memory flash with her generous offer but didn't ask. Years before, I'd invited my parents for a meal when I'd first moved into my apartment. After valiantly attempting to ingest the first few bites of the hamburger casserole I'd spent all afternoon making, we had to order pizza. Before they left that night, I could see that my mother felt sorry for me, and in an attempt to be encouraging, she left me with, "Trish, you can't have every gift."

Enough said.

"It smells so good in here, ladies," I commented while entering the kitchen. "Thank you so much." I looked at them and then at my mother.

I'd been introduced to the ladies earlier. They had come into the house with many of their own supplies and quickly made our kitchen their home. Anna and Veronica had been partners for years and worked like a well-oiled machine. Their reputation was excellent, and I suspected that my mother was paying a ridiculous amount, since she'd booked them on such short notice.

Anna looked at me and said, "It's fun to do. We usually get bigger jobs in smaller kitchens, so having all these people with all this space is a treat."

My mother had just helped herself to an appetizer off a beautifully stacked plate, taking one and moving others so that the presentation wasn't ruined.

"Oh ... that's good," she approved, dabbing the corners of her mouth with a pink napkin. It always amazed me how she could eat without affecting her lipstick at all.

"I told you, Helen," replied a smiling Veronica, "you made perfect choices."

I had no idea what "perfect choices" for a toddler's birthday party would be, but I suspected foods that babies liked were not involved.

I started thinking again of how different my mother and I were, but the thought was gone as fast as it had come with the sounding of the front entrance bell.

I threw open the door to find a beaming Trent and Melissa. Trent held a car seat that he swung gently back and forth. My eyes teared in anticipation of seeing their precious cargo, but I threw my arms around Melissa before they could enter.

"Hey! It's not warm out here," said Trent, smiling.

"Okay, okay," I said excitedly, breaking the hug and moving back into the house. I could hardly wait until the blanket would be pulled off the car seat.

"Wait!" I then blurted out. "Grant, come downstairs!" I yelled as I ran toward the bottom of the staircase.

Unfortunately, marriage hadn't cured my bent for tripping, and in my haste I didn't see the toy on the floor until it was too late. I tried to jump over it at the last second but then smashed into a table that had been moved from its usual place, for party reasons.

The crash was heard throughout the house as I, eventually, landed on my rump. I groaned as I peered at my immediately swelling ankle and then looked up as Grant came bounding down the stairs.

"Oh, good!" he said with relief when seeing that Kylie was nowhere to be found.

I knew why he had said it, and I smiled a little as he blushed.

"I'm sorry. That didn't come out right," he said as he kneeled down to examine my leg.

"I knew what you meant," I said, trying to smile as I held my bruised ankle.

Trent had moved quickly to the kitchen to ask for ice and came back with a little of that and my mother as well. He joined me and Grant on the floor.

"Oh dear," stated my mother, appearing as close to compassionate as I'd ever seen her. "What can I do?" she asked everyone in the room.

"Nothing, Mom," I said, looking up at her worried face. "Really. I'm fine. Just continue what you're doing. I'm fine." I was more embarrassed than anything and didn't need any dramatic attention.

Trent looked up at her and smiled reassuringly, and I recognized him going into nurse-mode. "It's probably nothing, Helen," he said. "Worse thing is a break. Not the end of the world."

Normally I would've agreed with him, but since it was my ankle and Kylie's party, I felt my world was at least ending a little.

"More ice would help," Trent suggested in my mother's direction, winking at me. She turned and went back into the kitchen, supposedly to find more.

I tried to move my foot but winced as Trent examined it.

"What do you think?" Grant asked Trent, as if I wasn't there.

"I don't know for sure. I think an X-ray will tell the tale. I think it might be broken, but..." Trent continued, finally remembering the person on the end of the ankle. "Try to stand, Trish."

They helped me up, and when I tried to bear weight, we all knew.

"Oh no," I groaned. "I can't go to the hospital, Trent."

I looked at Grant with pleading eyes. "We'll do the party first and then I'll go, okay?"

The men looked at each other and then back at me.

"See?" I said, leaning on Grant and putting a little more weight on the sore ankle. "It doesn't huuuurt." I groaned louder because of my pathetic inability to fake anything.

"We have no choice," said Grant, suddenly looking toward the opening front door.

Jack had just entered and stood in calm observation of the sight before him. We all talked at once, but a minute or two later it was decided that Jack would take me to the Emergency room. Grant wanted to go, but I insisted that it was imperative he stay with Kylie to welcome our family and friends and begin the celebration, for her sake.

I limped to the door on Grant's arm but stopped short. There Melissa stood with a smiling baby girl on her hip. She was a bundle of yellow lace and bows, including one on top of her head. She looked to be close to Kylie's age, but that could be asked later. Melissa looked at my smiling face with tears in her eyes.

"I'm so sorry about your ankle, Trish," she said. "It was because of us that happened."

"No, it wasn't." I shook my head, forgetting my ankle and moving to step toward her. I winced as Grant held me steady and told me to stop moving.

"She's beautiful," I breathed, wishing I could reach out to hold her.

"Her name is Abigail," introduced Trent. "Abigail, meet your Aunty Trish."

Abigail continued smiling but then, noticing everyone staring at her, turned her head to cuddle against Melissa.

I fleetingly noticed a birthmark on her cheek as Jack ushered me out the door.

• • •

Emergency rooms are all about priorities. Sore ankles, even if broken, don't rank high on the ER priority list. Heart attacks, breathing issues, and blood gushing from anywhere are at the top of the list, so I knew that if they were busy, I'd be waiting, which irked me greatly. I had argued with Trent that I thought it better to spend the hours I might wait in the waiting room enjoying the party for Kylie instead. He had, however, told me that the sooner the diagnosis was made, the better for my walking future.

Sitting in the Emergency waiting room with Jack was an interesting experience, however, which distracted me from thinking of what I was missing at home. A policeman entered with a handcuffed patient who had clearly had too much to drink and appeared to have gotten into a fight with someone or something that had gotten the upper hand. When the patient and the officer saw Jack, they both stared. The patient looked frightened and backed away, but the police officer looked at me with a question in his eye.

The strong painkillers the triage nurse had given me must have started to take affect, and my mind tripped. As I watched the policeman look at me, I wondered if Jack would think it funny if I started crying and said to him, "Please, sir, don't kick me again. I'll be good." But then I thought better of it. The policeman appeared to be on the edge of a breakdown as it was, and I didn't want him pulling a gun.

I know I'm a nurse, but I'm not a fan of sitting too long in either Emergency rooms or doctor's offices. If you're not seriously ill when you enter, you have a greater chance of contracting something that will make you so by the time you leave.

I work labour and delivery for a few reasons. The most important is that I love seeing and being a part of life being brought into the world. There is, however, a perk not really spoken of, and that's the fact that it's a low-risk environment for contracting a lot of diseases.

Because I work in that specialty, I know little about orthopaedics, except what I learned in nursing school. This bothered me as I sat and waited. I dislike being knowledge-challenged. It's a pride thing. I do know, however, that bruising and swelling aren't healthy, and my ankle was looking less and less healthy.

Noticing more of the strange looks Jack was getting from the patients and their care-givers in the waiting room, I asked him if he wanted to join me in the exam room. It would be just the two of us with maybe a nurse and the doctor. He shrugged like it didn't matter one way or the other but then decided to help me in and stay.

It seemed like an eternity, but it wasn't long until someone saw me. When the nurse assessed my ankle again and saw how much more swollen and bruised it had become, another ice pack appeared, and an X-ray was expeditiously done. Then we waited some more.

I was perched on the stretcher with ice on my ankle, enjoying whatever was in the pills I'd taken, as Jack quietly loomed large, standing next to me. He had no choice. It was a small room.

The ER doctors, as a rule, didn't deliver babies, so I knew I'd be a stranger to whomever I saw.

"Trish Holmes?" said the older doctor, glancing over the top of his glasses and then reading from his clipboard. "So ... you tripped?" he inquired. He then looked up, noticed Jack, and jumped back a step. He recovered quickly, however, and cleared his throat, giving Jack a disapproving expression.

Jack stood, saying nothing, and stared back at the doctor with just the smallest smile on his face.

The doctor finally turned his attention to me then and asked his question more quietly, as if hoping Jack wouldn't hear.

"Tell me the truth, Miss," he said slowly. "How did this happen?" He purposely avoided looking Jack's way and stared me in the eye.

I knew what was going through his mind immediately. Since Jack seemed to be hovering, the doctor was strongly suspecting I'd been abused. As much as the pills were playing with my mind and I would've loved to play the comedian, thankfully my ankle pain won out and I just wanted to get the diagnosis and get out of there.

"I tripped," I heard myself say, slowly and succinctly. "All by myself," I added, almost proudly.

The seasoned doctor smirked then. "You're sure?"

I nodded. "I'm sure. I'm the biggest klutz around."

In my head, it sounded like I was slurring my words and I knew that wouldn't look good. What had I been given? Had I even asked the ER nurse what it was? Now I feared the doctor would think me an abused drug addict. I did the only thing I could think of in my haze.

"Ask my best friend, Trent Bellamy. He used to work here."

Let's face it—it pays to throw a name around in an opportune circumstance sometimes, and I'd use Trent's if I had to. Besides, I thought it wouldn't hurt if we shared a mutual friend who, the doctor would know, was sane.

The doctor's demeanour changed instantly, and I knew I'd made the right decision.

"You know Trent?" he exclaimed, grinning now. "We miss him around here. He's a good nurse."

"He's the one who told me to get in here tonight after I'd fallen ... *all by myself*," I explained slowly, trying to focus.

"Okay, okay," laughed the doctor. "What's Trent up to?"

I felt at that point that he should focus on my sore ankle, but I'd opened the can, so I answered, "He's working in Emergency in our small town, and they adopted a baby, but you don't know that. Do you want to hear all about it?"

"Wow," the doc said, smiling. "Those pills are really working for you, huh?"

I was glad he realized it was the analgesia and not a drug problem that was making my brain mush.

He continued, "If you remember later, just tell Trent hi from all of us here and that he'd be welcomed back anytime. Okay?"

I nodded, feeling less pain and more tired now.

"Back to your ankle, Trish," he said, looking at the X-ray he'd accessed on the computer in the room. "Can you see here?" he asked as he turned the screen toward me. "You've got a common type of ankle fracture. You've broken your lateral malleolus, the end of the fibula, but it's a minor break."

I don't care who you are. Nothing is "common" or "minor" when it involves you personally. I wouldn't have cared at that point if he'd told me it was the "worst" break. All I heard was "break," and I fell apart.

"Oh nooooo!" I blurted out. "I don't have time for this. I have a party to get back to. This can't be happening!" I looked at Jack. "Jack!" I demanded, grabbing his arm and attempting to move off the stretcher. "Take me home. I'll stand on my good leg and come back tomorrow for the surgery. I have no time for this tonight! Besides, it feels fine now."

Jack, who easily held me back from jumping off the stretcher, spoke for the first time, quietly but firmly. "You'll do what the doc says. We aren't leaving until he tells us you can."

The doctor and I both startled a little.

"Thanks, man," said the doctor, looking at Jack.

I thought that a bit out of line but kept quiet.

"Trish, you won't need surgery," the doctor informed me, talking as if I was a small child. "Like I said, it's a small break. We'll splint it tonight and give you some crutches and you'll be on your way. I'll give you a prescription for an anti-inflammatory, you'll ice it at home overnight, and come back tomorrow if there's no improvement, but I honestly think it will heal fairly quickly. You'll be off your foot, though, for a few weeks."

I took that news better, but I wasn't looking forward to telling my manager that I'd be off sick from work after I'd just recently been away for my honeymoon.

The sun had just set in the sky by the time we left the Emergency room. My meds had levelled off, and I was more myself.

Jack had said little more as my ankle was splinted but had laughed when I first tried the crutches.

"Have you never used those before?" he'd asked. He'd caught me again before I fell trying to manoeuvre my way to the car.

"Never," I admitted, feeling somewhat embarrassed.

"You've never shown a patient how to use them?" he inquired.

"No," I answered, feeling irritated by the question and even more so by my ineptness. "We don't get a lot of broken bones on the Labour unit," I added, dryly.

He laughed as he closed my door and walked around to the driver's seat.

"I'm sorry this happened to you tonight," he said as he pulled out of the parking lot.

I smiled up at his profile as he drove. "At least it's not worse, I guess. I hate being a klutz. As much as I've always been, I've never broken a bone before. That really surprised me."

"I know what you're sayin'," he smiled. "I was like that when I was a kid too, but I took some martial arts classes and got my balance."

I smiled at him. "I think it's a little late for me to learn that."

"It's never too late to learn something new, Trish. Life's all about learning." He paused and then added, "And life is always about surprises too. That's what makes it worth living, I guess. You never know what's around the corner."

He let that sit with me as we drove home.

"I hope there's at least some cake left," I said as I hobbled up the walk.

Jack laughed as he swung open the front door and ushered me in.

# Chapter Forty-Four

WHEN WE ENTERED THE HOUSE, JACK EXCUSED HIMSELF TO RETRIEVE THE GIFT he had made for Kylie, saying he'd be back shortly. He said he wanted to bring it in just when it was time for Kylie to open her gifts, since he hadn't wrapped it.

Grant saw me first and rushed over to help me to the couch so that I could continue elevating my splinted ankle.

Family and friends poured into the living room, and I felt embarrassed by the unsolicited attention. My ankle throbbed more now, but when Trent suggested I take one of the pills we'd picked up at the pharmacy on the way home, I declined it. Until that point in my life, I hadn't needed many painkillers because I hadn't experienced a lot of serious pain.

"It's fine," I said. "It's not too bad."

"Trish," he explained in his nurse-toned voice again, "you know you should take something sooner rather than later. If the pain gets too out of control, it's harder to get on top of it."

Shauna had come into the room also and was whole-heartedly agreeing with Trent.

"I know that, you guys," I said, gritting my teeth and trying for patience, "but I don't need any more yet. I want a clear head."

I didn't appreciate being told what to do, and I was tired. I just wanted to see Kylie, sing "Happy Birthday," have a piece of cake, and go to sleep.

Grant brought Kylie over to see me and then my heart melted.

"What happened to Mama?" he crooned to her. "Did she get an owie?"

"Ow," mimicked Kylie, pointing to me as we all burst out laughing. She'd just started saying some simple words, and we were so proud. "Dada" had been learned while we were away, and Grant beamed any time she said it.

"Yes," I said, as Grant sat her next to me on the couch. "I have an ow."

He knelt in front of us and told me, "We waited with the cake until you got here."

"Thank you." I smiled at him, feeling warm all over.

I declined his offer of dinner foods as Trent and Melissa came closer with Abigail. I greeted them and their new addition, and we gushed over her. I had so many questions, and I knew Melissa would be excited to share all the details about their precious daughter, but it would have to wait.

A loud chorus of "Happy Birthday" was sung by all as Anna brought the cake into the living room. Kylie looked as if she might cry when the singing started, so Grant stood and picked her up. She stared at the brightly lit candle as he blew it out for her, and we all clapped. We thought she'd dive into the beautiful swirls of pink frosting, but she simply pointed at it. When Grant put a little of the icing on his finger and placed it on her lips, she licked it, scrunched up her nose, and squirmed to be put down.

Grant and I looked at each other and shrugged, a little surprised.

"She'll learn to like it." I smiled confidently. "She's our daughter. She must like cake."

Anna carried the cake back into the kitchen for cutting and then she, Veronica, Sandy, and my mom passed out the pieces.

Kylie had scooted back to her place on the couch next to me, and Grant moved to sit on the floor facing us again. He tried to feed Kylie small chunks of cake, which she would have none of. The living room was packed with people sitting and standing, and the noise of conversation and laughing filled the air.

My mother had been upstairs serving the people there, but now she descended the staircase. I looked up, smiled at her, and mouthed "thank you" as she smiled back, nodding.

In that brief moment, the woman who'd raised me and with whom I had struggled so often seemed ... different. As in some of the special moments we'd shared surrounding the finding of my sister, I felt in this glance that, perhaps, we'd finally found a real understanding. We were both very different women, but we also loved the same people and the same God. And maybe, just maybe going forward, we would learn to love and appreciate each other on a much deeper level.

I looked around the room and saw all the people I loved. I looked down at the little girl who, although my niece by blood, had become my daughter. Although I fought it, my eyes teared as I looked at Grant. He was staring at me intently with a question on his face. My mind went back to the very first time I met him—when he spoke with such conviction about the goodness of God.

"I was just thinking," I said, talking loud enough for just him to hear. He smiled and waited as I looked at him.

This man had experienced some of the greatest losses anyone ever could, but still he saw it—God's love and grace. That had brought us here. So often I'd heard people talk of God's goodness, but Grant believed that truth, even through his unimaginable trials.

I sighed as I smiled back at him. "You were right, Grant." I paused as a tear fell down my cheek. "Only God can see it all, and He is good. All the time."

## Epilogue

JACK WAS RIGHT. LIFE WAS ALL ABOUT SURPRISES. HE HAD COME BACK A FEW minutes earlier carrying the baby cradle he'd made for Kylie's dolls and was standing in the entrance with Joe. He'd placed the gift down and now was laughing in the low, thunderous way he did at something Joe had said.

Helen had been smiling at her daughter as she descended the staircase and was feeling glad that the party had been a great success. Thankfully, she'd reached the bottom of the stairs when she heard the distantly familiar sound. She looked up and saw ... him. Her breath left her and she suddenly paled. She clung, white knuckled, to the bottom of the bannister, trying not to sway.

As though he felt her gaze, Jack's head slowly turned to face her. He halted in mid-laugh and took a small step back.

They stared at each other ... unmoving.

The noisy crowd at Kylie's party continued in their amusements, but for Helen and Jack, time stood still.

• • •

Somewhere in a city far from home, Stephanie tossed and turned. She couldn't sleep again—for too many nights to count. She got up and turned on the TV with the small remote that was housed beside her bed.

She had finished her college course and met her goal. She'd recently found success in a job she had always dreamt of and had moved away from home to start a new life and to ... forget. Unfortunately, her dreams wouldn't let her.

"God!" she cried out. "Just let me forget ... *everything!*"

• • •

The dream wouldn't leave. It had come so often that he knew when he was in it but couldn't tear himself from it. He prayed for consciousness. She held on, an apparition who gripped him in a trance. In the mist, with her beautiful hair blowing softly in a breeze he couldn't feel, she'd whisper.

"Grant." So far away but still so close. "You promised ... You promised me ..."

"I heard the message!" he yelled at the form before him. "I did! I did!" he'd repeat, trying to convince her.

When he'd reach for her, she would smile sadly and turn away. He couldn't take his eyes off her as she walked away from him but then, at the last moment, she would slowly turn to face him again. He knew she'd been weeping.

Then that whisper—always the whisper before he'd awaken ...

"Promise me ... you'll find her ..."

# About the Author

PATTIE JANZEN HAS LIVED IN SASKATCHEWAN HER WHOLE LIFE. AT NINETEEN, she married "a pretty fantastic guy," Brian, whose emotional stability, faith, and wisdom has been a blessing to her.

Together they had five children. Two were painful losses on earth but huge gains in heaven, and they look forward to meeting them someday. They were privileged to raise the other three children, who have given them many grandchildren—two digits' worth, as Pattie says.

Pattie has always found writing to be therapeutic, especially through the hard times.

When her children were small, an editor from a local paper liked her funny bone and gave her a weekly column in the paper, which she has returned to in recent years. She also felt called into nursing from a young age, spending most of her career on the maternity unit.

With God as her rock, Pattie stepped out in faith to write *Someone of Substance: the Goodness!* The book stands as proof that she finally listened to that "still, small voice." Her prayer is that readers hear His voice when they read the book because it came from Him.

God is *always* good—not only in the moments we see it, but especially in the moments we don't.